THE PATH TO DESTINY

The Destiny Series Book 2

EMMA EASTER

The Path to Destiny
by Emma Easter

Paperback Edition

CKN Christian Publishing
An Imprint of Wolfpack Publishing

6032 Wheat Penny Avenue
Las Vegas, NV 89122

Paperback ISBN: 978-1-64734-512-9
Ebook ISBN: 978-1-64734-511-2

THE PATH TO DESTINY

ONE

Keith shook the hands of the construction workers as he went around inspecting the new church building. He could not contain his excitement. The building was almost completed. This had been his dream for years and now it was finally coming true. And it was all thanks to Taylor, Rachel's brother, and the countless people from all over Denver and other parts of the country who had given generously. All the building equipment and workmen here were from Taylor.

On top of the two hundred thousand dollars Rachel's brother had given for the church building and for the town, he had sent a check for an additional two hundred thousand. That and the donations that had poured in through the relief fund set up for the town of Destiny had helped to rebuild the town as a whole, the church included. In a few months, the church would be completely finished, and Keith could not wait for the day he would open the doors to everyone in town and finally dedicate it to the Lord.

"Thank you so much, dear Lord," he whispered, and then made his way out of the building again. As he left the church grounds, still thinking about how God had miraculously provided for the town and all that He had done for him, his excitement increased. He finally felt like he was in the middle of God's will after such a long time of believing, despite not knowing what direction he was going with his life. He had never been more certain than he was now that God had called him to be the pastor, not just of this church, but of this town. He had been living in this constant state of excitement since the money and resources had begun to pour in. The only thing that put a damper on his excitement was Rachel. Not Rachel, exactly, because being married to her was much more than he ever could have dreamed of.

He began to make his way through town, looking this way and that. All around him were buildings in different stages of completion and the other construction workers from Taylor who were working side by side with many of the men in town, rebuilding the homes that had been destroyed.

He sighed sadly as he continued to think about Rachel. The excitement he had felt after inspecting the church just minutes ago began to fade away. He loved her with all his heart. As well as the Lord, she was the light and love of his life. They had a great relationship. But he knew she was unhappy in spite of how much she tried to hide it. And because of that, he felt guilty a lot of the time. She ached constantly for her daughter, Emily, and even though she regularly told him how much she loved being his wife, he could not help feeling that he was partly to blame for her separation from her daughter. After all, if they had not met, she would probably still be with Emily. In spite of how everything now seemed to be coming together for him, he knew he would never be fully happy until she was.

A young couple standing in front of a house waved eagerly to him, and he smiled in spite of himself and waved back. He walked towards them, keen to distract himself from his worries.

"How's it going, Adam?" he asked the man. "And Kelly, you look great. I'm glad to see you both looking really happy today." He looked at the small bungalow behind them, and then faced the smiling couple again. "I see that your house is almost finished."

Adam grinned. "All thanks to you and your wife, Pastor Keith. Those workers are really God-sent. Just take a look at Ben and Madison's down the street. Weeks ago, it was just rubble, now it is almost like it was before, only newer." He looked back at their home. "In a few days, I am sure ours will be ready for us to move back in again."

Kelly had tears in her eyes as she looked at Keith. "We thought it was all over after the hurricane destroyed our home and many of the houses in Destiny. We thought we would never be able to come back and live in this town we love so much ever again. But here we are, almost ready to move back. It's such a blessing that your brother-in-law sent all these construction workers and equipment to rebuild our town. We can't thank you enough, Pastor Keith."

Keith shook his head. "No, Kelly. It's not me. It's the Lord's doing and the generous donations from many, many people, not just my wife's brother."

"Still, we know how much Rachel loves you. It is because of you that all this is taking place." Kelly pointed at the men across the road working tirelessly on several houses, and Keith looked around him. This part of Destiny had had a lot of destroyed houses, but the men that Taylor had sent to the town had gone around rebuilding the homes with the superior equipment from their boss. Even Keith had not imagined that Destiny would be almost completely rebuilt in such a short space of time. The town was coming together once again and if not for the ache in his heart over Rachel's constant sadness, he would be the happiest man in the world.

He said goodbye to the couple and continued on. Someone else soon stopped him to thank him and, just like he had done with Kelly, he reminded the woman he was not the one responsible for the town being rebuilt.

He stopped to talk with a few other people before he finally got to his house. As usual, he entered through the kitchen so as not to disturb Rachel and the kids she took care of during the day. She had started a home daycare after getting her license two months ago, and there were about seven kids under the age of five whose parents dropped them off with Rachel every weekday. Keith had begun to use the small empty space beside the kitchen as his temporary office until the church was fully completed.

He could hear their exuberant little voices now. They were in the living room, singing a song about a lion and a tiger. He knew all the lyrics of the song now, having heard it for months. He smiled as he heard Rachel singing along with the children, and then he shut the door, mostly shutting out their singing.

He folded his hands on the desk and looked at his wristwatch. It was already noon. His heart skipped a beat and, as always, a thread of excitement ran through him. Any moment now, Rachel would walk through the door and take a seat facing him. She came to his office to spend time with him every day at about this hour while her eighteen-year-old assistant watched the children. He could not wait for her to come in and sit with him, even though it would only be for a few minutes.

"Setting up the daycare has been one of the best things I have ever done in my life," Rachel had told him a month after she started it. She had put her heart and soul into running it and loved each one of the children under her care. But he knew her so well that he could feel her pain when she sometimes talked about those children. They reminded her of her daughter.

Keith sighed. They both loved the life they shared together and their jobs. Their lives would be perfect if not for Rachel's separation from her daughter. Because of the hectic wedding planning, the wedding itself, and the pressures of helping with the whole town's renovation, they hadn't gotten around to hiring a lawyer until now. Keith's sister, Mary had gotten one for them. They were still in the process of discussing all the nitty-gritty involved with filing for sole custody of Emily.

He couldn't wait until the custody case went to court. The earlier they began to fight for Emily, the better. All he wanted was to see Rachel truly happy. These days, her smile hardly reached her eyes no matter how many times he told her he loved her or she said the same to him.

He sighed again, weary from thinking about Rachel's sadness, and opened his Bible to read in order to try to silence his worries. He remained absorbed in his reading until he heard the door open. He looked up and an aching joy ran through him as Rachel walked in. Standing up quickly, he went to her and gathered her into his arms. After a few seconds, he stepped back, took her hands, and kissed each of her fingers, his heart flooding with love for her.

She smiled at him and said, "I can't believe that you're mine now. I always feel like I am still dreaming whenever I wake up in the morning and find you right next to me."

His pulse quickened as he gazed at her. "I can't believe you are mine either," he said. "Sometimes I'm afraid that I'll wake up and find out you aren't really married to me and it was all a dream."

She put her palm on his cheek and said softly, "That will never happen, Keith."

He wrapped his arms around her and kissed her again, his heart beating wildly.

For a long moment, he held her close, savoring the taste and feel of her lips as they kissed. They separated for a brief moment and then he took her lips again and kissed her deeply, trying to show her through his kisses just how much he treasured her, how much she meant to him. When they separated again, he brushed his nose against hers and then went to take his seat.

She sat across from him and leaned forward with her elbows resting on his desk. She looked into his eyes and asked, "How are you doing?"

He grinned. "Great, as usual. I went to inspect the new church building again today. I'm so excited, Rachel. In a few months we will be able to hold church services there. It's what I've been dreaming and praying about for years. A place of worship big enough to hold every single person in Destiny if need be."

"I know," Rachel said, and took his hand. "I can't wait to see you standing in the pulpit in a suit to dedicate the church to the Lord."

He raised his eyebrows. "A suit? I don't know about that. I didn't even wear a suit on our wedding day."

She smiled. "Yes, but we had an informal wedding. I think a church dedication is a formal occasion."

"Maybe a white button-up shirt and pants. Not a suit."

"No, you will wear a suit," Rachel said, laughing. "At least for that day. After that you can wear whatever you want."

He chuckled and looked up thoughtfully. "You know what, Rachel? We have to start planning for the dedication ceremony now. I suspect it will probably be in about two to three months' time." She nodded with a smile on her lips, and he said to her, "Look at me going on about the church and my dreams. I haven't even asked how your day has been. I could hear you singing along with the kids when I came into the house. You all seemed like you were having a great time... as always."

The smile on her face suddenly melted away, and he groaned inwardly. *Great, Keith. You've reminded her of Emily again and now she's sad.* He squeezed her hand and said, "I'm so sorry, Rachel. I didn't mean to remind you about..."

"No!" she cut in. "It's okay, Keith. I'll be fine."

He was not sure about that. He searched her eyes, her face, while trying to figure out what exactly he could say that would make her feel better. "I was planning to call the lawyer after reading my Bible for advice concerning filing for sole custody, but I think we will have a good chance of winning when the case goes to court."

Rachel sighed loudly. "Are you sure, Keith? It all scares me. I mean, I can't wait to have Emily in my arms again, but almost every night I dream that Mike was given sole custody of Emily in the court and that he's disappeared with her to an unknown place." Rachel's face clouded up. "And then I never see her again. If that happens, I don't know how I'll be able to go on." She bowed her head.

Keith immediately stood up and went to her. He crouched beside her and wrapped his arms around her. "That will never happen, Rachel. I promise."

She raised her head and looked at him. "But how do you know it will never happen? Mike has all the money to hire the best lawyers, and he has all the resources of Fallow Creek at his disposal."

"I just do," he said. "And Mike might have all that, but we have the Lord on our side." He smiled as he studied her face even though he was hurting for her. He spoke with more confidence than he felt. "This is what will happen. We'll file for sole custody and we'll win the case in as short a time as possible, and then Emily will come here to live with us. She will grow up in Destiny where she will be free to be and do whatever she wants."

Rachel smiled sadly. "Apart from being separated permanently from my daughter, the other thing I fear the most is her growing up in a place like Fallow Creek. I can't stand the thought of her living in a place where women are looked down on, their gifts and talents stifled, and their lives only dedicated to sleeping with and producing children for men with multiple wives. I don't want that for her."

"And that will not be her life, Rachel," Keith said. "She will grow up here with us and have a great life, I promise."

For the first time in a long while, Rachel gave him a smile that reached her eyes as she leaned in and kissed him. He pulled her up from her seat and held her close as they kissed again. He blinked when someone cleared their throat behind him. When Rachel pulled away, he turned around and smiled at the sheepish look on Rachel's assistant's face.

"Billy is crying," Alice said, looking at Rachel. "I tried to comfort him, but he wants only you."

Rachel looked up at the clock on the wall and then looked at Keith. "It's time for me to go already." She held out her hand and he took it. He squeezed it and then said, "I'll see you in a few hours, sweetie."

After she left his office, Keith sighed and picked up his phone. They had to file for custody now. They already had enough advice from the lawyer on what to expect when they filed and how to improve their chances of winning. He dialed the lawyer's number and waited as the phone rang and rang. "Great!" he said when the lawyer did not pick up. He dropped his phone on the table in annoyance and looked out the window. He would have to try the lawyer in about an hour.

He stood up and went to the window to watch the construction workers who were rebuilding his neighbors' house just down the road. Rob and Trina's home had already been rebuilt before they'd come back from Trina's parents' place in Denver. They'd returned to Destiny immediately after Keith had called to tell them that the house had been rebuilt.

Keith turned away from the window again. Destiny was mostly back to its former self. Though a mix of conflicting emotions warred in his mind right now, he could not help feeling overwhelmingly hopeful about the present and the future. He could see him and Rachel growing old here with Emily and the other children that the Lord would bless them with in due time. He could just imagine how Rachel would look when they were old and grey. She would be even more beautiful to him.

The few months they had spent together as man and wife, despite the sadness about Emily, had been magical. He could only imagine how beautiful and joyful the coming years living here with her would be. He was married to the woman he loved more than life itself and he lived in the town that had his heart. In spite of all that was going on right now, he could not help feeling like the luckiest... no... the most blessed man in all the world.

TWO

Rachel closed her Bible and sat up on her bed. She closed her eyes and began to pray. She prayed about the scripture she had read, asking the Lord to help her lock the word in her heart and make it a daily part of her life. She prayed about the children that she watched during the day, asking the Lord to bless every single one of them and their parents, and thanking the Lord for giving her a job that she loved so much. With a smile on her lips, she prayed for Keith, who was still in his small office near the kitchen preparing for his sermon tomorrow. She thanked the Lord for bringing them together and for the astounding joy their marriage brought her, and then asked the Lord to protect him always.

Finally, with a heavy heart, she prayed for Emily. She asked the Lord to watch over her, to ensure that Emily would always be well taken care of, that their court case would be successful, and that she and Keith would ultimately be able to get full custody of her.

She opened her eyes and turned to look at the

door as she yearned for Keith. He was taking much longer than usual to come to bed. She tossed the covers aside and got out of bed, ready to go to his office to get him, and then smiled when he appeared at the door. He looked really tired and she held out her hands to him. When he immediately came to her, she wrapped her arms around him. She kissed his cheek and asked, "How is your sermon coming along?"

He gave her a weary smile. "It's coming along," he said.

She looked at him and immediately knew there was something on his mind that he was not telling her. Even though they had only known each other for less than a year, she knew him well enough to know exactly what it was. Sadness filled her heart. She was grateful for him; grateful for how concerned he was about her because he loved her so much. But she hated the fact that she was the cause of his constant worries. He looked like he had spent more time in his office worrying than he had studying for his sermon. He had the same look on his face now that he'd had during their time together this afternoon, when he'd thought he was the cause of her sadness because he had reminded her of Emily. He carried so much of her fears and burdens; those that she shared with him and those that she didn't, which he still found out somehow.

"Keith, I know you're worried about me. But you shouldn't be. I told you. I'll be fine."

"I know, Rachel. But knowing how troubled you are about Emily, I feel as though I can't rest until we finally have her with us."

She sighed sadly. "I feel the same way, but we'll

have to try to live as normally as possible while we trust in God that the custody case will go in our favor."

He nodded as he changed out of his clothes into his pajamas. He headed toward the bathroom and said over his shoulder, "I called the lawyer today."

She said nothing and climbed back into bed, waiting for him to finish brushing his teeth and come back to the bedroom. When he did, she gave him a smile as he climbed into bed beside her. She propped up a pillow against the headboard and they sat side by side, leaning their backs against the pillow.

His eyes studied hers. "You didn't ask me what the lawyer said."

"I already know he didn't say anything or you would have told me by now," she said, sighing.

He nodded. "I couldn't reach him, but I'll try again tomorrow."

She blinked back the tears threatening to fall down her cheeks and then snuggled up to Keith for comfort.

He said nothing more but held her tightly and kissed her; it was his way of trying to comfort her, to let her know that everything would be alright.

They stayed in each other's arms until minutes later when she looked up at his face. His eyes were closed and he was breathing deeply, clearly fast asleep. She slowly pulled away from him, careful not to wake him, and sat up again. Studying his face, she could not resist gently running her fingers through his hair. She kissed him lightly on his nose and whispered, "I love you with all my heart." Tears welled up in her eyes. He had tried to comfort her before he slept, but unfortunately her heart was still heavy, just as it was on the occasions when she allowed herself to obsess over Emily. The decision to start the custody battle now already brought her daughter constantly to the forefront of her mind, and she lived minute to minute, continually thinking about Emily, agonizing over the fact that her baby daughter was growing up without her.

Knowing it would be impossible to fall asleep now, she got out of bed slowly, still trying to make sure she didn't wake Keith up. She picked up her Bible from beside her pillow, walked to the bedroom door, and turned off the light.

In the living room, she settled down on the sofa and opened her Bible to read. Keith's close relationship with the Lord when she'd first met him had caused her to seek out the same for herself. Now that they were married, she watched him as he prayed passionately and fellowshipped with the Lord, and she tried to do the same. As a result, she had grown in leaps and bounds in her walk with God in spite of the wearying sadness over her daughter. Keith's encouraging words, as well as the words the Lord spoke to her during her daily Bible study, were the two things that got her through each day.

She continued reading her Bible from where she had stopped before she went to bed. A few weeks after she and Keith got married, she'd started reading the Bible from the very beginning, reading one to several chapters a day. Now she was in the book of Romans. She continued to read the eighth chapter, this time trying to memorize some of the scriptures that spoke to her heart.

Halfway through, she shook her head, sighed heavily, and closed her Bible. She could not stop thinking about the day she was taken to that Restoration House. The way Emily's face had looked. It was the last day she'd seen her daughter.

Emily was too young to understand everything that had gone on at that time or to know why her mother had been away, but the sheer joy on her little face when Rachel had woken up in Fallow Creek to find her on the bed had shown how much her daughter had missed her. At that point, she had only been away from Emily for a short time. Now, she hadn't seen her daughter in months. Rachel's greatest fear was that Emily would forget about her, and that her ex's wife, Olivia, or whoever else he decided to "marry," would take her place.

"Lord, please don't let that ever happen," she whispered brokenly.

Anger began to boil in her heart against her ex, Mike, for everything he had done to her and, most of all, for separating her from Emily.

"I hate him!" she said. It was not the first time she had felt burning anger toward Mike. She was constantly angry with him because he was the cause of all this sadness. She silently cursed the day she had met him and she cursed the day her mother had taken her and her brother to Fallow Creek. By the grace of God, when she won the custody case and Emily came to live with her and Keith, it would be the last time she would ever have to see Mike or any of the people in Fallow Creek. She would expunge them from her heart and her thoughts, and it would be as though she never knew any of the people there or ever lived in Fallow Creek.

Except for her brother, Taylor, every other person in that community, and the place itself, would be dead to her.

"Daughter, forgive!"

Rachel's mouth flew open and her heart began to beat in fear. *Who on earth said that? Was it the Lord, or have I started hearing things?* She looked at the entrance to the living room to see if Keith had stepped in, but she saw no one. Besides, that voice was not his.

She took a deep breath to try to calm herself and stood up from the sofa. She was probably tired and that was why she was hearing things.

The audible voice said again, *"Rachel, daughter, forgive Mike and all the people who wronged you in Fallow Creek."*

Rachel's jaw dropped and she slowly sat down on the sofa again. This time she knew she wasn't making up the voice. It was not a voice she'd ever heard before nor could she make it up. It sounded otherworldly and yet familiar. It reverberated on the inside of her and yet came from the outside also.

Her body began to tingle with both fear and excitement. She had never heard God's voice. Was that what she had just heard or something else? As much as she felt thrilled to hear God's voice so loudly and clearly, a part of her didn't want it to be His voice. She knew what the scripture said about forgiveness. She just wasn't ready to fully extend that to Mike or any of the people in Fallow Creek who'd had a hand in separating her from Emily.

And yet she could not shake the feeling of absolute certainty that the voice was indeed the Lord's and that He was asking her to forgive everyone who had hurt her.

She whispered, "Lord, I know you want me to forgive, but I don't know how." She sighed. How could she ever forgive Mike? And even if she wanted to, it would be hard, especially now that they were about to file the custody case. They would have to testify against Mike and point out how unsuitable he was to raise Emily.

She nearly jumped out of her skin when the voice said, *I want you to drop that custody case. Move with Keith to Fallow Creek.*

She leaned back in her seat, took deep breaths, and shook her head at the absurdity of the words she was hearing. If not for how scared she was, she would have laughed. This time, she knew she was imagining it all, because this could not be the Lord's voice. There was no way God would tell her and Keith to move to Fallow Creek.

And yet, as doubts ran through her mind, her skin began to tingle again with the presence of God. A supernatural peace settled in her heart. Again, she heard the instruction to move to Fallow Creek, but in her heart this time, and she knew without a doubt that it was God who was speaking to her.

Months ago, she'd had to make a decision between staying in Fallow Creek with Mike, which would result in her being allowed to stay with Emily, or leaving the town and her daughter so she could honor God. It had been an excruciating decision, especially as she had thought Keith was dead, but she had ultimately chosen to obey and honor God. She'd believed that someday she and Emily would be reunited, but the last thing she would ever have expected was for God to ask her to move back there… and with Keith.

She whispered, "Lord, you know I can't move back to Fallow Creek, and I especially can't move there with Keith. It's impossible. I want to get my daughter out of that place, not move back there."

She was breathing hard as she listened again to what the Lord would say to her. She waited for a minute, and then ten minutes, and then another ten minutes, but she heard nothing. After almost an hour of waiting, she finally stood up from the sofa. She slowly walked back to the bedroom, thinking about the words she had heard. She whispered as she went, "I can't move back to Fallow Creek. It's impossible!"

But if it was the Lord who had really spoken to her, and she was quite sure it was, she could not disobey. She was in a bind once more, just as she'd been all those months ago when she'd had to make that difficult decision. She had been so sure the Lord wanted her and Keith in Destiny. She had a job that she loved and finally the church that Keith had dreamt of for so long was almost finished. They both felt like they were right in the center of God's will for their lives. And Destiny had Keith's heart and soul. There was no way he would ever move away from his beloved hometown.

She felt dazed as she lay in bed once more beside Keith. The words she'd heard an hour ago now felt even more absurd as she stretched out beside him. How was it possible that the Lord would ask them to move to Fallow Creek, of all places? Many of the things done there were completely against what she and Keith believed in. Besides, she had been banished from the town. There was no way they would let her come back to live among them. And definitely not with a new husband. Having lived in Fallow Creek most of her life, she knew it would be an affront to the men there to bring a new husband into the community. Women were not allowed to do such things.

Words began to form in her mind, and she frowned at the strangeness of it all. In her mind's eye, she saw the words, *Your destiny is tied to Fallow Creek. I have called you and Keith to be a light in the midst of the darkness there.*

She bit her lip as the words settled on her and around her, overwhelming her. It was the strangest feeling she'd ever had; nothing had even come close. Even though they were not words she wanted to hear, not a shred of doubt remained in her heart that it was the Lord who was speaking to her. But still, she wasn't sure how she could bring herself to tell Keith that the Lord was asking them to move to a place like Fallow Creek. And if she told him, he might think she was so distressed about being away from her baby that she had unknowingly made it all up so she could be with her daughter again.

She turned her face to the wall and prayed in her heart. *Lord, you know how strange these words are and how weird it all feels. Please, Lord, if these words are really from you, and if this is what you want Keith and I to do, then please speak to Keith yourself.* She bit her lip again. Moving to Fallow Creek would be the very last thing on his mind. It had probably never even crossed his mind, especially now that she was with him and they were married. Rachel whispered, "If you speak to him about it, it would be a clear sign to me that these words are truly from you."

She listened, but heard nothing more. She sighed and prayed in her heart again. *Also, Lord, you know I was banished from the town. If you are the one speaking to me about this, you have to make a way for me to be allowed back to the town with Keith.* It would take a miracle to reverse the elders' decision and let her move back to the town with a husband that was not Mike.

She thought again about what the Lord had said moments ago. She and Keith were called to be a light in the midst of the darkness in Fallow Creek and their destinies were tied with the town's. The only joy she got from thinking about it all was that if indeed it was the Lord and if Keith agreed for them to move to Fallow Creek, she would have the chance to see Emily again. And yet, living in Fallow Creek was the last thing she wanted for herself or her daughter.

She turned around and faced Keith. She could not see his face well enough in the darkness, but still she reached out her hand and touched his hair. He stirred, and she smiled when he pulled her closer. She buried her face in his chest, but she already felt sorry for him. If the Lord did speak to him about moving, he would have to leave this town that he loved so much. And he would be moving to a place of which she had spoken nothing but ill; a place she despised and which he did too after all she'd told him. "I'm so sorry for bringing this on you," she whispered.

He stirred again. "Are you still awake, Rachel?"

"Oh, sorry, Keith. Did I wake you up?"

"It's okay. Get some sleep, honey," he said in a soothing voice. He ran his hand down her back. "We have to wake up early for service."

"I know," she said softly. If he knew what was going on in her heart right now, the words that the Lord had spoken to her, he would not be asking her to go to sleep now. She smiled sadly. His world was about to change completely, and hers too, if all she had heard was from the Lord. She only hoped that he would not resent her for it, because she knew one thing for sure: moving away from Destiny to somewhere else, no matter where it was, would be very hard on Keith. Moving to the place where the man who had tried to kill him lived and where she had gone through so much would be excruciating. And yet, that was exactly what they would have to do if indeed she had heard the Lord's voice.

In spite of what she knew for sure, that the voice she had heard was God's, she still hoped and prayed it wasn't. Because she wanted nothing more than for her new husband to be happy, and leaving Destiny would make him very miserable.

She tossed and turned, unable to find sleep, too worried to relax. She finally told herself that the only answer to this was to surrender completely to the Lord. A moment later, she nodded off.

THREE

The road Keith walked on was unfamiliar and yet familiar at the same time. It was a long stretch of road with no houses on either side, only sand and sparse grass. He kept walking, confused by how much the place looked familiar when he was sure he had never been here before. A blue Volkswagen crawled by, and a man with a bushy beard and brows popped his head out of the window. "Where are you headed?" the man asked Keith.

"To the border," Keith said. He frowned after he had spoken. He didn't even know where he was, and now he was talking about heading to the border.

"Get in," the man said. "I'll take you there."

Keith got into the front seat and buckled his seatbelt. He thanked the man and looked out the window as the stranger began to drive once again. Keith turned around to look at the man who had picked him up, and it was on the tip of his tongue to ask how far the border was, but he found he already knew. What was more, he knew exactly why he was heading to the border.

They passed by a big house with a red roof, and Keith blinked when he realized he knew who owned that house. It was a man named Dennis Hamilton. How he knew that, he wasn't quite sure.

His heart began to race when he spotted a group of young men in fatigues a short distance away. Their black SUVs were blocking the road ahead and they were staring at the Volkswagen he was in. The bearded man beside him did not seem as though he had spotted the men.

Keith turned to face the bearded stranger and said, "Those men there in fatigues... they are blocking the road. I don't think we'll be allowed to pass."

The man did not seem bothered at all.

"Aren't you going to slow down?" Keith asked.

"Why should I?" the man said. "It's just the security squad team ahead."

Keith shook his head as he stared at the man. He looked totally unconcerned. In fact, he seemed almost happy, as though the men in fatigues who were holding rifles were actually there to welcome them into the town.

They reached the men, and from the looks on their faces, they were not happy to see Keith and the stranger. The men gathered around the Volkswagen and stared intently at Keith, ignoring the bearded man beside him. "Where are you going?" one of the young men asked.

Keith did not know what to answer because he did not know where he was going or why. They had reached the border now and he wasn't sure why he wanted to enter the town ahead or where he was coming from. He asked the first thing that came to mind. "Where am I?"

The men looked at each other and then looked at Keith as though he had lost his mind. "You don't know where you are?" asked the man who had asked him where he was going. "This is Fallow Creek."

Keith's jaw dropped. Maybe that was why this place seemed so familiar. Rachel had told him a lot about it. So, these men were the infamous security squad guards that she had told him all about. He certainly didn't want to go into the town. He faced the bearded man beside him and told him he wanted to turn back.

The guard he'd been talking with shook his head and said, "You can't turn back anymore. You belong in Fallow Creek now."

Keith wanted to scream. Angry, he said to them, "I don't belong here. I live in a town called Destiny. I could never live here."

The men looked at each other, and then the one that seemed to be their leader said, "Fallow Creek is now your destiny." The men surrounded the Volkswagen.

Keith was getting more and more anxious to turn back. He shouted at them and told them to make way so they could drive away from here, but the men did not listen. His heart started racing and sweat began to run down his face. From what Rachel had told him, this was not the sort of place he wanted to live, and especially not without Rachel.

He argued vehemently, telling the men to give way so they could pass, but the men refused to listen, insisting that he was meant to be here. The more he argued with them, the more insistent they became. And then they suddenly started as someone... no, two people wearing jeans and white t-shirts began to approach. He noticed the woman looked familiar, and then his mouth flew open. It was Rachel, coming toward him with another man. He could not believe it. Her arms were wrapped tightly around the man. Keith turned angrily to the man she was with and his heart sank to his feet. It was *himself.*

"Lord, what is happening?" he whispered, unable to breathe properly.

The man... the *other Keith...* and Rachel came to stand beside the Volkswagen and stared at him through the window. "This is where you belong, Keith," they said. "This is your destiny."

"No, it can't be," he said. He turned to Rachel. "You of all people know how bad this place is. Surely, you don't want to live here."

The other Keith said to him, "This is where you are meant to be."

Keith opened his mouth to yell at him and then jerked awake. He gasped and looked around. He was in his tiny office at home, safely in Destiny. He had fallen asleep with his head resting on his desk, but the dream he'd just had seemed so real. And even now that he was awake, it still felt real.

Get yourself together, Keith! he chided himself, and then took a deep breath as his racing heart began to calm down.

He still could not shake the dream even now that he felt calmer. It was strange how real it felt. He rubbed his face with his hand, his heart beginning to race again as details of the dream flashed through his mind. "Lord, what could this dream mean?" he asked, and gasped when a small voice whispered in his ear, "It means your destiny is in Fallow Creek. I want you and Rachel to move to Fallow Creek and be a light for the people there."

"What?" Keith stood up from his chair. He had heard the Lord's voice enough times to know it was Him who was speaking, but he had never heard something so ridiculous. Still, he could not deny that the dream he'd had and the clear words he now heard, though strange, were from God.

He began to shake his head as he paced his tiny office, troubled. "Lord, no, no, no! My destiny is here. Right here in Destiny. I can't leave this town, especially for a place like Fallow Creek. And I can't take Rachel back there."

He heard nothing else and groaned. How could the Lord tell him to take Rachel back to that place? How could the Lord ask him to leave everything here — the church that he was pastoring, his grandmother's house, his friends, and the people of Destiny as a whole?

Last year, when he couldn't continue building the new church because of lack of finances, he had wondered about his future as a minister. When the hurricane destroyed both the old church and the new uncompleted church building, he'd thought he had lost his ministry for sure. Now that the new church was nearly complete and Destiny was being rebuilt, he was starting to feel like he was in the center of God's will. There was no better time to be in Destiny; to enjoy the town and relish everything he had prayed about for so long. Why would he abandon the town for somewhere like Fallow Creek?

He felt as though the Lord was playing tricks on him. At any moment, the Lord would tell him He was just joking! But he had still heard nothing more from God half an hour later.

He sat down once more and asked the Lord to take away this call to go to Fallow Creek. "Please send someone else, Lord," he pleaded. "I'm sure there's another couple who are at this time asking you to show them what their purpose in life is and who would be willing to go to Fallow Creek. Please send them and not me and Rachel."

He closed his eyes, repeating the plea he'd just made to the Lord. That was not the way the Lord worked, he knew, but he couldn't help praying that way. Anguish filled his heart. Destiny was his hometown. The place he had imagined growing old in with his wife, surrounded by their kids and grandkids. He'd never imagined living somewhere else.

The thought of telling Rachel that they would be moving to a place like Fallow Creek, a place where she had been forced to live as a sister wife and had gone through so much misery, struck him as insane. How on earth was he going to tell her that the Lord wanted them to move there?

He put his head down on the table and groaned again. Maybe he would do nothing about it. He would tell Rachel nothing and hope it all went away — the memory of the dream, the voice calling them to move, this burning certainty he felt in his heart that it was all from God.

He stood up once more, wanting to get away from God's presence. He needed to leave the house now. He needed to be out on the streets of Destiny.

He began to make his way to the door but stopped as it opened. Rachel walked in, and he had to stifle another groan.

"What is it, love?" she asked, standing at the door and staring at him. "What's wrong?"

He went to sit down again and glanced at his wristwatch. It was twelve fifteen, the time Rachel usually came into his office to see him. For the first time since they'd gotten married, he did not want to be with her right now. He was afraid that his dream and the words he had heard from God would spill out from his lips because he had never hidden anything from her. It was the last thing he wanted to happen, especially now. She had enough worries. If he told her about what he'd heard God say, she would be terribly upset.

Rachel sat across from him, her eyes on his. "Tell me what's wrong, Keith."

He forced a smile. "It's nothing. I'm just slightly worried about the progress of the new church building."

She raised her brows and said, "You are worried about the progress of the church building? But you told me a few days ago that you were happy about the way things were going and that the church would be completed in just a few months."

He put his hand on his forehead and murmured, "I did say that, didn't I?"

"Yes, you did." Rachel chuckled. "It's okay, Keith. Stop worrying. I'm sure the church will be finished just at the right time, and then the pastor can dedicate the church."

He raised his head and looked at her, frowning. "The pastor?"

She had a strange look on her face and her frown deepened. "Umm... I meant you, Keith... maybe."

He stared at her for a few seconds and said slowly, "Rachel, what do you mean, 'maybe'?" He studied her face, looking deeply into her eyes. She looked uncomfortable. Without a doubt, she was keeping something from him. He leaned back in his seat and folded his arms across his chest. "Rachel, baby, you're hiding something from me. What is it?"

She looked away and he leaned forward again, his eyes fixed on her. "Rachel, tell me. What is it? What's wrong?"

His heart began to race. The dream was fresh in his mind and he still worried about the words the Lord had spoken to him, but the look on Rachel's face worried him even more. There was something wrong. Something really wrong.

He got up from his seat and went to her. Lifting her from hers, he searched her eyes, trying to figure out what it was. Finally, he said, "You know we're not supposed to hide anything from each other," and immediately felt guilty. Wasn't he hiding something from her? He had made up his mind not to tell her about the strange dream and what God had told him concerning moving to Fallow Creek. There was no way he could hide anything from her. He had to tell her about it. He would let her know he did not expect her to move, but then again, knowing that the voice came from God, he wasn't sure how that was going to work. Right now, though, he had to first find out what exactly was wrong with her.

She looked into his eyes and pressed her lips together. "Keith, I have something to tell you. It's something that will sound really crazy..." she sighed loudly, "and it might drive you crazy as well. But I have to tell you about it."

He gave her a sad smile and said, "I also have something to tell you, sweetie. You're not going to like what I have to say, but..." He shook his head. "But please, go on."

She said softly, "You go first, then."

"No, honey, I want to hear what you have to say first." He brushed her hair away from her face, kissed her forehead, and went to take his seat again.

She sat down on the chair facing him and took his hands on the table. From the look on her face, he knew she was finding it difficult to speak. He squeezed her hands encouragingly and waited.

She gave him a nervous smile and began. "A few nights ago, I couldn't sleep and so I went to the living room to read my Bible and pray."

In spite of the seriousness of the moment, he chuckled. "Was that the day I woke up to find you staring at me and then asked why you were not asleep?"

"Yes," she said with a nod, and then smiled and arched her brows. "I was staring at you? It was dark. How did you know that?"

"I felt your stare," he said. "Please go on."

"Anyway, I began to read my Bible because I was so worried about Emily and the upcoming custody case, and then I heard the strangest thing, Keith. When I tell you, you might not believe it. At the time, I was sure the words I heard were from God, but now I am not so sure. Maybe I made it all up... though it really sounded like it was from the Lord then." She looked up with a thoughtful expression and looked at him again. "The experience I had still feels so real."

Keith's heart drummed as she spoke. What was she going to tell him? He felt like he could already guess what she was about to say, but he hoped he was wrong. He wanted to tell her that it did not matter anymore what she was keeping from him and that she did not need to tell him anything. But he knew he had to let her talk.

She continued. "I was praying about everything and then thinking about Mike and how much he had hurt me, and as usual I was angry at him. Really angry. And then I heard a voice." She stopped talking and her eyes searched his as though to try to find some confirmation in them that she wasn't crazy.

He could not breathe. He knew what she was going to tell him.

She went on. "I heard an audible voice telling me to forgive Mike and drop the custody case. And then, Keith, the voice told me something so absurd you wouldn't even imagine. It said we were both supposed to leave Destiny and move to Fallow Creek… to be a light in the darkness there."

Keith shut his eyes, overwhelming sadness settling on him. "Lord, no. Please, no." But there was no denying it. The Lord had spoken to him and to Rachel separately and in a way that left no doubt that He was the one speaking. If they decided to ignore His voice, it would be plain disobedience. He felt like screaming in outrage, but he held himself together. For Rachel's sake.

She stared at him with a surprised expression on her face. "Keith, did you hear what I just said?"

He nodded.

"And you're not surprised or in disbelief? Why? And why are you not saying anything?"

He threaded his fingers through hers and said slowly, "Because I know, Rachel."

She raised her brows, staring quizzically at him. "What do you mean?"

"The Lord just spoke to me about it now." He began to tell her about the dream and then about the explanation the Lord gave him concerning it when he woke up.

When he finished speaking, she briefly shut her eyes and said, "So, it's from the Lord, then. I asked Him to confirm it by speaking to you about it and He did." Tears slipped down her cheeks as she spoke.

He stood up once more, took her hands, and gently lifted her out of her chair. Wiping away the tears from her face, he hugged her tightly and said, "I don't know why the Lord would ask us to leave Destiny and move to Fallow Creek, of all places, but He knows best."

"I'm so sorry, Keith," Rachel said. "It's all my fault. If it wasn't for me, the Lord would not ask you to move to that awful place."

Her head was bowed as he drew slightly back from her, and he tilted her chin so she could look at him again. "Don't ever say that again," he said fiercely. "We are one now. It's not your fault. Why would you blame yourself?"

She opened her mouth to speak, but he shook his head. "We're in this together," he said. "If the Lord is asking us to move to Fallow Creek, then I believe he has a great plan for both of us. He wouldn't ask us to go there if He didn't." Keith continued to whisper encouraging words to her, but he didn't even know if he believed anything he was saying.

"But Fallow Creek can be a dangerous place," Rachel said. "I lived there for almost all my life. At best it will be terribly inhospitable, and at worst our lives would be in danger. Also, I have been banished from the town. I don't know how I can move back there when I'm not even allowed in."

He ran his hands down her arms and took her hands in his. "At least you'll get to see Emily again."

She shook her head. "You don't understand the way that town is. I might not be allowed to see her, especially when I show up with a new husband. Women aren't allowed to do that at all. Men get new wives, not the other way around."

He shrugged. "So, this time you did something different. Maybe that is part of what God meant about shining our lights into the darkness there."

She sighed. "I vowed never to step foot in Fallow Creek again, except maybe to get Emily to come live with us."

"You know, Rachel, since you were banished from that place, I guess the Lord will have to perform a miracle in order for us to be able to stay there. If he does, and we're allowed to stay in Fallow Creek, then I'm sure he will do more for us." As much as the thought of moving to Fallow Creek caused him agony and assailed him with a myriad of doubts, he knew he had to hold himself together and speak encouraging words to Rachel. "Everything will be okay. I'm sure of it."

"Keith, you are forever optimistic."

"No, Rachel. Not optimistic. Trusting. I choose

to believe in God's unceasing faithfulness."

She gazed at him for a long moment and said, "I want to be like you when I grow up."

He chuckled and gently caressed her cheek with the back of his hand. "I love you just the way you are." He chuckled again. "Never change."

She smiled and then her expression turned sober again. "Seriously, Keith, this is not good, not good at all. We are supposed to move to Fallow Creek!"

He knew exactly how she felt. He still could not imagine himself moving away from Destiny. But now that they knew without a doubt that the Lord wanted them to move to Fallow Creek, there was no point mourning over it. Their complaining would not change God's mind. The only thing he could do now was encourage Rachel and himself. Before he could say anything, though, she spoke. "Did the Lord tell you when we are supposed to move?"

"No, He didn't. Did He tell you?"

She shook her head.

"Well then," he grinned. "Let's just hope that the Lord takes His sweet time in telling us."

She snorted and he chuckled along with her. It felt good to laugh when they were both clearly out of sorts, but her mirth soon died as she looked at him. "Just look at us laughing at something so serious. I feel utterly devastated."

Her eyes welled up again, and he shook his head and placed his hands on her shoulders. "Rachel, please don't cry. Remember that we have to trust that God always has a perfect plan for us. We'll be fine."

"But how can you say that?" She stepped away from him. "You'll have to leave this town that you love, your grandmother's house, the church. Everything. Doesn't that scare you?"

His heart thudded, but he refused to give in to his fears because it would accomplish nothing. "Yes, but we are following the Lord on our way to our destiny, and that is the greatest adventure anyone could ever hope for."

She reached out and took hold of his hands. "You're the greatest man that I have ever met. What would I do without you? I love the way you trust the Lord in everything, and that is the way I want to be, too."

He held her closely, but his heart ached as he thought about moving away from his beloved Destiny. If Rachel knew how frightened he was, how uncertain, she would not say what she'd just said about him. He was simply holding together because of her. Like she'd told him months before they got married, they had each other and the Lord, and that was all that mattered. At least that was all that should matter now. He might not get to continue to live in the town he grew up in and loved, but he would still continue to live with Rachel. No matter where he made his home, she would be there with him. She was his home and his life now.

FOUR

Taylor Dalton opened the door to the pharmacy and walked in. He began to make his way to the counter to get the medications he needed for his wife and stopped in his tracks when he spotted Andrew Lowery.

"No," he muttered. He backed away slowly and groaned when Andrew turned around.

Andrew gave him a hard look as Taylor reluctantly walked toward him. He got to the counter and forced a smile as he turned to Andrew. "I haven't seen you in a while, Andy. How are you?"

Andrew scowled at him. He was at least ten years older than Taylor, but they were friends — or at least they had been. "How do you think I am? I came here to get Sarah some medicine because she hasn't been feeling well. You haven't even bothered to ask about her in months. And now you still don't care to find out how she is doing."

Taylor groaned inwardly but said nothing.

"My wives are taking care of their children, and so I have to come here personally to get my daughter's medication. The least you could do is to ask about your wife-to-be. That is, if you're still planning to take Sarah as your wife."

"I'm sorry, Andy."

Andrew narrowed his eyes. "I don't need your apology. You showed all this interest in marrying my Sarah. You let her become all worked up about it because, according to her, she would be marrying the richest and most handsome man in Fallow Creek. It was all she could talk about for a long time. And then you suddenly stopped coming to the house or showing any interest in her. Sarah told me that she saw you around town a few times, but that you ignored her."

"If you would only allow me to explain," Taylor said. "You know my wife, Faye, is pregnant. She's been having a very difficult pregnancy, and so I didn't think it was appropriate at this time to marry a second wife."

Andrew stared at him as though he had lost his mind. "What does your wife's difficult pregnancy have to do with marrying Sarah? Besides, I would think as your wife isn't well, you would need another woman to take care of you and your son."

Taylor looked away. As much as he and Faye were not exactly in love, he did love her in his own way and had some decency in him. This was not the best time to add to Faye's discomfort by marrying a second wife. He knew none of that mattered to most of the men in this community, but he just couldn't bring himself to act that way. Maybe it was because he hadn't been born here. To him, it was just basic thoughtfulness to wait until his wife delivered safely before he thought about marrying

Sarah.

"You have nothing to say, do you?" Andrew said.

Taylor faced Andrew again and looked him in the eye. "I promise, Andy. Once Faye safely gives birth to our baby, the wedding plans will start again."

Andrew glared at Taylor before grabbing his bag of medicine and walking out of the pharmacy.

Taylor quickly bought the medicine the midwife had prescribed for Faye and left the pharmacy. On the short walk back to his house, he thought about Sarah and his plans to marry her some months ago. But that was before Faye became pregnant. He'd married Faye six years ago because she was a friend's sister. His friend, Mark, had thought they would be a great match. Since he wasn't into any particular woman at the time and many in the community were breathing down his neck about getting a wife, he thought there was no harm in it and married Faye. Faye was just two years younger than he was. They'd gotten married when he was twenty-four, and she twenty-two.

Sarah, on the other hand, was much younger and had personally shown her interest in him the first time he'd gone to Andrew's home. Because at the time he and Andrew were involved in a business deal, he had been preoccupied and had not paid her much attention. But Andrew had noticed and had pushed her toward Taylor. She was young, pretty, and vivacious, but when Andrew had told Taylor that she would make him a great wife, he had not been too excited about taking a second wife. He wasn't sure why, especially since many men his age in this community had at least two wives. Many of them had even pushed their sisters and daughters towards him. Maybe it was because, for some reason, he'd always believed it would not be fair to Faye.

But he'd agreed to Andrew's suggestion because he liked the man. They had a good business and personal relationship. Besides, Sarah was beautiful. He'd decided to make a go of it, but when Faye became pregnant and they were told it was a high-risk pregnancy, he couldn't bring himself to go on with the wedding plans. But he understood Andrew's anger. His mind was made up. As soon as Faye gave birth to their child, he would go ahead and marry Sarah.

He got to his house and found his five-year-old son, Joshua, playing outside with their neighbors' child. Josh immediately ran up to him, and Taylor hugged him. "Is your mother still asleep?" Taylor asked.

Josh shrugged, and Taylor shook his head and smiled down at his son. When Josh went back to his playmate, Taylor entered the house. He climbed the marble stairs and went to the bedroom he shared with his wife. She was still lying on the bed, fast asleep. The midwife had told them she had to be on bed rest for the few months leading up to her due date. Usually Rebecca, their efficient housekeeper who cooked their meals and got whatever they needed, also attended to Faye, especially on days like this when Faye was too tired to do anything. But today was Rebecca's day off. She came every day except on Sundays. He sat down on the bed beside Faye and touched her shoulder. He gently woke her and smiled when she sat up.

"I've bought your medicine, Faye," he said. "I'll go and get you some food so you can eat and then take it."

Faye smiled weakly. "Thank you," she said. "What would I do without you?" She looked past him. "Where is Josh?"

"He's outside playing with his little friend, Ben."

Faye nodded and lay back down on the bed.

"No, Faye. Sit up. I'll go and get your food. After you've eaten and taken your medicine, you can go back to sleep."

Faye moaned. "I'm so tired, Taylor."

Fear and worry coursed through Taylor. He gently ran his fingers through her hair and touched her face. She looked so much paler and thinner than usual. She had been curvy and robust with health when he had married her and even up to six months ago. Now, despite being pregnant, the only weight she had gained was in her belly where their baby lived, unaware of how much suffering the baby in utero was causing his mother.

"Stop looking at me like that," she said to him.

"I'm worried about you," he told her.

"Stop worrying. I'll be fine and then you can marry your second wife."

He winced. He had not known that she'd paid attention to his marriage plans. He had told her nothing about it. Even though he knew she would eventually find out, because Fallow Creek was a tiny town, he didn't think she would mention it to him. Usually, most wives pretended they did not notice that their husbands were in the process of marrying an additional wife even if he had already married several before.

"It's okay, Taylor. I just want you to know it's okay with me," she said to him. "I know you are a bit reluctant to do so, but I don't mind."

Again, he searched her face. She certainly did not look like she did not mind. "I just want you to be completely well again before I ever think about marrying someone else."

"I know you are more than thinking about marrying someone else," she said to him. "You are already in the process of marrying Sarah Lowery."

There was mirth in her voice but also a hint of accusation. He said nothing.

"In the six years we have been together, you've been the perfect husband," she said to him. "Most men in this town would have at least one more wife by now. But not you."

He blurted out, "I am not a perfect husband!"

She took his hand. "To me you have been the perfect husband, Taylor. You're not like the other men in this town. You are the kindest and most thoughtful man I have ever met. I thank God every single day for giving me a man like you." She smiled mischievously. "You are a bae."

He raised his brows in confusion. "A bae?"

She chuckled. "A boo bae."

He frowned. "What does it all mean?"

"I am not sure myself, but I overheard Sarah Lowery and her young friends talking about you some months ago and that was what they called you. That was how I found out you were planning to marry Sarah." She chuckled again. "I think it means you are some kind of dazzling prince... or a tiny babe."

He shook his head. "It's amazing that as weak as you are you still have enough energy to make jokes."

She laughed softly.

"But I'm serious, Faye. I want you to get well and have our baby safely. Nothing else matters."

"And he said he is not the perfect husband," Faye whispered.

Guilt gripped him. In spite of her cheery attitude, he could see that the idea of him marrying another wife bothered her. But his mind was made up. He would marry Sarah once Faye had their baby safely. He'd already promised Sarah's father that he would, and Sarah was counting on him as well. Plus, most of the men in town were already wondering about him having only one wife, even though he had been married for six years.

Abruptly, he stood up and moved away from Faye. She looked like she was about to call him back, but he said, "Let me go and get your food," and hurried out of the room.

***

Lily Hunter stepped out of the Restoration House and looked up at the blue sky. It was a perfect day, neither hot nor cold. It was a great day to finally be released from the House after months of being held here and forcefully made to repeatedly recite quotations that were against all she believed, and scriptures that had been twisted and taken out of context.

For months, according to the tutors here, she had been unwilling to be "restored" or her mind "renewed." She'd been left in the House, chafing under the forceful imprisonment and all the brainwashing. But as she'd told Rachel Dalton some months ago, no one left the house, especially after staying for so long, without having their minds broken. It was only after she agreed to marry some man that her parents wanted her to wed did they agree to release her from this place.

She bit her lip as she made her way off the grounds of the Restoration House. She had promised herself and God that she would not get married, especially to someone she did not love, and definitely not to someone who was already married. It was why they had brought her in the first place. She had refused every suitor that came her way, knowing she loved none of them. Besides, some of them were already married.

But now, not only had she agreed to marry some mysterious man who her parents had arranged for her, she was almost sure the man was married to at least one wife. Her mother had mentioned something like that when she'd come to visit for the first time since Lily had arrived at the House. But she had been desperate to be released and had not even asked who it was or tried to find out how many wives the man had. Not like it mattered anyway if the man had one or several wives. She had broken the promise she'd made to herself and was going against everything she believed in. But she could not stand one more day in the House.

And you think living in some man's house you don't even love with several other wives will be better?

She sighed. None of the options were better. But she had decided that leaving the Restoration House would at least give her a chance to find a way to escape this terrible town. Rachel Dalton had escaped.

Lily smiled sadly as she walked through the gates. Rachel had not actually escaped… at least not the second time. That time she had been banished from the town, but still, that was what Rachel had wanted. She'd wanted not only to leave the Restoration House, but also to leave the town. Lily had heard what happened from a few of the women who had been talking in hushed tones in her room. One of her roommates had said, "I was shocked when I heard that a woman asked for a hearing with the elders and her request was granted."

Lily had probed one of the women who seemed to know a lot about it and was told that Rachel wanted her daughter to go with her but instead had been banned from ever setting foot in town and from ever seeing her daughter again.

Lily hurt for Rachel, but unlike her friend, Lily did not have a child to keep her here or worry about. Yes, it would be almost impossible to escape town, but she would try. For now, she had to head home and submit to her parents and their wedding preparations. Hopefully, she would find a way to escape before she actually got married to whatever man her parents were planning for her to wed. But if not, she would continue to make her plans until the right time came and she could successfully escape.

She trudged on, carrying her small bag with the few clothes and personal items that she'd been allowed to bring to the Restoration House.

She was passing by a house that was under construction when she noticed a man standing a few feet away, looking up at the unfinished house. The man looked familiar. When he turned in her direction, her stomach flipped. It was Taylor Dalton. When they were growing up as neighbors, she'd had a huge crush on him.

He was still as handsome as ever. If she was truthful to herself, she still had a crush on him. They had been friendly as kids because she was his younger sister's friend, but she had not spoken to him in years, even though she saw him a couple of times a year. She knew she had never lost her crush because every time she saw him, even though he didn't seem to remember who she was, her heart always skipped a beat. When she saw Rachel at the Restoration House, her mind had immediately gone to Taylor. And yet she knew the man was married. It was wrong for her to stand here, gawking at him.

He looked at her with a slight recognition in his eyes and she hurried away.

What were you thinking, gaping at him like that? She scolded herself. She put him firmly out of her mind and hastened her steps all the way to her parents' house.

She stood in front of the house she'd lived in all her life. She looked at the three-bedroom bungalow, so similar to many of the houses here, and groaned. If only women did not have to remain in their parents' homes until they were married. If only women were allowed to live alone, she would get a house of her own.

Get a house of my own? She chided herself. She did not even have a job — at least not a paid one. Women were not allowed to because it was not their role in the family.

Reluctantly, she entered the house and slowly sat down on the sofa. Thankfully, her parents were nowhere around. Her younger sister was already married and living a short drive away in her husband's house. She groaned when she heard heels clicking on the tiled floor. That had to be her mother's footsteps.

"Lily, you're back! I thought you would be released this evening."

Lily smirked. "Yes, Mom. I am back. They couldn't wait to get rid of me."

Mom snorted. She came and sat down next to Lily and searched her eyes. "I know you don't like the idea of marrying someone you say you don't love, but love grows in a marriage if…"

Lily cut in. "Not if it is shared between more than two people."

"That isn't true."

"Yes, it is. Most men don't have enough love for a single wife let alone sharing their affection with more than one."

Mom sighed and said, "I just want you to be happily married…"

"Please, Mom. Stop! I agreed to marry the man you said was interested in me, but please let us not pretend that it will be anything but a business contract between him and Father."

Mom frowned. "I don't understand you, Lily. I don't know where you got all these strange ideas."

Lily narrowed her eyes. "What strange ideas? The ideas in Fallow Creek are strange. In case you don't know, there are other people in this world who don't live in this weird town and don't believe the strange things we do."

Her mother tilted her head towards her and studied her face. After a short moment she said, "And how did you come to the conclusion that our ideas are strange and weird?"

Lily wanted to tell her mother that there was such a thing as the internet, but there was no point. Fallow Creek had Wi-Fi, but most people never connected to it because using the internet was generally frowned upon. So was watching TV, though some young people still watched secretly. In general, owning cell phones was also discouraged. The people who owned them were men the elders decided needed them for one reason or another. But there were also some young people who found a way to get them and a way to get on the internet.

Lily had grown up not watching TV and had not gotten a cell phone until three years ago, given to her by a good friend who'd had it smuggled in with the help of a security squad guard. The squad guard had also helped them connect to the internet. On there, she had learned many, many things. The more she learned, the more she wanted to be independent and free, and she knew in order to do that she had to leave Fallow Creek.

"I will leave this town someday soon," she mumbled.

"What did you say?" Her mother raised her brows and stared quizzically at her.

"Nothing! So, who is this man you're planning to marry me off to?" Lily asked, praying that somehow she was wrong and that the man was, at least, single.

Her mother smiled. "You will be surprised, but quite pleased."

Lily's stomach flipped. She didn't like the smile on her mother's face. "Who is it?" she asked suspiciously.

"Well." Mom smiled widely. "You're getting married to our great leader."

Lily's heart stopped. "No! Mom!"

"Yes!"

"Dennis Hamilton? Mom, no! Please tell me you're joking!"

Her mother sat back and said, "You should be happy, Lily. Dennis Hamilton owns Fallow Creek, including this very land our house sits on. He is a powerful man and rich. You will lack for nothing."

Lily sprang up from the sofa and stared down at her mother. "He has about a hundred wives!"

"Stop exaggerating, Lily. He doesn't have a hundred wives. He has only seven."

"And I'm supposed to be happy to be his eighth? Why have you and Father done this to me?"

Mom stood up and faced off with her. "I don't know what I did to deserve such a stubborn daughter. No girl in this town behaves or even thinks like you do. Every single girl in Fallow Creek would be ecstatic to be in your shoes right now."

"First of all, Mother, I am not a girl. I am a woman. A twenty-five-year-old woman. Secondly, you've said it already. I am not like the other women in this town. I know better. I want better for myself."

Mom folded her arms across her chest. "And that's my point. You are getting too old. Soon no one in this town will want you. You need to settle down now… or is being single for the rest of your life what you want for yourself?"

"Yes, Mother. At least I'd be independent."

Mom laughed. "Independent? What woman asks for independence? You know what the Bible says about women being…"

"Please, Mom! Don't talk to me about the Bible. Everyone here thinks that they can twist the scriptures to suit whatever perverse beliefs they have. You are all lying manipulators!"

She winced in pain when her mother slapped her hard across the face.

"You will not talk to me like that!" her mother said, and marched out of the living room.

Lily sat down slowly on the sofa, cradling her cheek. She turned around when her mother marched back towards her and said, "Change out of that horrible gown you're wearing and put on something cleaner and nicer. Dennis will be coming this evening to see you."

Lily shook her head. There was no way she was going to marry Dennis Hamilton. And yet, what choice did she have?

Maybe she did have a choice. As much as she hated the Restoration House, it was better than marrying Dennis. Not only did the fact that the man had seven wives disgust her, she would never escape this town if she married him. His house was more heavily guarded than the Restoration House. But what was most revolting was that his forebears were the ones who had made up all the rules and regulations of this town, which were degrading to women and which he'd joyfully perpetuated. She would die before she married him… or, at least, go back to the Restoration House. She looked up at her mother and said, "I am not marrying Dennis

Hamilton."

Her mother propped her hands on her waist and chuckled. "Yes, you will."

"No, I won't. Do whatever you want with me, but I won't marry him."

"That means you're going back to the Restoration House, because apparently your mind has not been renewed and is still as wicked as ever."

Lily shrugged and her mother marched out of the living room again. She sighed sadly and groaned. She was going back to that awful place. This time, they would probably keep her there for an indefinite period of time, especially since she had rejected the almighty Dennis Hamilton. They would increase her chores and maybe even separate her from the other women. It would be a living hell unless she found a way to escape.

She whispered, "Lord, please help me," and opened her eyes as peace settled in her heart. She smiled, albeit sadly. In spite of how difficult her life was going to be soon, she was certain she would be alright. God was pleased with the decision she had made, she was sure, hence the peace in her heart. One day, when the time was right and she'd gathered enough money somehow, the Lord would make a way for her to escape the town and then she would truly be free.

FIVE

The yard sale was supposed to have started an hour ago, but no one had shown up. Keith looked around as his stomach squeezed with worry. He turned to Rachel, who was arranging the books they had brought from the house for the umpteenth time. They had set up the yard sale right in front of their house and almost all their belongings were here. They had to sell their things in order to raise money to cover their living expenses in Fallow Creek until they found their feet. But if no one came, they would be in big trouble.

Keith picked up one of his favorite books, a large historical novel which he had read a couple of times. "I can't believe we have to sell off all our things." If only they were not so sure that God wanted them to leave Destiny immediately, they would not be out here planning to sell off all their belongings.

Rachel grimaced. "I'm so sorry, Keith," she said. "Most of the things here are yours. I wish I had more things to sell."

Keith put his arm around Rachel and said, "No,

they're not, Rachel. Everything here is also yours because all I have became yours when we got married." He looked around. Rachel had found a big wooden table somewhere, and they had arranged many things like his books, some table lamps and paintings, random things like mirrors, and even some of Rachel's makeup. On the floor were bigger items like stools and armchairs, standing fans and air conditioners, and his two television sets. There were also duvets and bedspreads, throw pillows, blankets and rugs, plus pots and pans and other kitchen items. Many of their clothes were hanging on a large clothes-stand. Virtually everything they owned was here. He'd decided, though, not to sell his grandmother's living room furniture because they were dear to her when she was alive and they had sentimental value. He had told Mary, his sister, over the phone about his plans to move and she had been incredulous. When he'd told her he was leaving the house to her for now, she had laughed and then gone silent.

"You're really serious about moving, Keith?"

"Yes, I am. The Lord wants Rachel and me to move."

"And you say you are moving to the small town your wife comes from?"

"Yes," he answered. He did not tell her anything specifically about Fallow Creek because he didn't want her to worry or try to discourage him from going.

"And when are you coming back to Destiny?"

"I don't know," he said. "I just hope the Lord tells us to come back soon. I will be overjoyed if He does."

Mary had been full of doubts and she had tried to talk him out of moving to some small town she'd never heard about. She didn't have a problem with him leaving Destiny. She'd always wanted him to leave because, according to her, Destiny was dying, but definitely not to an even smaller town than Destiny with a strange name. "You will end up wasting away in that place," she had said.

Keith had laughed at that. "You told me I would die alone if I stayed in Destiny, but see? I am married now to the love of my life."

"Yeah, yeah!" she had chuckled. "Still, you will have a lot to gain if you just move here with me and..."

He had cut her off. "I promise to call you once I get to Fallow Creek," he said, before he ended the call.

Another wave of doubt and uncertainty washed over him as he looked around at their belongings again. Yesterday, he had sold his car to his friends, Eric and Paula. They'd tried to talk him out of leaving once more, and Paula had even shed a tear as she'd hugged Rachel before they left the house. As he'd told them before, he reminded them that he couldn't change his mind because God had told them to move. But now, with no one here to buy their things, they might end up with no money at all when they left Destiny.

He told Rachel about his worries and gave her a small smile in spite of it. He also told her it was strange that nobody had come since he'd told everyone he knew about the sale. "But it might be a good thing because then it will be our excuse for staying here. After all, we can't leave if we don't have any money."

Rachel said, "Well, we have the money from the sale of your car."

"Yes, that's true. So, I guess we won't have any excuses. That money won't last very long, though."

His Honda was very old and he had not gotten much for it. Eric had tried to give him a bit more, but he'd refused. Eric was only buying the car because they were good friends. His friend didn't have that much money and did not particularly need the car. Keith had taken only what he had asked for, which he thought was fair for such an old car.

Even with money from the sale of the car, they had to sell more things. If they were not going to live off Taylor in Fallow Creek, they needed as much money as they could get. Taylor would be providing them with accommodation, at least until they could get their own place, but Keith did not want him to have to do everything for them.

Rachel smiled at Keith. "Don't worry, Keith. People will come."

"But the yard sale was supposed to start at one o'clock this afternoon." He glanced at his wristwatch. "It's almost two-thirty."

"They will come," Rachel said. "You always tell me to trust God; now I am telling you the same thing."

"Thank you."

She arched her brows, "For what?"

"For being such a blessing and source of encouragement to me. What would I have done without you?"

She said cynically, "Probably still be looking forward to dedicating the new church without all the uncertainty and sadness of leaving the town you love."

"Stop it, Rachel! We are in this together, remember? Don't ever talk like that again."

Rachel said nothing, and Keith drew her even closer. His heart suddenly soared with happiness when two men began to approach, and behind them a couple.

Rachel whispered, "Steve and Jude are coming, Keith. And is that Phillip and Jennifer behind them?"

"Yes," he said, not knowing how to feel. On one hand, he felt relief. They would not have to leave the town empty-handed, but on the other hand he felt slightly afraid. Almost everything they had was on sale.

More people began to arrive and soon the place was bustling with buyers. Every time someone bought one of his books or a well-loved item, he winced inwardly. But he put on a bright smile for everyone, hiding how he truly felt.

Almost everyone who came to buy something asked why he was leaving, even though he had already explained to as many people as he could that it was God's will for him and his wife to move. Many of them looked sad, and a few had tears in their eyes.

"We will miss you so much," Elaine, a white-haired elderly lady, said as she bought a shiny red and silver jewelry box Keith had bought for Rachel just after their wedding.

He sighed as he looked at Rachel, handing the box over to Elaine. She had loved the box so much when he'd given it to her and it broke his heart.

When she came to ask if they could also sell the box since it was brand new and expensive and would definitely bring in a good sum of money, he had asked if she was sure she wanted to sell it.

"Yes," she said with a nod. "I'm sure."

"Well then, it's yours to do as you please," he'd told her.

He turned to sell one of his wristwatches to a church member named Allen, and then turned back to look at Rachel. She was smiling brightly at a teenager who had come to buy a pair of her shoes. She had very few and his heart ached with love and concern for her. Unlike her, he had mixed feelings about moving to Fallow Creek. He was happy for her because she would be in the same town as her daughter, but he worried that Mike might not allow her to see Emily, which would leave her devastated.

He sighed again, turned his eyes away from her, and put his concerns temporarily out of his mind. He smiled as another man came by to buy the expensive set of fountain pens Mary had given him for his birthday last year.

The more people bought their belongings, the more pain he felt in his heart. It was not just about losing many of the things that had sentimental value, but selling off everything they owned made their impending departure even more real. Each time someone bought something he particularly loved, he told himself he should be happy about it. That meant more money to tide him and Rachel over until he could get a paid job in Fallow Creek. But what that would be, he didn't know.

About an hour later, the front of his house was empty of people and their possessions. He was not really surprised about that. Most of the people in Destiny had come specially to support him, even though they didn't want him to leave. Most of the things they put up for sale had been bought at bargain prices, except for a few new items. He couldn't help but beam when Eric and Paula walked up to him and Rachel.

"The yard sale went really well," Eric said, looking around. "This place is almost empty."

"Yes." Keith sighed wearily.

"The people of this town have been so supportive," Rachel said, her voice choked with emotion.

Paula held Rachel's hands and smiled sadly. "Are you both sure you want to leave?"

Eric said, "Keith, man, are you sure that God really spoke to you about this?"

Keith groaned. "Please, Eric. Not again. I thought we had talked about this before."

"You heard what almost everyone who came here today said." Eric shook his head. "I am just echoing their sentiments. We're all going to miss you both terribly. We don't want you to leave."

"I wish you guys didn't have to go," Paula said.

Keith moaned inwardly. His friends were making it even more difficult and painful than it already was. He shifted his eyes away from Eric and Paula when a young couple with their three-year-old daughter approached him. Apart from Paula and Eric, they were the only people still around.

Sheila, the wife, greeted Eric and Paula and then beamed at Rachel and Keith. Matt, her husband, said to Keith, "How come you're leaving now... just when our new church is nearly finished? Who will be our pastor?"

Eric nodded eagerly. "Yes, Pastor Keith. Who will be our pastor when you leave?"

"You know Alec will do a good job," Keith said to Eric and smiled at Sheila and Matt. "You'll all do just fine without me." He patted their daughter's head affectionately and grinned at the little girl.

Matt gave him a sad smile. "You are the best pastor this town has ever had."

Keith was too overcome with emotion to speak.

Sheila lifted their daughter into her arms and said, "Anyway, we want to buy this for Allie, Pastor Keith." She showed him a small box that contained a collection of multi-colored pebbles. "I wish we could buy more, but we can't afford to right now."

Keith smiled. "That's okay," he said, and looked at her husband. Matt had never had much to begin with, but he did have a job working at the confectionery store in town. Unfortunately, the place had been destroyed by the hurricane. The owner had left Destiny and Matt was unemployed now. For the first time, Keith realized how old their daughter's dress looked and noticed a hole in Sheila's blouse.

Some people in Destiny who had been left with no jobs after the hurricane were going back to them now that their places of work were rebuilt and open again. But a few still didn't have employment. He looked at Matt and Sheila and said, "You can take the marbles for free, guys." He smiled at their daughter again. "I hope she enjoys playing with them."

When Matt and Sheila began to protest, Keith said firmly, "Please. It's a gift from Rachel and me to little Allie."

They both smiled warmly at him and Rachel. After he hugged them, they left.

"So, what about your store, Keith?" Paula asked. "What do you plan to do with it?"

Keith swept his hand around and said, "We've sold most of the things from the store already. I told Mary she was in charge of it." He looked at Eric and Paula as an idea came to him. "But I think you guys are in a better position to take care of it. And if you need to use it for anything, don't hesitate to do so. I will hand over the keys to you before we leave."

Eric shook his head. "Nope! I don't think we need it." He faced his wife. "Do we, Paula?"

Paula didn't say anything for a second and then nodded. "I don't think so."

Keith studied them both briefly and said, "I'll give you the keys to the store anyway. You might need it for something someday." He shook his head when they refused again. "Guys… it's me, Keith. Use the store whenever and for whatever you want. You don't have to feel guilty about that. I'll feel much better if it's in the care of people I trust."

Eric pounded his back and smiled. "You're a good man, Keith. Since you won't change your minds about leaving, I wish you guys the best. But I hope you hurry back here soon."

After Keith hugged Eric and Paula, Rachel hugged them too. The four of them made plans to have dinner together the next evening, the day before they would leave Destiny. When Eric and Paula left, Keith turned to face Rachel. "Well, that's that," he said, feeling emotionally exhausted. He looked around the place again.

"We still have to find out how much we made,"

Rachel said.

He followed her into the house and they sat side-by-side on the couch. Rachel opened her purse and brought out the proceeds from their yard sale. She counted the money while he held his breath, anxious. The quality of life they would have in Fallow Creek, at least when they first arrived, depended on the amount they'd made. Considering they'd sold most of the things they had put up for sale, he hoped they had made enough to live on comfortably until he found a job. He had a rough idea about how much they had made, but there was a chance he was way off in his initial calculations.

Rachel finally turned to him and said, "We have two thousand, seven hundred and fifty-three dollars."

He closed his eyes and sighed. It was not very much, but it wasn't terribly small either. He said, "We got three thousand five hundred dollars for my car. So that is, umm…" he calculated briefly in his mind, "a total of six thousand, two hundred and fifty-three dollars."

"That's not bad."

Keith nodded. "It depends on how quickly I'm able to find a job. If I don't find something quickly, then we will have to depend on your brother for much longer than I would like." The thought of doing that left a sour taste in his mouth. He had never been rich, but he'd always had enough; not for luxuries, but for his daily needs. The thought of depending on someone else to provide for him and his wife made him queasy and, frankly, a little annoyed.

Rachel put her arm around him and said, "The

Lord will provide for us before the money runs out. Don't worry. And Taylor is a great guy. He's different from most of the men in Fallow Creek. He will not resent helping us until we're able to become financially independent."

Keith forced a smile for Rachel's sake. He did not want to add to her worries. "You're right, honey," he said. "So, this will be sufficient for our plane fare to Fallow Creek and our basic needs there."

Give the money to Matt and Sheila!

Keith's jaw dropped and his heart twisted in fear. "What? No, Lord."

Rachel frowned. "Keith! What is it?"

Keith did not answer for a long moment. The still small voice spoke to his heart again, telling him the same thing. He could feel Rachel's eyes on him as he struggled with the instruction he'd just received from the Lord. How would they survive if he gave all their money away?

"Keith, what's wrong?" Rachel asked again, but he didn't answer. He silently asked the Lord what they would do for money if he gave theirs all away, but he heard nothing. Finally, he sighed in resignation. He turned to Rachel and searched her eyes for a long moment, reluctant to tell her what he had just heard. Since they'd gotten the word from the Lord to move to Fallow Creek, she had been worried but also very hopeful. Even full of faith, given the circumstances. But this would shake her faith. He was deeply worried about how she would take it, but he had to tell her what he had heard.

She put her hand on his arm, looking at him with an alarmed expression. "Tell me what you're thinking!"

He said slowly, "I think the Lord wants us to give this money to Sheila and Matt."

Rachel blinked and tears welled up in her eyes. For a long moment, neither of them could speak, and then she said, "I guess we have to learn to completely rely on God now."

He said nothing, but there was nothing else to say. If the Lord wanted them to go to Fallow Creek empty-handed, then there was nothing they could do but trust Him completely, as Rachel had said.

SIX

Lily closed the book she was reading, sat up on her bed, and sighed. Her heart pounded with worry. The thought of going back to the Restoration House made her sick, but the thought of marrying someone like Dennis Hamilton made her feel even worse. She closed her eyes and sighed again as she thought about the miserable months she had spent at the Restoration House. The only time she had been happy there was when Rachel Dalton had come, but Rachel had not stayed for long. After she'd left, Lily had gone back to feeling miserable. Without a doubt, she would soon be back there, as she would never consider marrying the leader of Fallow Creek no matter what her mother said.

Her heart began to pound even faster when she heard the roar of an engine outside and then car doors slamming shut. Slowly, she stood up, went to the window, and drew back the curtains. Looking through the window, she bit her lip. As she had suspected, it was Dennis. She stared in distaste at him as she wondered why at fifty-something, with more than half a dozen wives, he still wanted her for his bride. How many wives did one man need in order to be finally satisfied? She frowned deeply. It was just disgusting.

Two security squad guards stood behind him. Her parents went out of the house to greet him, and Lily shook her head in annoyance. She left the window and went to sit down on her bed again. She closed her eyes and took a deep breath to try to calm her nerves. This time for sure, she would be spending years rather than months in that Restoration House. No one rejected the leader of the community without severe consequences. Her mind would be broken and her life would be wasted in that house. And yet, even with that dreary thought, she could not bring herself to consider marrying Dennis Hamilton.

She curled up on her bed, knowing that any minute now her mother would come in and try to force her to go and meet the man. Her stomach hurt from worrying for hours, and she wrapped her arms around her belly. Less than a minute later, her mother walked in.

"Lily, you have a visitor," her mom said cheerily.

Lily pressed her lips tightly together, revulsion running through her as she pictured Dennis Hamilton waiting in the living room for her, probably already making plans to take her as his wife. She remained curled up on her bed, determined not to move, no matter what her mother said.

"Lily, did you hear me?" Mom called out again. This time she sounded slightly irritated. "Dennis Hamilton is here to see you. You need to stand up right now and go out there to see him."

Lily ignored her mother. She would have to be physically carried out of the bed and out of this room because she was not going to stand up.

"Lily, get up right now!" Mom yelled and came and grabbed her hand. She pulled Lily up and tried to pull her out of the bed, but Lily resisted.

Her mother sat on the bed and stared at her. She groaned. "Why won't you stand up, Lily? Why?"

Lily sighed loudly. "Mom, I told you I will not marry that man. I'm not even going to come out to meet him. My things are still packed and I'm ready to go back to the Restoration House."

"Lily, you're going to get us in trouble if you refuse to marry him. And besides, why would you not marry him? Do you know how many..."

"Please stop!" Lily glowered at her mother. "We've talked about this before. You and Father can do anything you want with me, but I am not marrying Dennis Hamilton."

Mom glared at her and said exasperatedly, "It's not what your father and I will do to you that you should be afraid of. You know that refusing the leader of this community will be considered almost an abomination."

Lily narrowed her eyes as she stared at her mother. "I don't care," she said. "There's no way I'm marrying that man." She clenched her jaw as a grim determination entered her heart. "And not only that, Mom. I'm not going to marry any man in this town who already has a wife. That's not the plan I have for my life."

Her mother didn't say anything for a full minute, and then she stepped back from Lily. "I'm going to get your father to try to talk some sense into you."

"You already know that there is nothing either of you could say that would change my mind. There's nothing anyone can say to make me think differently."

Mom marched out of the room, and Lily pressed her back against the wall, her heart drumming. Her mother was right. Refusing the leader of the community would not be without serious consequences, and not just for her, but for her parents. But her determination not to give in did not lessen. Instead, it grew. She would refuse him and anyone else she did not want to marry. It was her right to do so, no matter what the people of this community said.

Her father walked, or rather, stormed into the room, his face red with anger, his eyes blazing and fixed on her. He looked down at her and roared, "Get up from the bed right now! You're going to meet your future husband!"

Lily turned her back to him. She knew how angry her father could get, but his anger was not going to intimidate her today. She winced in pain when he grabbed her hand and jerked her out of the bed. "You'll come out right now to meet Dennis or you'll pay for your rebellion," he threatened.

She cried out when he squeezed her wrist hard.

Mom stepped in and said, "Wait, Cliff. You're hurting her and it won't help matters. You know how stubborn Lily can get. It's not like we can force her to marry Dennis, at least not in this way."

Her father let go of her hand and turned to her mom. "What do you suggest we do?"

"Let's try to reason with her." Mom faced Lily. "Please reconsider, Lily."

"No," Lily said firmly.

"Do you see what trying to reason with her gets you?" her father said, glaring at Lily. "There is no reasoning with this one."

"Okay, Lily, what do you want? We'll give you anything if you only agree to marry Dennis," her mother pleaded. "Please, Lily. For our sake. You know how everyone will treat us if you reject him."

Lily sighed. She felt sorry for her mother. Her mom was right. Her parents would suffer for her rejection of the leader of the community. That was why her father was so angry. But she could not marry the man. Her parents would have to bear whatever consequences of her rejection came their way, just like she would.

"Please," her mom pleaded again.

"Listen, Lily, you will marry Dennis Hamilton. Do you hear me?" her father yelled. "If you don't..." Her father's eyes suddenly grew wide, and he stopped talking as someone walked into the room.

Lily turned and her heart jumped into her throat. Dennis Hamilton stood at the door, staring at them.

Father walked over to Dennis and said, "Please, just give her a little bit of time. She will come out to meet you now."

She stepped back slightly as Dennis Hamilton walked into her room. Her turned to look briefly at her parents, and they moved away to the door. He stood in front of Lily and his eyes ran down the length of her. She felt sick with worry, revulsion, and a hint of hatred as she looked at the leader of Fallow Creek. His father had been the leader of the community before his death, and his grandfather the founder. This was the man responsible for all the sick rules that this community had. She squared her shoulders and looked him in the eye, even though her heart was pounding with fear.

He studied her face for a long time as though he was trying to find something on it. Something that had eluded him. Finally, he chuckled. He turned to her parents and said, "Your daughter is lost."

Lily frowned and her parents did the same.

"What do you mean by that, sir?" her mother asked.

"I mean I can see into her. She's completely lost. There is no hope for her. I heard everything you all said before I came in here. You were trying to force and beg her to marry me, but I'm not the kind of man who will ever marry someone on those terms." He turned back and faced Lily again. "Every single girl in this town would sell everything they had for the chance that you have been given and which you have spurned."

Lily glowered at him. It was the same thing her mother had been telling her since she'd come back to the house. And it was the last thing that would convince her to change her mind. In fact, it only strengthened her resolve to not give in. Someone in this town had to do the right thing and show these people that it was okay to break the ridiculous rules in this town no matter the cost. If she had to be the one to do it, then so be it. Girls in this town had been groomed from childhood to think of themselves as property to men and nothing more. She was determined to be different, even if she spent the rest of her life in the Restoration House. She said a silent prayer to God asking for strength.

Dennis turned back to her parents and said, "I have made a decision about her."

Lily blinked. What decision? She was going back to the Restoration House. Was there any other decision to make?

He faced her once more with a smile and slowly walked up to her as she backed away. "You must have heard about Rachel Cadwell. She wanted to ruin our way of life and we couldn't allow it. *I* could not allow it." The smile melted off his face as his eyes pierced Lily's. "Since you've decided to tread the same path, you will suffer the same consequences for your rebellion as she did."

Lily widened her eyes as she stared at the man. She couldn't breathe, knowing exactly what he was going to say.

He went on. "Today... no... now, you will leave Fallow Creek. You will never be allowed back here again so that you will not spread your rebellion and lies to the rest of our community. You will take nothing except for your clothes, and no one is allowed to help you. You will never step into Fallow Creek or see your parents again."

Her mother cried out. "Please!" she pleaded with Dennis. "Please just give us time to speak to her. She will change her mind about marrying you."

Dennis frowned and shook his head. "It's not just about her refusing to marry me. Just like I told you, I can see into her. She is full of rebellion. I can't allow her to stay here any longer."

Father stood before Dennis. "Can you not just give us a little time to get her to change her mind?"

"No, I can't!" Dennis said firmly. The two security squad guards that had come into the house with him entered Lily's room. He said to them, "You will make sure that she leaves Fallow Creek right now. She must not be allowed to speak with anyone and no one is to approach her or help her."

They nodded and Dennis turned back to Lily. He looked down at the small bag she'd brought from the Restoration House. It was still packed and she had been ready to take it with her when she was bundled back to the House. "I see you are packed already," he said. "You'll take that bag with you and nothing else."

Lily's mouth was dry and she felt confused. Never had she imagined that she would be asked to leave the community since they never allowed anyone to leave permanently. But after what happened with Rachel, she should have known there might be a possibility that she would be banished as Rachel had been.

Her feelings were all jumbled up. She felt exhilarated. She would finally be free of this place and she could go on an adventure to discover her purpose and destiny. But she also felt dread and panic. The thought of leaving her parents, her sister, her friends, and never seeing them again made her sick to her stomach. In spite of her parents' blind dedication to the rules of this place, she loved them dearly. Tears welled up in her eyes as she looked at her mother, who was pleading again with the leader of the community, trying to change his mind. It was a waste of time. No one could change Dennis Hamilton's mind once he made a decision.

She looked at her father. He knew what she already did — that there was no point pleading with the leader of Fallow Creek. His eyes were fixed on her. They pleaded silently with her, begging her to reconsider.

She looked at Dennis, who was now almost at the door. He glanced casually at her father and then shook his head at her mother. "Stop begging!" he said harshly. "You should have raised your daughter better." He walked out of the room while the squad guards moved closer to Lily, their faces devoid of emotion.

Her father faced her fully, his face a mask of agony. "What have you done, Lily?"

Mom rushed out of the room, probably to go and continue pleading with Dennis Hamilton.

Lily said nothing to her father. The exhilaration she'd felt earlier had melted away, leaving just confusion. *Where will I go? What will I do for money? How will I survive outside this community?* She had never lived anywhere else; never even been anywhere else.

As though her father could read her mind, he asked her the same questions she'd asked herself. "You have nothing to your name, Lily. What are you going to do outside of this place?"

The squad guards stood over her, watching silently as she picked up her bag and looked at her father again.

Lily swallowed the sob rising up inside her. For the first time since she could remember, her father looked like he was about to cry. She took a deep breath to calm herself and felt a fresh rush of determination settle on her. With God's help, she would survive. As for whether she would ever see her parents again, she was determined that she would, no matter how long it took. When she was well established, she would find a way to return one day and free her parents from the clutches of this town.

And how are you going to be established outside here when you have nothing at all? a voice in her head mocked her.

"Hurry up!" one of the guards said, glaring at her.

She knew for sure that Dennis Hamilton would be waiting outside the house in his car to make sure that she came out of the house quickly. She shouldered her bag and then said to her father, "I'm sorry for the pain I have caused you, Dad." She reached out and hugged him.

At first, his body remained rigid and he refused to hug her back. Then he put his arms around her and held her. He whispered in her ear, "What have you done to us, Lily?"

She pulled back and stared into his eyes. He looked so broken. She apologized again, not for refusing to marry Dennis Hamilton, but for the pain that her impending departure would cost him. She smiled sadly and then stepped away from him and followed the guards out of her room. There was no point lingering any longer. It would only make everything more painful.

In the living room, her mother wept, grabbing at her clothes in despair. She rushed up to Lily, grabbed her, and held her tightly. "Why, Lily? Why have you done this to us?"

Lily said nothing as tears streamed down her face. There was nothing to say. Her heart was breaking, just as her mom's clearly was. And yet she sensed a tiny glimmer of excitement and anticipation within her. She felt her mother's hand in her pocket and felt something drop into it. She stepped away from her mother and followed the guards out of the house without looking back.

As she had guessed, Dennis Hamilton was still in his car. His windows were rolled down and he stared at her with a look of derision.

She turned away from him and continued walking, two guards beside her. She walked down the long road, glancing at the houses that lined the streets of Fallow Creek and taking mental pictures of the town. She had lived here since she was born and she had never experienced life outside of this place. She wasn't sure how life anywhere else would be. All she knew was what she had seen on the internet.

Her heart began to pound again as she thought about her future, uncertain about what she was supposed to do when she left Fallow Creek. Where she was supposed to go. She felt like Abraham in a way: she was leaving the land of her birth to a place she did not know. Like Abraham, she would have to depend on God totally.

She had always believed in God — how could she not when she was born and lived in this place where daily life revolved around a host of religious activities? But she had known from a young age that the religion of this place did not match what was in her heart. She had questioned everything since she was a teenager, and about five years ago, she had found her own personal faith in Christ. Thankfully, her many questions about God had not led her further away from Him, but closer. She had found a personal relationship with God that was different from the rigid religious rituals she'd been taught growing up.

She kept walking with the guards. The more she walked, the wearier she became. Her bag, though not initially heavy, was now beginning to weigh her down. Neither of the guards offered to help. She didn't expect them to anyway.

She thought about Rachel as they approached the edge of town. Where was her friend now? If only she knew where Rachel was, she would head there. The only thing she knew was that Rachel had told her about a place called Destiny. She had constantly talked about the town and the man she loved who lived there but who had been killed. Lily remembered that Rachel had told her Destiny was in Colorado. There was no way she could get there and she did not even have the money to make it there.

Fear gripped her again. She had never had any of her own money. All her needs had been provided for by her parents. She suddenly remembered that her mom had put something in her dress pocket and dug her hand into it. She gasped as she brought out three one-hundred-dollar bills. The guards were still with her. No one was supposed to help her with anything, not even her mother. She quickly put the money back into her pocket and looked down. She whispered her thanks to God. The money wasn't a lot, but it was better than nothing. She knew if her mother had had more money on her, she would have given all she had to Lily. Tears filled her eyes as she thought about her mother weeping as she left the house.

Her feet began to hurt, but she continued on.

She still had a long way to go after she left Fallow Creek. They finally got to the town's border and the guards stopped, and so did she.

There were a few other squad guards at the border. They stared at her, but none of them spoke to her. She turned and gazed at Fallow Creek once more and bitter tears stung her eyes. When this day started, she could not have imagined that it would end with her permanently leaving the town of her birth and everyone she loved here. A firm determination entered her heart. She would find a way to see them again, and soon, too.

She looked at all the guards. In spite of their hard stares, she said, "I will miss this place and you, too."

None of them replied.

She smiled sadly. It was not the squad guards as a team that she would miss, but the people behind the fatigues and stern faces. She knew them all and was even acquainted with a few of them. She turned around and began to walk away, her heart heavy. The road stretched on before her. There were no houses anywhere, but she knew from a few people who were regularly allowed to leave Fallow Creek for business that the next town was not so far away. However, she did not know how long she would have to walk in order to get there.

Five minutes later, she brought out the money her mother had given her. Once more tears fell down her cheeks as she remembered her mother putting the money into her pocket. She suddenly broke down and began to sob. She would miss her parents and her younger sister, Allison, so much. Her heart was broken and she could not stop crying, but she thanked God again for the money.

If nothing else, she would have enough to take her to Phoenix, which was where she had already set her heart to go. She wanted somewhere completely different from Fallow Creek. A big city rather than a small town. She wanted to experience a different life from the one she'd led until now.

The next town was much farther than she had thought, but she finally got there and sat on a bench on the side of the road, exhausted. The town, as far as she could see, was nothing more than a few old houses with a small store that sold an assortment of things. It seemed as small as Fallow Creek, but definitely not as prosperous or organized. She thought about Taylor again and the big buildings he had constructed in town, and then she pushed him out of her mind. She went into the store and bought some snacks and drinks. After she had eaten what she bought, she asked the storekeeper how she could get to Phoenix.

"Phoenix," the storekeeper said. He told her where to get a bus that would take her to Tucson and from there, she could take a bus or train to Phoenix.

She thanked him and left the store. Even though she was tired, she kept walking until she got to the small bus station and climbed aboard one of the buses to take her to the next town. There were only a few people on the bus as it left the station. She took a deep breath and whispered a prayer of thanksgiving to God.

Gradually, the heaviness in her heart began to dissipate and she felt herself smile. Leaving her loved ones back in Fallow Creek was hard, but she was on her way to her destiny. She was sure of that. For the first time in her life, she felt truly independent and free.

She got out of the bus in the next city and gave a long sigh. She didn't know exactly where she was. All she knew was that she was heading to Phoenix and she had to find a bus going there.

She asked for directions to the bus station where she could get a bus to Tucson. A woman directed her to a nearby station and she went there. After paying for her fare with the money she had left, she settled on the bus and soon fell asleep, tired. When she woke up, she was in Tucson.

She exited the bus, left the station, and stared at the huge impressive structures and skyscrapers with her heart thudding. She started to cross the road with her bag, staring at a particularly tall skyscraper and wondering where on earth she was going to go now, and then her eyes widened in horror as a car raced down the road toward her at top speed. She stood frozen for a few seconds and hurried to move out of the way. But it was too late. She felt herself flying through the air and she hit the ground hard. Everything went black.

SEVEN

On the outside, Keith wore a big smile as he waved a final goodbye to Eric and Paula and the small crowd who had gathered at the bus station to see him and Rachel off. But on the inside, he wept at the thought of leaving his beloved Destiny, the town he'd grown up in and where he'd thought he would live for the rest of his life.

Mayor Winston shook his hand and patted his back. "We'll all miss you, Pastor Keith," he said.

Keith could not speak, overwhelmed with emotion.

With tears in her eyes, Rachel went to hug Paula and Eric's kids and then hugged the children who she had taken care of for months while their parents were at work. Just before they both got on the bus that would take them to the airport in Denver, where they would fly to Phoenix, Eric put his hand on Keith's shoulder. He opened his mouth to say something, but Keith shook his head. He already knew that Eric was going to ask him again if he was sure he wanted to leave the town for good.

"No, Eric. Please don't ask me to stay again."

Eric sighed loudly but said nothing.

Keith got on the bus quickly, his heart shredding. There was no point lingering and getting himself and Rachel and all the people here worked up further than they already were. There were tears in the eyes of almost everyone who had come to see them off. He sighed again as he looked out of the window and waved to them.

Rachel put her hand on his arm, and he turned to face her. "Are you okay?" she asked.

He nodded. He knew that she hurt for him because of how much he loved Destiny. She loved the town, too, but it was not the same. He looked out once more at his beloved town and then drew in a harsh breath. "I hope we will be able to come back here soon," he said. He did not tell Rachel that he hoped they would be sent back at the border in Fallow Creek so he could come back to Destiny. From everything that had happened, he was pretty sure it was God who had sent them. But there was still a tiny shred of doubt in him, a voice that constantly questioned his sanity for selling off everything he had, giving the money away, and moving off with his new wife to a town he'd heard nothing but evil about.

"Are we doing the right thing?" he whispered to Rachel, and then chided himself for doing so. It was not right for him to burden her with his doubts. This mad venture they were already on was enough to drive anyone up the wall. And not knowing how they would survive now that they had given away all their money was enough burden for her to bear.

She did nothing except give him an encouraging

smile. He knew her well enough to know that the smile meant that she was certain they were doing the right thing, but like him, she harbored a tiny shred of doubt.

The bus began to move, and Keith chuckled and said with forced humor, "This is our last chance to get off the bus."

Rachel shook her head and grinned. In spite of the sadness he saw in her eyes, he also saw hope and anticipation.

He said to her, "By God's grace you will soon be reunited with Emily."

The smile did not leave her face, but he knew she was also thinking about the possibility that her ex would not let her see her daughter. He also knew his presence with her in Fallow Creek would be an affront to Mike Cadwell and most of the men there.

He had thought about it long and hard, knowing that being with her as a husband would drastically reduce her chances of being allowed to see her daughter. However, the Lord had sent them to the town together and told them not to pursue the lawsuit for full custody of Emily. Surely, the Lord's grace would follow them and He would make an open door for Rachel to be able to see her daughter as regularly as she wanted. Maybe in due time, Emily could come and live with them wherever they made their home in Fallow Creek. All that was his hope and his constant prayer.

The bus ride took hours. Keith passed the time talking with Rachel, their arms around each other, their voices full of fear and hope. After a while, Rachel fell asleep, leaving Keith to his own thoughts. His mind tormented him continuously about every bad thing that could happen when they got to Fallow Creek. Maybe Taylor would not be in town, and then they would find themselves living on the street. Maybe because they had no money they would eventually starve, as no one in the town would help them.

His mind kept going around and around every scary scenario he could think of until he groaned, shut his eyes, and began to pray. It was the only way he knew to stifle the fears assailing him.

Rachel woke up half an hour later and, as always, she took his hand again and smiled at him. "Are you okay, Keith?" she asked.

"I'm fine." He smiled at her.

"Did you sleep at all?"

"No, I just couldn't. Maybe I will sleep on the plane."

She pressed her lips tightly together and said, "My mind is filled with all kinds of confusing emotions."

He nodded. "I understand how you feel."

She said nothing more except to squeeze his hand encouragingly and smile at him. She put her head down on the back of the seat in front of them as though to go back to sleep. But a minute later, she raised her head, sighed loudly, and then looked out of the window.

Keith had hardly looked out since they'd begun their journey from Destiny, but now he did and saw they were approaching Denver. He glanced at his wristwatch. They had been on the road for almost seven hours. He looked at Rachel and said, "Finally."

They exited the bus about thirty minutes later and took another bus to the airport.

All through the ride to the airport, Keith stared out of the window at the city. He hadn't been out of his small town in ages and he couldn't help but gape at the tall buildings and wide streets in Denver. But all of the glitz and glamour could not compare to Destiny in his heart.

They got their luggage out of the bus once they got to the airport. They didn't have much since they had sold most of their possessions. All their things fit into a single suitcase.

After booking a flight to Phoenix, which would leave in about two hours, they checked in and sat waiting for their flights. Keith got restless a few minutes later and asked Rachel if they could go get something to eat. He needed something to distract him from his constant worry, and nothing could do that more than sharing a meal with Rachel.

They found a small restaurant a short distance from where they sat and went inside. The place was empty, but it was the way he liked it so that he could have Rachel all to himself. They could talk without having to watch what they said or how loud they spoke.

As they ate, they talked about everything but Fallow Creek. They talked about their friends in Destiny, about the church, and about his past assistant who would now become the head pastor. He could see how much Rachel had loved taking care of the children in Destiny and how much she would miss them. Hopefully, she would find something similar to do in Fallow Creek. She had told him that women did not hold paid jobs there, but still he knew she would watch the children for free because she loved kids.

They finally left the small restaurant and then went to sit in the departure lounge. An hour later, they boarded the plane and buckled their seatbelts. Just before the plane took off, Keith turned and said to Rachel, "We have to trust God completely because we have nothing." He wanted to tell her how uneasy he felt, but he withheld his anxiety.

But as always, Rachel guessed what was on his mind and said firmly, "God was the one who sent us to Fallow Creek. He will provide everything we need. At least we have a place to stay, and Taylor will help us out until we are financially independent."

"And what if we aren't allowed into the town?"

"We will be."

He marveled at how confident she sounded and how strong her faith was. He said to her, "I'm so glad you're with me, Rachel. Your faith in God is so strong, while I am filled with doubt right now."

She smiled again. "I've had a good teacher."

He smiled at her.

Her eyes studied his. "I have learned how important it is to trust God fully just by watching you every day," she said. "But don't be fooled by my confident words. I'm just as scared as you are." She touched his cheek. "But like you always tell me, God is in charge and we are in His hands."

He nodded. "Yes, Rachel. You're right. We're in God's hands now, and we'll trust Him to supply all our needs."

For the rest of the trip to Phoenix, every time his heart pounded and doubts assailed him, he drew strength from Rachel's words and from the unwavering confidence he had always had in God's faithfulness, no matter what situation he was in.

***

Throughout the flight to Phoenix, Rachel stared wide awake while Keith dozed off and on. Left mostly to her thoughts, she could not help but worry. Keith had said that she was full of faith, when he had doubt. But the truth was that she was scared. Very scared. She believed the Lord would make a way for them somehow, but that did not stop her from being afraid.

She was not afraid of not being allowed into Fallow Creek, because she was sure the Lord had sent them to live there, neither was she afraid of what they would do for money, because at least they would have a roof over their heads and food to eat. Taylor would see to that. What she was afraid of was that she would not be allowed to see Emily. She and Keith had abandoned their plan to fight for custody of Emily because the Lord had told them to. It was a great risk to take in hopes that following the Lord closely would lead not only to the purpose He had for them but also to seeing Emily again. But what if Mike would not let her see her daughter?

Stop being so afraid, Rachel! she chided herself. The Lord would touch Mike's heart so he would let her see Emily as much as she wanted. She pushed away her concerns and looked down at Keith. His head was slightly bent as he slept and his hair fell across his forehead. She tenderly brushed his hair back and gently ran her fingers through it, her heart overflowing with love for him. He was her world now. Her life with him was so different from the way her life had been with Mike. Unlike Mike, he treated her as an equal. He let her make her own decisions, which at first had been totally new and strange to her.

She smiled as she remembered the weeks after they'd gotten married. Like she had done with Mike, she had asked him constantly for every single thing she wanted to do, every decision she wanted to take. "Can I go and get groceries now?" Or, "Can I go and see Paula?" she would ask him.

Every time she asked, he looked at her with surprise, his eyebrows raised. "Yes, Rachel. Of course you can go. You don't need my permission every single time you want to go out, you know."

But she soon forgot and asked his permission to take a stroll around the town the next day. He never lost his patience or became angry with her. But he always firmly reminded her that she could do whatever she wanted. "Go on, Rachel."

Sometimes, when he wasn't busy with his sermons, he joined her on her walks. They had many walks around the town, memorable ones like the one they had taken the day they'd confessed their love for each other. The day she knew she wanted to spend the rest of her life with him.

They had already talked about having more kids and with everything in her she wanted a little baby with Keith. But they had said they would try to get custody of Emily before they started having other children. Now that their lives had been turned upside down, having children was the last thing on her mind Still, if Keith told her today that he wanted a child with her, she would agree immediately. She found that with him, even though he never required anything of her, unlike Mike, she wanted to do everything for him. She loved him dearly and fiercely like she had never loved anyone else except for her daughter. It hurt her to see him so sad about leaving his hometown. A fierce determination entered her heart as she gazed at him. She would do all she could to make him happy in Fallow Creek.

Her mind went back to her last day there, the day she was sent packing from the town. At that time, she had thought Keith was dead and, even though she knew she was going to return to Destiny in order to help the town with the money Taylor had given her, her heart was full of sorrow. Keith had been the light of her life and, apart from God, the only thing that kept her from descending into depression because of her separation from Emily. She could not believe that she was going back to Fallow Creek, the place she had vowed never to step foot in again except to get her daughter from Mike.

She sighed softly. Fallow Creek, with its rules that subjugated women. Its false piety. Everyday life was ruled by religion and yet the true gospel had not touched the hearts of most of the people there. It was probably why the Lord was sending them to the town. At least, she was sure it was partly because of that.

She did not realize that she'd dozed off until she felt a hand on her hair. Someone kissed her cheek and she opened her eyes to find Keith looking intently at her. "We've arrived, Rachel," he said. "We're in Arizona."

After they had gotten their suitcase at the airport, they walked out to find a taxi that would take them to the train station and from there to Prospect, and then the long bus ride to the town near Fallow Creek.

"How long will it take for us to get from here to

Fallow Creek?" Keith asked her as they got into a taxi.

"About eight hours," Rachel answered.

Keith groaned and she laughed. "I am weary of traveling."

She smiled and rubbed his shoulder. "You will have me for company, Keith. The time will fly by pretty fast."

He grinned at her. "You're the best companion anyone could ever ask for."

After they got to the train station and boarded a train, Keith said, "Rachel, tell me everything you know about Fallow Creek." He was sitting across from her, close to the window. He leaned forward, staring intently at her, his elbows resting on the small table between them.

"But I have told you most of what I know," she said.

"Yes, you've told me a lot about the town, like the daily life there and the way the town looks. I don't want to know about that. Tell me how the town was founded, by whom, and the leadership there."

She took a deep breath and took his hands on the table. She began, "I remember my mother telling me when I was nine that Fallow Creek was founded by our leader..." She stopped talking and then corrected herself. "By *their* leader, Dennis Hamilton's grandfather. I don't know where he came from initially, but he came to Fallow Creek when the place was mostly deserted. I think there were a few people there but most of the original people moved out."

"And how did it become the religious polygamous community it is now?" Keith asked.

Rachel shook her head and sighed. "Dennis Hamilton's grandfather was a wealthy man. He bought up the whole community and then invited some of his friends to see the place. They were already part of a church that believed in polygamy, but they left that so they could form their own little kingdom." She pressed her lips together as she recalled the story everyone in the town knew. Most people told it with a hint of reverence, but the story deserved to be told with nothing but disgust.

She continued. "They settled in the town and began to indulge their wildest fantasy, which was to marry as many wives as they wanted under the guise that God's plan was for them to populate the earth with more righteous people." She gave a harsh laugh. "Which, of course, meant they had to have multiple wives to do that with."

"And where did the many wives come from since there weren't other people there?" Keith asked.

"They already had wives. Some had two, but they found gullible women in other towns who swallowed their false teachings, drawn by the men's charisma and wealth. Other like-minded people soon joined the community. Dennis's grandfather and his friends believed they were chosen by God to form a separate and pure community, and they exercised complete control over the people who live there using scriptures. But their interpretation of scripture was and is totally twisted." She sighed wearily. "In Fallow Creek, their religion is actually about control and dominance."

"Wow!" Keith looked up with a thoughtful expression on his face. "That explains why the leaders there have the power to decide who stays and who leaves. It is actually a private property owned by one person."

"Yes. Dennis Hamilton inherited the land where that town is built from his grandfather. And just as you've said, he decides what happens in the town, who stays and who doesn't. The problem is that once you're allowed to stay, you're never allowed to leave, at least not permanently, unless you're banished like me." She squeezed Keith's hand. "That's why we have to be careful. We'll be trespassing unless we're given permission to stay."

Keith leaned back on his seat and whispered, "The Earth is the Lord's and the fullness thereof."

"What?"

"It's a scripture from the Bible, Rachel. Surely you know it."

"Yes."

Keith said, "Ultimately, Fallow Creek belongs to the Lord, and He will decide who stays there."

She began to tell him a lot more about Fallow Creek, revealing details that she had not told him before. He listened intently, asking her questions once in a while, but mostly letting her talk. Finally, when she stopped speaking, he said, "You told me there are guards posted at the town's border. Since you were banished from the town, how are we going to get in? Maybe we will have to wait until it's nighttime and try to sneak in."

"Nope! We can't do that," Rachel said. "First of all, the guards are also there at night and even more vigilant then. In your dream, the man who drove you to Fallow Creek drove straight toward the guards unbothered by their presence at the border."

"Yes."

"Then that's what we'll do, Keith," she said. "We'll go straight to the guards and tell them to let us through. I know that sounds crazy, but can you think of any other way for us to get in? I think the Lord gave you that dream partly to show us the right way into the town."

Keith looked up thoughtfully and looked at her again. He sighed. "You're right as usual, Rachel. There's no other way in, at least none that I can think of. And since you know the town really well, if there was another way in, you would know about it."

"There's no other way that I know of," Rachel said. Fear rose up in her again. Not only was she planning to return to the town where she had been banished, she was now planning to come back with her new husband. Their experience at the border with the guards would determine whether they had truly heard from the Lord. If they were allowed in, then God had truly spoken to them, but if not, then they would know that the Lord had not sent them. Keith would rejoice since that would mean he could go back to Destiny. She, on the other hand, would despair at the thought of being so close to Emily and yet not being able to see her.

Hours later, they stopped in the small town called Prospect, and alighted from the train. They walked with their suitcase to the bus station. Their trip reminded Rachel of her departure from Fallow Creek months ago. If anyone had told her then that she would be back here just a few months later, she would not have believed it.

They got onto the bus that would take them to the town near Fallow Creek. Once they were there, they would have to find someone willing to drive them to the edge of town or they would have to walk the long distance there. Rachel hoped it would not come to that. She'd had to walk when she'd left, and the walk was a long and tiring one.

They spent another three hours on the bus, still talking about Fallow Creek and their plans once they got there. They were not sure what the Lord specifically wanted them to do in Fallow Creek except that He'd said they were to be lights shining in the darkness. Since Keith was a pastor and had been for years, she was sure he would figure it all out. Whatever he decided they were supposed to do, she would follow.

EIGHT

Keith turned to look at Rachel as they exited the bus in the small town called Black Valley. "So, you're saying that if we don't find someone to drive us to the edge of Fallow Creek, we'll have to walk all the way there?"

"Yes," Rachel said.

Keith groaned. He was bone-tired after traveling for almost a full day.

"Maybe we should rest?"

"I'm sorry, Rachel," he said. "I just wanted to get there as soon as we could, but if you're tired, we definitely should rest."

"No," she said. "I am a little tired, but I think it's better we continue on so we can get to Fallow Creek before nightfall."

They began to walk away from the small bus station, and Keith said, "Where will we find someone who would be willing to take us to Fallow Creek's border?" His eyes traveled around the area they were in. "There aren't many people in this small town." He saw a few people walking around but no cars.

"I've never actually come this way by car. At least, not on my own. When I was leaving Fallow Creek, I had to walk all the way from the town to this one. But I remember someone telling me that they hitchhiked from Black Valley to Fallow Creek when they had to leave temporarily for some brief business in Phoenix."

They continued to walk slowly through the tiny town as they were both tired, and Keith pointed at an old petrol station. There was a man pumping gas into his truck. "Do you think he would be willing to take us?"

Rachel turned to the direction he was pointing and shrugged. "Let's ask him."

They walked over to the man while Keith prayed, asking the Lord to grant them favor. The man turned his eyes to them, staring curiously at them. He was the typical kind of man Keith had always imagined he would find in a place like this. He had on dirty faded jeans and an old, sleeveless T-shirt that might once have been white. His hair was long, his beard and moustache bushy. But his eyes looked kind.

Before they reached him, the man said, "You're not from here, are you? Are you headed to that weird town next to ours?"

"Yes," Rachel answered before Keith could say anything. He smiled at how neither of them corrected the man on his evaluation of Fallow Creek. From everything Rachel had told him about the town, the man was right on the money.

"If it won't be any trouble for you, can you take us there?" Keith asked.

The man looked up thoughtfully for a few seconds and then faced them again. He said cheerfully, "Sure, why not? It's a short drive from here."

"Thank you so much," Keith and Rachel said in unison.

After the man had hurled their suitcase into the trunk of his old truck, they got in. Keith sat in the front seat beside the man while Rachel sat in the back. All through the ride, Keith's heart hammered. Not even the man's ceaseless questions about Fallow Creek distracted him from the warring emotions in his heart.

"I don't know," he said constantly to the man in answer to his many questions. Once in a while, Rachel supplied an answer, but mostly she kept silent. Keith knew that, just like him, she was consumed with thoughts about their future in the town they were heading to.

They turned a curve and Keith immediately recalled his dream about Fallow Creek as the road they drove on now looked like the one he'd seen in his dream. Before they spotted them, he knew immediately that they would soon see the infamous Security Squad Rachel had told him so much about.

And just as he guessed, a minute later, he spotted them — a group of young men in fatigues, holding guns and standing close to half a dozen SUVs. He turned and said to Rachel, "This road looks like the one I saw in my dream and those guards are exactly as I saw them." He smiled and said sarcastically, "It will be something if they start shooting at us."

Rachel chuckled and said, "They won't shoot, Keith. Not unless we trespass."

"Great!" Keith said, shaking his head. "That makes me feel a lot better."

Rachel chuckled again as Keith turned and faced the road once more. The closer they got to the guards, the faster his heart raced. All the guards turned to look at them, their eyes full of curiosity. A few feet away from the squad team, their driver stopped and said to Keith, "This is as far as I can go, guys. Those ones down there look kinda scary." He turned to look at Rachel and then turned back to Keith. "Are you sure you want to go on?"

Keith said nothing, but Rachel nodded and said, "Thank you for your kindness, sir."

Keith gathered up a smile for the man and thanked him for bringing them this far. It was nothing but a miracle that someone had agreed to drive them from the next town to this one.

After they got out of the truck with their suitcase, the man drove away and Keith took a long, deep breath. He put his arm firmly around Rachel's waist. With his other hand, he lifted up their suitcase and then with grim determination he faced the security guards. He whispered a short prayer asking the Lord for help and said to Rachel, "I guess it's time for the Lord to show up. This is the time we see if God really sent us here."

They both walked slowly to all the guards who were facing them, their eyes fixed firmly on them. Most of the men soon locked their gazes on Rachel as recognition lit up in their eyes.

"They are all frowning at me," Rachel said. "I'm not supposed to be here. From the look on their faces, I can see they are wondering what on earth I am doing trying to come back to the town while clinging to a man who isn't Mike."

Keith partly expected her to pull away slightly, but instead she held on even more tightly to him. They got to the men and stopped. Keith brushed aside the fear that rose up in him and said as boldly as he could, "Hi! We need to get into the town."

One of the men, who appeared to be their leader, came out of the ranks and stood before them, glowering at both of them. He turned his gaze to Rachel and said, "What do you want here? You've been banished from Fallow Creek!"

"Good day, Daniel," she said politely. "I just want to speak to Taylor. Surely, you will allow me to visit my own brother?"

Daniel shook his head. He turned to look at Keith with curiosity and then disdain and turned back to Rachel. "You have no brother in this town. You lost everything, including your relatives, when you were sent away."

She sounded frantic as she said, "At least send someone to get Taylor here so I can speak to him."

"No, I won't." He tapped his rifle and said, "I suggest you both leave, right now. If you don't, whatever happens to you will be all your fault."

Keith ran his fingers through his hair, slightly confused. "Lord, what now?" Once again, he said a brief prayer, asking the Lord for wisdom and then spoke the first thing that came to his mind. "We are here to deliver a message from God. Let us into the town now!" He blinked after he said that. He had planned on pleading with the men to let them through, but the words that had just escaped his lips were definitely an order rather than a plea.

All the guards laughed, and Rachel held his hand

tighter. On his own, he would have been glad to turn around and go, but he knew Rachel wanted to see Emily with all her heart. Plus, the certainty that God had indeed brought them here had grown even more during their journey to the town.

The one called Daniel said again, "If you don't leave now, we'll have to shoot you for trespassing."

"Lord, please help us," Keith whispered wearily, and then said once more, "We have a specific message for your leader, Dennis Hamilton. We were sent by a great authority." He blinked. *Where did that come from?*

The guards frowned; their faces full of surprise. None of them said anything for a short while, and then Daniel spoke. "By the authorities, you say?"

Keith did not answer. He had said "by a great authority" and not the authorities, but Daniel could believe whatever he wanted.

Daniel looked him over. "We keep the law here. What business do the authorities have with us?"

An otherworldly boldness settled on Keith and words formed in his mind. He spoke the words out as they did. "Dennis Hamilton's life is in danger, and the only way he will survive is if he hears the message we have for him."

Daniel stared at Keith with eyes as round as saucers, and then he turned to glare at Rachel. He finally said, "Wait here!"

He beckoned to one of the guards behind him and whispered in the man's ear. The guard hurried away, and Daniel faced Keith and Rachel again. He began to tap on his rifle, his eyes on Keith, clearly trying to intimidate him. Keith ignored him and looked away. The road behind the guards and in front of them was familiar, same as the one he had seen in his dream. A strong sense of destiny came over him, and with it alarm and a hint of excitement. Since the Lord told him and Rachel to come here, his emotions had been all jumbled up. But what he felt now was different and strange and confusing. He felt more confused than he had ever been.

Some of the men were now staring at Rachel lustfully, and Keith glared at them. He began to pray silently once more as he wrapped his arm possessively around her. About five minutes later, the man Daniel had sent on some errand came back and whispered something in Daniel's ear.

Daniel turned to Keith and said, "Our leader will speak to you... alone."

Keith shook his head vehemently. "What do you mean, he wants to speak to me alone?"

Daniel glanced at Rachel. "She is to remain here because she was banished from the town. She is never allowed to enter Fallow Creek again."

"I'm not going into *your town* without my wife."

Daniel arched his brows and stared at Keith and Rachel with distaste. He shrugged. "Your choice."

Rachel moved slightly away from Keith. "Don't worry about me, Keith. Just go. I'll be waiting for you here."

"I can't leave you here with these wolves."

Rachel smiled. She turned to Daniel and said, "I've known Dan since we were children. He will ensure that I am safe. Won't you, Dan?"

Daniel frowned and then nodded. "None of my men will touch her. We are not animals here," he said, his voice loaded with accusation as he looked at Keith and then at Rachel.

Keith turned away from Daniel and hugged Rachel. He whispered in her ear, "I'll be right back, sweetie." He kissed her and then followed one of the guards into town.

NINE

As they approached the leader's house, Keith wasn't surprised to find that it looked like the one he had seen in his dream. Nothing surprised him anymore after the strange words he'd spoken earlier at the border. The house was a two-story, Spanish-style home with a red tile roof. He entered behind the guard and immediately moved out of the way as three small children ran past him, shouting and chasing each other. He continued down a wide foyer and entered what seemed like a family room. There were three women sitting there, two of them holding babies, while the third was wiping the nose of a little boy. Keith could hear more shouts and laughter clearly made by children from somewhere in the house. The women stared curiously at him and then quickly turned again.

Keith continued to follow the guard as they climbed up stairs. Once more, he moved out of the way, pressing his back against the wall as two other women came down the stairs, one of them holding a set of twin girls who looked about five years old.

Rachel had told him that many of the men in this town married multiple wives and had many children, but seeing everything in living color was jarring. He continued up the stairs after the women and children had passed, still following the guard. They finally stopped at the top of the stairs and then walked toward a door that was shut. Keith's heart kept beating with panic... and a feeling akin to excitement. He had given Daniel a clear message for the leader, saying that the man's life was in danger and that he had more to tell him. But he had nothing else to say. He continued to pray silently, asking the Lord for something else to tell the leader when he stood before him.

The guard knocked, and when a commanding male voice said, "Enter," opened the door.

Keith entered with the guard and his eyes fell on a man whose back was to them as he looked at stacks of books on a large bookshelf. He picked up one book after another, either looking for something to read or stalling. The room was clearly the leader's study. There were bookshelves loaded with books and a chair behind a polished mahogany desk where more books were piled high.

The man, clearly the leader of the community, turned his piercing green eyes on Keith. A bushy beard like Mike Cadwell's and a moustache framed his face. Keith had imagined someone with an imposing height, but the man was small. Not what he'd expected at all. However, his face and bearing radiated authority. Keith wanted to dislike the man after all that Rachel had said about him, but he felt nothing but pity. He paid little attention to his feelings, though, as all his emotions were too confusing to sort out right now.

Dennis Hamilton walked to his desk, lifted a tome from the chair, and placed it on the desk. He sat down and pointed at the seat facing his. "Sit," he said to Keith.

The guard stepped back as Keith went to sit down.

"So, I was told you have a message for me. A message from the authorities… or from God?"

"A message from God."

Dennis Hamilton blinked. "A message from God," he said incredulously.

"Yes," Keith nodded. He was still panicking on the inside even though he put on a brave face. *Lord, this is where you speak*, he prayed silently again. Still he heard nothing.

The leader raised his eyebrows. "You have no message from God for me, do you?" Dennis Hamilton's eyes appraised Keith and he chuckled. "Of course you don't. I sent for you only because I wanted to see the crazy man who decided to come here and make such an audacious statement."

Keith's heart began to pound as the leader stood up. "I have no time for this nonsense," Dennis Hamilton said, looking down at Keith with disdain. He looked past Keith and beckoned to the guard at the door. The guard came closer and Dennis Hamilton said, "Escort this man out of my town!"

Keith groaned inwardly. They were going to be thrown out of town. Did that mean that the Lord did not send them here? If He hadn't, what were those words that Keith had spoken to that guy, Daniel, at the border? He gasped as words began to form in his mind again. Without waiting to consider what the words meant, he said to Dennis, "You recently got a call from a man who had been blackmailing you years ago but left you alone after you gave him money."

The leader's mouth fell open and his eyes widened with obvious shock. He turned slightly away from Keith and said in a shaky voice, "How... how did you find out about that? I haven't told anyone about it."

Emboldened by the prophetic words he had just spoken, Keith continued, "Your blackmailer is back and threatening to expose you for what you did years ago."

"Stop talking!" Dennis narrowed his eyes as he stared at Keith and slowly sat down in his chair. His eyes scrutinized Keith's face. "Who told you all this?" he asked, and the surprised expression on his face suddenly turned to suspicion. "No one knows about any of this except me and that blackmailer. Are you working together?" he asked accusingly. "He sent you, didn't he? You've come to continue the blackmail, haven't you?"

The supernatural boldness that had come over Keith a minute ago melted away, leaving only fear and amazement; fear of the implications of Dennis's accusations, and amazement at the fact that the words he had spoken had actually been true and had deeply affected the man before him.

Dennis said again, "That blackmailer sent you, didn't he?"

"No, I don't know who he is. I got the words I spoke only now and they are from God."

Dennis's eyes frantically searched Keith's, as though he could discover the full truth in them. He said, "You expect me to believe that it was God who told you all that?"

"Why would I come here if…?"

"Because you and my blackmailer work together and you want more money from me," Dennis cut in.

From the look on Dennis's face, Keith knew the leader was beginning to think about what to do with him. Dennis did not believe that Keith had truly heard from God and wasn't working somehow with his blackmailer. Keith pressed his lips together, worried. His life was in danger now. Unless the Lord gave him something else, something that would prove that he was not working with Dennis's blackmailer and had really been sent by God, he would be in serious trouble, and so would Rachel. Once again, he silently prayed for help, and sighed with relief as more words formed in his mind.

"Last night, you were so troubled by everything that you couldn't sleep. You got up from your bed and asked the Lord to help you. You told Him that if He helped you get rid of your blackmailer, you would clean up your act and do whatever He asked of you."

Dennis's face turned white as Keith spoke. When Keith finished, he said slowly with his voice trembling, "Even my last wife, Helen, who shared my bed last night, was fast asleep when I woke up to pray and didn't know that I couldn't sleep. And she certainly didn't know what I prayed for… especially since I prayed to God in my heart, as I was afraid she might hear if I prayed out loud. No one could have known what I asked God except…"
He shook his head as he stared at Keith with a look

of wonder.

Keith took a deep breath. He was sure he looked just as perplexed as Dennis Hamilton did. Never had he heard God's voice so clearly and accurately. Since the Lord had told him and Rachel to come here, it was as if his ears and heart had been unplugged and heaven opened up to him. It was what he had been praying for, for such a long time — to hear the voice of God clearly. And yet, now that it was happening, he didn't know if he wanted it anymore.

Dennis continued to stare in wonder at Keith and finally whispered, "Everything you say is true. I told God I would 'clean my act up' and do whatever He told me to. The problem is that I don't know what He wants me to do. I simply know there's something He's been wanting me to do for a long time."

Keith was surprised. "You don't know what God wants you to do?"

Dennis groaned. "I'm not a prophet like you. I don't hear God's voice except what I am told in the scriptures."

"I'm not a prophet either," Keith said incredulously. He wasn't surprised when more words came to him again. He repeated the words he was sensing in his heart. "The Lord wants you to know that He will tell you everything He wants you to do gradually."

"Will you tell me who exactly my blackmailer is and what to do about him?" Dennis asked eagerly.

Keith neither knew who the blackmailer was, nor did he hear anything more, but he knew that God's will was for them to stay here. He added, "I will tell you everything I hear from God if you let Rachel and me stay here."

Dennis leaned back against his chair and frowned. "Rachel Cadwell? She was banished from this town. She can never step foot in here again."

"Do you want to know who your blackmailer is or not?"

Dennis looked conflicted. He said nothing for a long moment and then gave a long sigh. "I will let Rachel stay here… but on one condition."

"And what is that?" Keith asked.

"That she goes back to her husband, Michael Cadwell."

"I am her husband," Keith said, annoyed. "And her name is Rachel Thorn now."

Dennis Hamilton shook his head. "No, Mike Cadwell is her husband."

"He's not!" Keith said, exasperated. "Mike Cadwell already has a wife. He was living with Rachel, but wasn't married to her… no matter what any of you in this town say."

Dennis opened his mouth, clearly to protest, but Keith said firmly, "Either Rachel lives with me as my wife here or we don't stay in the town at all. You won't know who your blackmailer is or what the Lord wants you to do." His voice was nonchalant. "You will have to deal with that blackmailer on your own." After he had spoken, he winced inwardly. He had spoken more boldly than he normally would, and his words did not sound like what he would say. He was turning into someone else.

Dennis stared thoughtfully at Keith for a long moment and then sighed loudly. "All right, then," he said. "But everyone in this town, especially the men here, will want to know why I allowed you to stay in this town with a woman who is already married."

Keith sighed wearily. He was tired of explaining his relationship to people like Dennis and even Mike Cadwell. "She wasn't and is not married to anyone else but me! How many times do I have to say that?"

"So you say," Dennis told him. "I don't know how you can be comfortable living with a woman who has a husband. And you say she's your wife."

"For the last time, she doesn't have any husband other than me, and yes, she's my wife! But I won't sit here and argue with you. Are you going to let Rachel and me live in this town as man and wife, or should I leave?"

The leader rapped his fingers on the desk for a long moment and then nodded at last. "Fine! You and Rachel can stay here. But let me warn you. Everyone in this community will be angry with you and Rachel, and I will not be blamed for whatever happens to either of you. Mike Cadwell particularly will be justified in whatever he does to you." Dennis shook his head. "Of course, I don't want anything to happen to you as I need you to tell me what God is saying about my blackmailer. I will have to assign guards to you two."

"God will protect us," Keith said, even though his heart was racing.

"Very well, you can stay. We'll meet here tomorrow so that you can share with me whatever God tells you."

He shook his head slowly. "I can't just snap my fingers and get a message from God."

"I don't know how you do it, but you told me that if I let you stay here, God would reveal everything I need to know about the blackmailer."

Keith did not answer. Those were not his exact words, but... He stood up and said, "I'm going to get my wife now."

"I'll see you here in my office first thing tomorrow!" Dennis Hamilton ordered. "And I don't have to tell you that you can't mention anything we've said here to anyone."

"Who do I know in this town?" Keith said.

Dennis called to the guard, who was standing just inside the door, and told him to let Keith and Rachel enter the town unharmed.

Keith turned around and walked out of the study. The guard stepped in front of him as he made his way down the hallway and then down the stairs. He left the house quickly and hurried past the guard as he could not wait to get to Rachel. His hands felt clammy as he ran through his mind all the words he had uttered in that study to the leader. His life was getting stranger and stranger by the day.

His heart flooded with joy when he spotted Rachel on the side of the road. Except for Daniel, the guards were on the other side of the road, well away from her. When he got to Rachel, he hugged her tightly and then pulled back.

She smiled at Keith. "I can see your meeting with Dennis went well."

"Yes, better than I could have imagined. But I also committed myself to something I don't know I can continue to do."

She lifted her brows. "What did you commit yourself to?"

"I'll tell you everything after we settle in your brother's house."

"So, we're allowed to enter the town?"

"Yes."

Daniel stared at both of them. "You can go into the town, but you have to hand over your phones; by order of our leader."

"Why?" Keith asked, slightly irritated.

Daniel shrugged. "You can't enter until you've both handed over your phones."

"Let's just give them to him," Rachel said.

They both handed over their phones to him. Daniel frowned as they wrapped their arms around each other, but Keith ignored him. They began to make their way down the road. Similar-looking bungalows lined the streets. From time to time he saw a different-looking house, but most of the homes looked the same.

"Taylor's house is on the other side of Fallow Creek," Rachel said. "It's a long walk from here but we've been through so much today. What is another few miles of trekking?"

Keith chuckled. "At least we have a place to rest our weary legs now and a roof over our heads until we're able to get our own house." He raised his brows and gasped as once again words formed in his mind. "No, no, no! Lord, please, no!"

Rachel stopped walking. "What is it?" she asked in alarm.

Keith shut his eyes briefly and then opened them again. He breathed, "God doesn't want us to stay at your brother's house or ask him to help us in any way."

Rachel's mouth dropped open. "Where are we

supposed to stay, then?"

He pursed his lips and shook his head. "I have no idea. The Lord didn't say."

TEN

Rachel took his hand as they made their way farther down the road. Her emotions roiled; they didn't know where they were going to live or even sleep tonight. She looked this way and that. The houses still looked the same from the last time she was here. *Of course they look the same. You left here only months ago.*

She sighed and began to pray silently for wisdom. Surely, God had not led them to Fallow Creek to become homeless vagabonds. And yet, she couldn't think of anywhere apart from Taylor's house where they could stay. She was close to no one in the town except maybe for Lily, her childhood friend, who she had gotten reacquainted with at the Restoration House. But knowing Lily, she was probably still there if she had not escaped.

Rachel felt Keith squeeze her hand, clearly to encourage her, and she turned to him. He had a silly smile on his face, and she could not help but laugh in spite of the way she felt. They soon both began to laugh together, despite their dire situation... or maybe because of it. But probably because she felt a supernatural peace descend on her soul and knew Keith had felt it too. And then she blinked as an idea entered her mind.

"What is it?" Keith asked, still smiling.

"I just remembered something," she said. "There's a tiny abandoned building not too far from here. It was owned by a man who used it to store some goods. I think he was sent away from the town for some undisclosed reason. The building has been empty and abandoned for a few years now. It's not much of a place, but at least we can stay there in the meantime until we actually find somewhere suitable to live."

With Keith pulling their suitcase behind him, they began to walk toward the building, Rachel leading the way. They walked past more and more houses as they went deeper into the town. A few people glanced at them, but she was thankful that most people were indoors now. It was a Sunday afternoon and most people had probably gone to the general service and then, as usual, stayed in their houses with their families.

"I haven't seen the place in a while," she told Keith. "I wonder what state it will be in now." She didn't have to wonder for long. They turned a corner and she spotted the building and bit her lip. It looked more dilapidated than she remembered. Shame washed over her, and she could not look at Keith. What would he be thinking right now? Maybe he would be wondering why he had married her because, without a doubt, if he hadn't, the Lord would probably not have sent him here to the town she grew up in, and now to live in some tiny abandoned building.

There was no door and the windows were broken. She entered the building first, followed closely by Keith, and looked around. It was nothing but one large room. The floor was bare with holes in it and the walls also had holes in them. There was nothing around they could sit on or lie down on. She took a deep breath and finally found the courage to look at Keith. He was not smiling as his eyes traveled around the room.

She opened her mouth to tell him how sorry she was once again, but he drew her close and kissed the top of her head. "Well, I guess it will have to do for now," he said.

"I wish we had something soft to lay on the ground so we could lie down," she said.

He pulled away from her and bent down to open their suitcase. Curiously she looked on as he searched through it. They had sold most of their things and had only a few clothes in there, so she didn't know what he was searching for. She looked on in surprise when he pulled out a grey blanket she thought they had sold and then proceeded to brush aside some of the dirt on the ground with his palms. He dusted the dirt from his hands and laid the blanket on the slightly cleaner floor. Sitting down on the blanket, he took her hand and said, "Sit, sweetie."

She smiled sadly as she sat down beside him. How on earth were they supposed to make a life in this place? Her stomach rumbled with hunger, but she ignored it. It was not as if there was any food around anywhere. And they had only pennies left of the money the Lord had allowed them to keep. She said to Keith, "So what now? What are we going to do?"

"I'm not sure," Keith answered. "But let me tell you everything that happened when I went to see Dennis Hamilton. Maybe after that, we can figure out how to move on and what exactly we're supposed to do now that we're here."

He began to narrate his experience to her and she could not have been more surprised if he had told her he'd just discovered an oil well. When he finished speaking, she was silent for a long while, pondering on what he had said.

She finally said to him, "So Dennis Hamilton has this terrible secret from his past that he doesn't want anyone to know about?"

"It appears so," Keith said.

"I'm amazed at how the Lord let you in on that."

"I used it as an open door for us to stay here. I don't know how long we'll be allowed to, though. Dennis told me that I had to go back early tomorrow morning to tell him whatever the Lord speaks to me about his situation."

"Can I go with you tomorrow?" she asked. Then she shook her head. "What am I even asking? Of course Dennis won't want me to come with you. First off, he banished me from this community, and I'm guessing he'll want to keep whatever you both talk about a secret."

Keith chuckled. "Well, I hope he knows that I can't keep secrets from you."

"Still, I shouldn't go. I wouldn't be welcome there. Besides, I want to visit Taylor tomorrow morning and try to figure out a way to see my Emily."

This time, Keith's stomach rumbled, and he

put his hand on his belly. He gave her a silly smile. "Well, we can use our lack of food as a reason to fast and pray."

Rachel laughed and then quickly sobered. "Seriously, though, Keith, we have nothing to eat."

"God will provide somehow," he said, but he didn't sound so convincing.

She sighed and stretched out on the blanket. Keith lay down beside her and pulled her close.

"What have we gotten ourselves into?" she whispered.

"No, Rachel. We didn't get ourselves into this. God did. And since the Lord was the one who got us into all this, He will find a way out for us."

She wanted to tell him that it would take a real miracle for anyone apart from Taylor to help them out in this community. Most people had probably heard about her and what she'd done and why she was banished from the town. They would not be particularly fond of her and the way she had threatened their way of life. Even the women here had been brainwashed from their youth. She was sure, like the men, they wouldn't be too happy that she'd returned. She held her peace, however. There was no point telling Keith all that and painting an even more scary picture of their situation right now.

They continued to talk about what their future might look like in Fallow Creek while the room began to grow dark as night approached. Soon, Keith began to snore lightly, already asleep, and Rachel couldn't help but smile. It was just like him to put aside every troubling situation because he was forever positive, fully trusting God in everything.

If only she could be the same way and fall asleep as easily as he had done. With all he'd told her about his experience with Dennis, it was even more clear to her that the Lord had brought them here. She had to trust Him fully.

And yet she couldn't sleep. Her mind roiled with a myriad of concerns and worries, from how she would be able to see Emily despite Mike's hostility, to the fact that they had nothing to eat at all.

"Stop worrying, Rachel. God will provide," she whispered and shut her eyes tightly.

After a few minutes of struggling to fall asleep, she opened her eyes again. When Keith left tomorrow, she would go and see Taylor. Unfortunately, she could ask nothing from him, as the Lord had told them not to. "I'm starving," she said, and for some reason, she chuckled as she found that funny. Even though she disliked Fallow Creek, she had never gone hungry in this place, or during the months she'd lived in Destiny. This was a first. She pulled her mind away from her hunger and the discomfort she felt from lying on the hard floor and focused on her daughter. After she visited Taylor tomorrow, she would go to Mike's house and ask to see Emily. She couldn't think of any other way to see her daughter except to just go and ask to see her directly. It was not likely that Mike would let her see Emily, but she had to try.

She whispered a short prayer, asking the Lord to touch Mike's heart so he would allow her to see her daughter. Mike was heartless and he would no doubt try to punish her for leaving him by keeping Emily away from her just as he'd done in the past. Her desperation to see Emily grew and she soon began to panic. She told herself to calm down. God had already done miracles for her and Keith. There was nothing He couldn't do now. Since He was the one who'd told them to drop the custody lawsuit and come here, she had to believe He was already planning to reunite her with her daughter.

She put her arm around Keith, drew closer to him, and prayed that morning would come quickly.

***

The next day, with his stomach still protesting from hunger, Keith held Rachel's hand and prayed, asking the Lord for His guidance, protection, and provision. He was not as concerned for himself about his hunger as he was for Rachel. Even though he sounded confident and full of faith as he prayed, he felt slightly afraid. There was still no food this morning and no way to get any. They had to have a miracle now.

They rounded off their prayers by committing their future in this place into God's hands. Keith wasn't sure what the day would bring. All they knew was that the Lord had told them to be lights in this dark town. There was, of course, the open door the Lord had made with Dennis Hamilton. In just a few minutes, he would stand up and prepare to leave for the leader's house. But first, he had to make sure that Rachel was okay. He knew she was hungry now, just as he was. He put his arm around her and assured her that the Lord would provide for them no matter how it seemed.

She smiled and nodded. "So, I guess since the Lord has made an open door for you to speak to

Dennis, that is what we've been called to do here, at least for now."

"Yes," he said. "I'll have to see where that leads me. And you plan to visit Taylor after I leave, right?"

"Yes," she answered. She'd also told him about her plan to go to Mike's house after she'd visited Taylor. "I have an aching need to see my daughter right now."

"Are you sure it's a good idea, Rachel? You know how Mike is. I don't think you should go to his house alone. In fact, I don't think you should go to Taylor's alone either. I want to come to both places with you."

She raised her brows and he added, "I need to thank Taylor for all the money he sent to help rebuild Destiny. As for Mike, I don't think I need to tell you how dangerous he is. He tried to kill me, in case you've forgotten. I don't want to tell you what to do, Rachel, but in this instance, I'm asking you not to go alone. Please wait for me. We'll find a way for you to see your daughter when I come back."

Rachel sighed loudly and shook her head. "Please let me go, Keith. I'll be careful. I promise. If you go with me to Mike's house, you know it'll only make things worse."

"If you're going to Mike's, then I'm going with you," he said firmly. "Besides, we can't just march up to his front door and demand to see Emily. That will probably not work and you know it."

She groaned, and he put his arm around her again. "We'll figure it out when I get back," he said.

He opened the suitcase and quickly changed into a plain black T-shirt and a pair of blue jeans. Before he left, he bent down to kiss her and asked if she would be okay. "Should I wait for you to change so we can leave the house together?"

"No, I'll be fine," she told him. "Besides, we're going in different directions."

He smiled and kissed her again.

"I'll miss you," she said.

"I'll miss you, too. I'll try to come back as soon as possible."

She nodded.

He stepped out of the house, praying again that God would provide for them because he didn't know how long they would survive without food.

ELEVEN

After Keith left, Rachel looked around the empty space in which they'd spent the night. In the bright morning light, it looked filthy. She brought out a small cloth from their suitcase and began to clean the ground with it, using it as both a broom and a duster. After she finished, she looked around their sleeping area again. It was basically clean now.

She glanced at the doorless entrance, and the reality of their situation crashed in on her. She was starving and this was no way to live. Why did the Lord tell them to give away all their money and then tell them not to ask Taylor for anything? There was no food or even water for her and Keith. Soon, she would have to go begging anyone she saw for something to eat and drink.

"Lord, please help us," she said. "You brought us here. Now we need a miracle."

In answer to her prayer, her stomach rumbled again. She groaned and closed her eyes. She opened them again, having pictured an image of a large burger in her mind, and sighed. *Why am I torturing myself?*

She blinked and stood up when she heard footsteps approaching. Her heart began to pound as Daniel appeared in the doorway holding his gun. He didn't enter, but he fixed his eyes on her and smiled slightly. "Hey, Rachel! I have something for you."

Curious, she moved closer to him, and he held out a small bag to her. "Food," he said.

She could smell a tantalizing aroma as she took the bag from him and her stomach rumbled again.

He looked back as though he were trying to make sure no one was coming and then turned to her again. "I thought you would be hungry so I brought you some food."

She looked at him and then down at the bag. She was surprised that he had brought her food after the way he had acted at the border yesterday. Without thinking, she blurted out, "Why did you bring this, Daniel? And how did you find us?"

He raised his brows, and she shook her head. "No, you don't need to answer that. Thank you so much for the food. You're right. I'm starving." She opened the bag and looked inside. There were two covered plastic bowls and two small bottles of water. She brought one of the bowls out, opened it, and smiled widely. "Spaghetti and meatballs!" she exclaimed. "One of my favorites."

"I remember you liked spaghetti and meatballs when were kids, and since it was what I had for dinner yesterday, I decided to bring the leftovers for you."

The food was too plentiful to be just leftovers, but she said nothing about it. She thanked him again, giving him a big smile.

He looked back again and then turned to her. "I need to go now, Rachel. I don't want anyone to know I came here." Before she could thank him once more, he hurried away.

She sat down on the blanket and shut her eyes to pray, her heart full of gratitude to God. "Thank you so much for the food, Lord." She opened the bag again and opened one of the plastic bowls. She guzzled up the food and didn't stop until she'd finished the bowl. She drank one of the small bottles of water and sighed with relief and contentment.

Once again, she thanked God for the food. A scripture flashed through her mind and she said it out loud. "Give us this day our daily bread."

God had provided breakfast. She would trust him to provide their lunch and dinner. There was another pack left and she would reserve that for Keith. She sighed. They would have to live every day trusting God for their next meal.

She thought about what she was supposed to do here as she packed up her empty bowl and kept it aside. "Lord, Keith has an open door to share your word with Dennis Hamilton. What about me? What am I specifically supposed to do in this town?"

She chided herself after she'd finished praying. Of course she was here to help Keith with whatever the Lord wanted him to do. She was his... she blinked in surprise as someone called her name. The Lord had been speaking to her more clearly than He ever had in her life, but was that the Lord's voice she'd just heard? She instinctively looked at the entrance to the building and her mouth fell open in surprise. "Olivia! What are you doing here?" Rachel stood up. "How did you know I was here?"

Like Daniel, Olivia, Mike's wife, looked behind her as though she was afraid of anyone seeing her, and then she turned back to Rachel. "The whole town knows you're here."

Rachel pursed her lips. This place was not safe for her and Keith if everyone in town knew where to find them.

Olivia said, "Mike is at home, raging. Since he found out you came here with some man who people say is your new husband, Mike has been behaving like a rabid dog." Olivia looked into the distance. "He's married someone else, Rachel. Did you know that?" Olivia looked incredibly sad. She said, "It's like he doesn't even see me, but he hasn't seen me for years. Now he's taken someone else to replace you. A girl even younger than you."

Rachel felt sorry for the woman. She'd been ridden with guilt when she was with Mike, knowing that she was sleeping with someone else's husband, right under the woman's nose. It had been so wrong and, even now, she felt guilt wash over her again. She wanted to reach out and hug Olivia to comfort her, but she didn't know if the woman would welcome that. She thought about telling Olivia to leave Mike, but Olivia would never do that. She loved him too much and she was too wrapped up in the rules and traditions of this place to even think about doing so.

Rachel brushed away her concerns for Olivia and opened her mouth to ask about Emily, but Olivia spoke again. "Mike has been really angry, wondering why Dennis allowed you and that man you came here with to stay in Fallow Creek and live as husband and wife when you are married to him still."

Rachel felt her stomach boil with anger. "I'm not married to him! What are you saying, Olivia? You are his wife… not me."

It was as though Olivia had not heard her. She continued. "How did you convince Dennis Hamilton to let you stay here?" She was looking at Rachel as though she had just dropped down from the sky. "It makes no sense," she said. "You were banished from this town. You're not supposed to be here."

Rachel narrowed her eyes angrily as she stared at Olivia and then her anger melted away. It was clear Olivia was worried that she would go back to Mike and his already divided attention would even be more so. She said to Olivia, "I'm not interested in Mike. In fact, I never was. Thank God I am married to a man I love with everything in me. Keith would give his life for me if he had to. I wish you had the same kind of love that I do."

Again, it was as though Olivia had not heard her. She asked again, "How come Dennis Hamilton let you and a man you claim is now your husband to stay in Fallow Creek?"

Rachel didn't answer her question. "How is Emily, Olivia?" she asked, desperate to know. "How is my daughter?"

Olivia kept looking at her as though she had never seen Rachel before.

Rachel asked frantically, "Please tell me, Olivia. How is my Emily doing?"

Olivia smiled slightly. "She's growing bigger and bigger every day." She arched her brows. "You know what you and that man did... are doing, is unheard of here. How did you...?"

"I need to see Emily now!" Rachel cut her short.

Olivia looked back again and then stepped into the house. "You know Mike will never let you see Emily again, Rachel. Especially as you are here with your..." She shook her head, leaving her sentence unfinished.

"I have to see Emily, Olivia! You have to help me! I'm her mother and I have a right to see her!"

"But Mike will be angry if he finds out I helped you see her," Olivia said. "He will be raving mad. I don't know that I can help you in any way, Rachel."

Rachel shook her head. "There has to be a way to help me without Mike knowing."

Olivia's eyes studied Rachel's for a long moment, and then she finally said, "You have no plans to return to Mike?"

"No, Olivia. None whatsoever. I told you, I'm married now to the man I love."

Olivia looked shocked.

Rachel couldn't help but ask if Olivia was sure she wanted to stay with Mike. "You know how cruel..."

"Stop it!" Olivia glared at Rachel. "I will not let you bad-mouth my husband. Just because you left and now say you're married to someone else doesn't mean that I have to leave him, too. I married him before you came with..." She stopped talking and looked away.

Once again, Rachel felt overwhelming sympathy for her. She came close and put her hands on Olivia's shoulders. "You have nothing to fear from me, Olivia." She showed Olivia her engagement and wedding rings. She knew how much Olivia loved Mike and how she was hurting. Again, she felt like telling Olivia to leave Mike, but she stopped herself from doing so. It was not her place to keep insisting.

"She's nothing like you," Olivia said, sounding distracted again.

Rachael raised her brows. "Who?"

"Mike's new wife. You were nice to me, and I could see you tried not to flaunt the affection Mike had for you in front of me. But this girl… She seems to think that she owns the whole house and since she now shares Mike's bed, she completely ignores me and thinks that she alone is married to him."

Rachel listened, hurting for Olivia. This would be how Olivia would spend the rest of her life unless something changed in this town… or she did. She would continue to pine for a man who hardly knew she existed even though they lived under the same roof. Maybe he would marry even more wives, and then she would be totally forgotten. Just a fixture in the house.

As Rachel looked at Olivia, she wished with all her heart that she could convince the woman to leave Mike, but she already knew she couldn't. Besides, it was not like Olivia had the choice to leave Mike as long as she lived in Fallow Creek. The way of life here did not support or tolerate a woman leaving her husband. And just like most women here, she had no connections outside Fallow Creek.

"Something has to change in this town," Rachel whispered.

"What? What did you say, Rachel?"

"Nothing," Rachel answered. She looked deeply into the woman's eyes. "Will you help me, Olivia?

Will you help find a way for me to see my daughter without Mike finding out?"

Olivia was silent for a full minute, and then she nodded. "Okay, Rachel. This is what I can do. Come to the house around midnight. Mike will be asleep by then and so will Davina, his other wife. I will bring Emily out to you so you can see her. It will have to be only for a few minutes because I don't want to risk Mike waking up and finding out what we're doing. Now that he knows you're back here, he will probably start to keep close vigil over Emily the way he did when you ran away months ago." She added, clearly more to herself than to Rachel, "That man is so paranoid now."

"Thank you so much, Olivia," Rachel said, and gathered the woman in a hug. Olivia felt stiff as Rachel hugged her, but Rachel squeezed her tight and then let her go.

Olivia stepped back and said, "I have to go now, before Mike notices that I'm gone." She snorted. "But then again, he might not even notice if I didn't go back all night. He's so preoccupied with his new bride."

She turned around and began to hurry away and Rachel called out, "Midnight, then?"

"Yes," she said, without turning around.

After she left, Rachel sat back down on the blanket and heaved a sigh of relief. Hopefully, she would be able to see Emily tonight and Mike would not find out about it.

Hope and excitement flooded her heart at the thought of seeing Emily again. She smiled and said, "Thank you, Lord. Now, about what we were talking before Olivia showed up. Keith has the open door to share your word with Dennis now. What am I meant to do here?"

She listened, but heard nothing. Sighing, she lay back on the blanket. There was nothing else to do but wait for Keith to come back and then tell him about Olivia's visit. They would both go to see Emily together tonight. She couldn't wait for Keith to finally meet her daughter. Hopefully he would bond with her and love Emily as much as she did. She could see that happening quickly because Keith had such a large heart. One day, she hoped Emily would finally be able to come and live with her and Keith and he could be a father to her as well.

Rachel looked out of the entrance of the building as though Keith would walk in at any moment. She couldn't hold in her excitement. "Lord, let it be midnight quickly," she whispered. "And please let everything work out so that one day, Lord, she will be able to come live with me and Keith, and then we'll never be separated again."

She shut her eyes. For now, she would have to be satisfied with seeing Emily intermittently, until the Lord did the miracle she was praying for with all her heart. He had already done one huge miracle for her — bringing Keith into her life, a man so kind and loving that she would never have dared to dream of finding him and the kind of love she now had. When she was reunited permanently with Emily, her life would be perfect.

She looked around her at the empty, dilapidated building and chuckled. "Well, almost perfect. And, Lord, please help us find somewhere else to live," she prayed.

***

Keith sighed as he looked at Dennis Hamilton, who was staring at him from across the table. He still had nothing to tell the man. The Lord had not revealed anything to him concerning who Dennis's blackmailer was or what Dennis was supposed to do about it. Dennis kept staring expectedly at him, and then a frown creased his forehead.

"Please tell me what God has told you," Dennis insisted. "Who is my blackmailer and what am I supposed to do in order to get rid of him?"

Keith said a desperate prayer in his heart, asking the Lord for just one word, but still he got nothing. He sighed again. The Lord had said that they were to be lights shining bright in this dark town. Perhaps all he could do right now was pray for Dennis to come to receive the true gospel. According to Rachel, most people here had a form of religion, but they did not have a true relationship with God. "Can I pray for you to come to know God better?" Keith asked him.

Dennis looked distracted. "You can pray, but afterwards you tell me who my blackmailer is."

Keith pressed his lips together and asked Dennis to tell him everything that had happened with the blackmailer and why he was blackmailing Dennis. Nothing Dennis told him about the blackmailer would help Keith know exactly who it was or what Dennis was supposed to do. He was just curious.

"Everything?" Dennis stared at him.

"Yes, everything."

"And then you'll tell me who it is?" Before Keith could say he wasn't sure about that, Dennis said off-handedly, "I know it's someone who's jealous of me because I'm the leader of this place. He's been accusing me of taking something that doesn't belong to me, but that isn't true."

Keith leaned forward, staring at Dennis. "Is that all?"

Dennis sighed and then waved his hand as though everything he said had fully explained all that Keith wanted to know, when in actual fact, he'd really said nothing at all.

Keith shook his head. "Is that all, Dennis?"

"Yes," Dennis said and pounded the table with his fist. "Now I want to know who the blackmailer is and how to keep what's mine!"

Keith bristled at the man's commanding tone. And he wasn't just offended that the man was commanding him to speak. It was the fact that it was the Lord he was actually commanding to speak. Dennis reminded him of Mike Cadwell. Both of them were such arrogant men.

Keith's mind immediately traveled to Rachel and what she had told him this morning about going to Mike's house in order to see Emily. She was desperate to see her daughter and he was desperate for her as well. He knew how the separation from Emily had affected her, but he also knew that the likelihood of Mike agreeing for her to see Emily was small. The man was brutal and heartless. He recalled how Mike had tried to kill him in Destiny and shuddered. He would have to ask Dennis for guards to accompany them when he and Rachel went to see her ex. He folded his hands on the desk and said, "I have a request."

Dennis groaned. "Another one? What is it now?"

"My wife has been grieving for some time since she had to be separated from her daughter when she left Fallow Creek. Now that she's back here, she wants to see her daughter again. But the thing is, we're certain Mike Cadwell won't let her see Emily. But if you intervene..."

"No!" Dennis cut him short. "I cannot interfere in another man's private affair. It wouldn't be right for me to instruct Michael Cadwell about what he is supposed to do with his wife..."

"Rachel is not Mike's wife! She's mine!"

"I will not intervene," Dennis said flatly.

Once again, Keith asked the Lord to touch Dennis's heart so he would reconsider. The words, *Feed my sheep!* flashed through Keith's mind and he groaned. What did that have to do with the request he'd just made? He didn't know what the words meant or what the Lord wanted him to do. He'd been a pastor for years before he was sent here, but...

He blinked. Was that what the Lord wanted him to do in Fallow Creek? He felt the Spirit tugging at his heart, telling him to ask Dennis for a place to start holding regular services. But that was the last thing he wanted to ask the man right now. What he really wanted now was for Dennis to help them convince Mike to allow Rachel see Emily regularly. Finally, he couldn't resist anymore and said exasperatedly, "Can you arrange a place where I can start to hold services... maybe every week?"

Dennis blinked rapidly. "You want to form a church here?"

"I wouldn't call it a church. Just somewhere people can gather and fellowship together."

Dennis shook his head and waved his hand. "No. We already have a general church service here."

"I'm just asking for a space to hold Bible study and prayer meetings. Around once a week. It's not going to interfere with the general church service, I promise."

Dennis looked up thoughtfully for a few seconds and said, "I can't allow it!"

"It's important that you allow me to hold those services." He wasn't sure why, but holding the prayer meetings was important. That he was sure of.

Dennis narrowed his eyes. He said nothing for a long while and Keith's heart drummed. Finally, he leaned back against his seat and said, "Is that part of what God wants me to do?"

"Yes, I believe so."

Dennis pressed his lips together and threaded his fingers together. "Okay, then. You can start your services. There's a small room at the back of the town hall. It's empty. You can use it for your services, but just make sure it doesn't interfere with ours or any other activity in this place." Dennis shook his head. "I can't believe I just agreed to let you start holding services here."

Keith bowed his head in thanks.

Dennis added. "Remember that you must keep all the rules of this town."

Keith's stomach rumbled from hunger.

"Now, tell me who the blackmailer..."

"What in the world is going on here?" someone roared behind Keith.

Keith turned around and stared into the face of Mike Cadwell.

TWELVE

Keith glared up at Mike as he roared, "Dennis Hamilton, what on earth do you think you're doing entertaining this man here, in your home?"

Dennis narrowed his eyes and said in a cold voice, "Michael Cadwell, remember who you're speaking to! And also remember that you are standing on shaky ground. I allowed you to come back here even after you fled the town with your wife without any consequences, but don't think you can speak to me any way you want. And you are in my home just as you said. I can invite and entertain anyone I want to here. Besides, I don't remember inviting you here."

Keith's heart burned with anger and revulsion as he stared at Mike, the man who had treated Rachel so badly and had almost killed him. Hatred raged in his heart, but he knew it was wrong, and he asked the Lord to take it away from him. No matter what the man had done they were here to be a light and that included loving those who had treated them badly.

Mike stood his ground and said, "It's not right, Dennis, and you know it! This man took my wife away from me and I hear they're insisting that they're married. How can you let such a man into your house, let alone give him an audience to speak with you?"

"I will speak to whomever I decide," Dennis said. "And you have no right to question me."

Mike's face turned red and then, without warning, he swung at Keith. But Keith was prepared for any display of violence from Mike and dodged the blow.

Dennis grabbed Mike and held him tightly to prevent him from trying to hit Keith again, and Keith shook his head. It reminded him of the day Mike had appeared at his house in Destiny uninvited and threatened him and Rachel. Rachel had arrived at his doorstep some days before drenched from the rain and had consequently fallen ill, but had made a full recovery at his house. She had refused to go back to Mike, but Mike had tried to drag her away by force. He had not succeeded in doing so, which had sparked his anger and led to his planning to kill Keith. Later, he had kidnapped Rachel.

"Listen, Mike, stop this nonsense right now," Dennis said as Mike struggled to free himself from Dennis's hold.

"Let me go!" Mike yelled. "Let me go right now!" He lunged at Keith, but Dennis grabbed his hands and held them securely behind his back. For a fifty-something-year-old man, he was remarkably strong.

Two squad guards appeared at the door, and Mike yelled, "You're breaking the rules of this place,

Dennis!" Mike struggled to free himself again.

Dennis let him go and the two security squad members immediately grabbed him. Dennis glowered at him and said to the squad members, "Escort him out of my house."

Mike glared at the squad guards and roared, "Let me go!"

They let go of him but stood beside him ready to grab him if he tried anything again. Mike shot a deadly look at Keith and walked out of the office, the guards following closely.

After they left, Dennis went to take his seat again while Keith shut his eyes, relieved that Mike had left at last. The man was a truly dangerous person, and he was afraid not so much for himself, but for Rachel. Rachel had told him how jealous Mike was, and he had experienced it firsthand on that day that Mike came to his house spewing threats, furious that Rachel was staying in his house. Now that he was actually married to Rachel and they were back here in Fallow Creek, who knew what Mike would try to do to him and Rachel because of his jealousy? Keith said a silent prayer, asking the Lord once more for protection. He brushed away his fear and fixed his eyes on Dennis again.

Dennis threaded his fingers together and looked pointedly at Keith. "The elders of this town will soon call for a meeting to find out why I let Rachel back into town as she was supposed to never set foot here again. Worse, they will want to know why I let you, a man who stole another man's wife, into this town and actually gave you a place to stay here."

Keith shook his head. "I don't know what to say."

"I'm not asking you to say anything. I just want you to understand the risk I am putting myself in by allowing you and Rachel to stay here as man and wife. You understand now that you must follow the rules of this place strictly."

"I don't know how much I can abide to the rules here. I guess Rachel and I have broken a lot of them by just our presence here. And that's not going to change, because I'm married to her."

"Listen," Dennis said. "I told you all this so you would know that you and Rachel can't stay here for much longer. You made a request for me to speak to Mike on Rachel's behalf, but as you can see from what happened right now with Mike, it'll be virtually impossible to reason with him in any way. Especially as it concerns his own child. For your safety and that of Rachel, you both will have to do whatever it is you came here for and then leave." Dennis leaned forward and looked intently at Keith. "But first, you have to tell me what you've heard from God. Do you know who my blackmailer is and what I'm supposed to do about him?"

"I've heard nothing more today than what I already told you," Keith said, feeling emotionally drained. "Tomorrow, I'll tell you everything I hear." There was a possibility that he would hear nothing even by tomorrow, but that was all he could think to say.

Dennis gave a long sigh and then said, "Okay. Tomorrow, then. But tomorrow you will have to tell me something or you and Rachel will have to leave this town immediately. I have attracted a lot of anger because of my decision to let you both stay. If you have nothing of value to say to me, then there's no point allowing you to continue on."

Keith's heart drummed as he said, "Can I ask for something else?"

"Go ahead."

"My wife and I are staying in an abandoned building that has no door and is unsafe. And we have no food. Can you give us food and somewhere to stay?"

Dennis stroked his beard and then gave Keith a curt nod. "I will give you a place to stay, but I can't let you and Rachel live together. From Mike's reaction just now, you can see that wouldn't be possible. If I give you both a house to live in together as husband and wife, I might have a revolt on my hands."

Keith frowned.

"You understand my situation, don't you?" Dennis said. "You can't stay together. You'll have to live in different places."

"I can't live separately from my wife, Dennis."

"You'll have to. My decision is final. There's no way you will stay in the same house as Rachel. It's also for your safety."

"I will not…"

"Stop! You have no choice. You will live in different places or you will have to leave Fallow Creek and I can see you don't want that. Frankly, neither do I, at least not for now."

Keith stared at Dennis, trying to get control of his emotions. It wasn't his idea to come here and if he couldn't stay with Rachel, if he could not live in the same house as his own wife, then he would not live here at all. He opened his mouth to tell Dennis that he would be leaving town unless he was allowed to live with Rachel, but he felt the Holy Spirit stop him. He sighed in resignation and nodded. "Okay, we'll stay in different places. For now at least."

"Don't worry about it," said Dennis. "I will find a good place for her. You can stay in another empty room close to the one I'm giving you for your services. It is small but furnished and comfortable."

"And where will my wife stay?"

"Rachel will stay at a place called the Restoration House. It's a great place and there are many other women there as well to keep her company."

Keith flinched and his stomach flipped. He recalled clearly the place that Rachel had told him about where she had loathed. She had called it the Restoration House. He shook his head. "No! My wife won't stay in that Restoration House. She told me how much she hated the place. And I remember her saying that the leader... or is it housekeeper, there hates her. She said the woman told her that she would make her life a living hell. I can't let my wife stay in that kind of place."

"There's no other place for Rachel in this town," Dennis said. "No one in Fallow Creek, except maybe for her brother, would allow her to stay in their house. Or you, for that matter."

Keith sighed as he remembered God's instructions concerning living with Taylor and said, "She can't live with her brother."

"Well, then, you see? You have no other choice. I've gotten both of you good places to stay."

"Dennis, it's impossible for Rachel to stay in that House."

Dennis groaned and said, "Fine! I'll transfer Margaret out of there and put someone else in charge so that Rachel will be comfortable."

"That's not enough." Keith shook his head. "And comfortable will definitely not be what I would use to describe that Restoration House from all that Rachel's told me about it."

Dennis narrowed his eyes and glared at Keith. "What exactly do you suggest then? Because I have given you the best option for Rachel."

"I want you to put Rachel in charge of that House," he blurted out, and then pressed his lips together in alarm. Where had that idea come from?

"Impossible!" Dennis stared at him with an incredulous expression on his face. "What on earth!"

Keith groaned on the inside. Why had he said that? Dennis would think he was crazy.

And yet, somehow, he knew that the words had come from God. He definitely did not want Rachel staying anywhere near that Restoration House, even as the head of the house.

"Are you insane?" Dennis exclaimed. "How can you ask me for such a thing?"

"I didn't plan to say that," Keith said slowly, his mind roiling in confusion. "I think those words were from God."

Dennis stared at him for a long moment. "So, you're saying God wants Rachel to be the head of the Restoration House?" he murmured.

"I think so," Keith answered, still confused.

Dennis didn't say anything for a long while and Keith's heart pounded. Rachel would definitely be better off staying at the Restoration House if she was in charge rather than someone else. At least she might not have to attend those horrible renewal classes she'd told him about or be subjected to a tyrant like Margaret. Still, he didn't want her to stay in the House, but it wasn't like they had a choice. He waited nervously for Dennis to speak again.

"You have asked so many things of me today," Dennis said, glaring at Keith. "I think you're taking the kindness I have extended to you so far as an excuse to ask all this of me. The next thing I know, you'll be asking me for the whole town."

Keith frowned.

"I would have asked you to leave town immediately if not for the fact that I know you truly hear from God. If you say that God wants Rachel to be head of the Restoration House, then I believe you and will oblige. Hopefully, now that I've done what God wants, He will speak to you about my blackmailer."

Keith didn't know whether to be relieved or worried. The man thought he could buy God's words with favors. He finally chose to be relieved for Rachel's sake and gave Dennis a smile of appreciation. "Thank you," he said.

Dennis held his hands up. "Putting Rachel in charge of the Restoration House is huge. There will be consequences for me, for you, and for Rachel. But she'll be put in charge of the House for now." He shook his head. "I wonder what you'll ask of me next."

Keith wanted to tell him jokingly that the next thing he was thinking of asking for was the town, but he thought better of it. That would be pushing it. "Thank you," he said again.

"I will have to find Rachel an assistant who understands everything about the Restoration House and how it should be run. I will also have to get a bodyguard for her."

Keith raised his brows in surprise. "A bodyguard?"

"Yes. And for you as well. Just like I said before, you both might be in danger here. Many people are not very fond of Rachel and now, probably, of you."

Keith sat back and looked at the man. He said, "The bodyguards will really be there to report everything we do back to you rather than for our protection, isn't that right?"

A smile touched Dennis's lips and he nodded. "You're right. Anyway, I expect that by tomorrow morning, you'll have something substantial for me; something from God that will help me know who my blackmailer is so I can know how to deal with him." He waved his hand as he looked at Keith. "For now, you can go."

But Keith didn't move. He sat there, perplexed by everything that had gone on for the past few days with this man in front of him.

Dennis arched his eyebrows and gave Keith a quizzical look.

Keith finally asked if he could have one more night with Rachel at the abandoned building.

"Fine," Dennis said.

"Another thing. Can we have some food and water? Rachel and I haven't had anything to eat since yesterday." That he was able to speak to Dennis for hours without food was another amazing thing.

Dennis called out to one of the guards and whispered in his ear. The guard left and a few minutes later, one of the women Keith had seen downstairs came into the office and handed Keith a paper bag.

Keith's stomach grumbled at the smell of the food and he thanked the woman. She hurried away and he turned to thank Dennis. He stood up immediately so he could hurry back to Rachel and share the food with her. When he got to the door, Dennis called to him. "Remember. Tomorrow morning, you'll have to tell me everything I want to know. Do whatever you have to in order to hear God's voice clearly, but you must have word for me tomorrow. No excuses."

Keith stared at the man in annoyance. He wanted to ask him if he controlled God's actions. It wasn't like he could just snap his fingers and get the Lord to speak clearly to him anytime he wanted. Instead, he shrugged and left Dennis's office.

He hurried out of the house and virtually ran to the abandoned building to get to Rachel quickly. For some reason, maybe because Mike had come to threaten him at Dennis's house, fear raced through him as he ran to the abandoned building, praying that Rachel was safe.

He heaved a huge sigh of relief when he saw Rachel lying on the blanket, asleep. He slowly lowered himself beside her and smiled down at her, his heart flooding with love. He reached out and ran his fingers through her dark hair. She did not wake up and he gently caressed her cheek and then her shoulder. "Rachel, sweetie, wake up," he said softly.

Rachel opened her eyes and looked up at him. She smiled and immediately sat up. "You're back," she said, her voice filled with relief and a hint of excitement.

He kissed her and then drew back and smiled

widely. "What's up? You look excited about something."

"I'm glad you're back," she said. "I'm just really happy to see you." He shook his head and she chuckled and then added, "Okay, also Olivia came."

He tilted his head and asked, "Who is Olivia?"

"Mike's first wife. You remember. I told you about her some time ago."

"Ah, yes, I remember. And you won't believe who came to Dennis's house raging with anger. Mike Cadwell."

Her mouth dropped open. "Mike? What did he want?"

"Let's talk while we eat," he said, and opened the bag of food. "I'm starving."

She smiled as she looked at the food, but she did not seem eager to eat. He asked her if she was not hungry, knowing that she was.

"Someone brought food for me just after you left. The leader of the squad guards at the border. Daniel, the one I told you I grew up with."

He looked at her as she got up and went to get a plastic bowl from the other end of the room. She returned and sat beside him again. "I guess we have something for this evening as well," she said.

"About that…" He began to tell her about his talk with Dennis.

They both ate as he talked and when he came to the part where Dennis told him they had to live in different places, her eyes widened with horror and she shook her head. "No! I can't live without you, Keith. I refuse to live somewhere else other than with you."

He dropped his fork and put his hands around

her. "It's only temporary, my love. We have no choice for now." He told her everything that Dennis had told him. "We're not so safe here, Rachel. Dennis said it might spark some kind of revolt if people here, especially the men, find out he gave us a house to live in together as husband and wife."

"Keith, we're married. We shouldn't give in to anyone who will try to intimidate us."

"Remember that the Lord sent us here to be lights and draw these people to Him. For now, we will have to keep the peace if we want to have any kind of influence on these people for God. I'm pretty sure the Lord will make a way for us to be able to live together again soon."

"So, where will you stay?" Rachel asked, staring at him with tears in her eyes.

He told her about the room Dennis had offered him behind the town hall and also that he had been given another space near there to hold Bible and prayer meetings.

"And where will I be staying?" she asked. "Here… all alone?"

"Certainly not!" he said. He didn't say anything for a long moment, knowing how she would react when he told her that she was to stay in the Restoration House. She hated that place.

Rachel put her hand on his shoulder and asked again, "Where, Keith? Where will I live?"

He said reluctantly, "At the Restoration House."

Her mouth flew open and for a long moment she stared at him. And then she laughed harshly. "The Restoration House! I'm not staying there!"

"Listen, Rachel. I told Dennis the same thing, but we worked something out for you."

"What?" Rachel frowned. "You remember all I told you about that place. It's the last place I could possibly want to stay."

Keith took her hands in his and looked into her eyes. He told her what he had asked of Dennis and what Dennis had promised him. "He promised to transfer Margaret to somewhere else and to make you the head of that place."

"What? Are you serious, Keith?"

"I am," Keith said. "I think it was the Lord who dropped that request in my heart. And it was confirmed when Dennis agreed."

She slowly removed her hands from Keith's. "How can I be the head of the Restoration House? That place and all that goes on there is against everything I believe in."

"Everything?" Keith said.

"Okay, not everything. But a lot of things like those awful renewal classes, the endless chores, the way women are treated like numbers…"

"And that's why you will be the best leader for that place. You know the things that need to be changed. They need you, Rachel. Can you not see the Lord's hand at work in this? Would you have ever imagined in your wildest dreams that you would be made the head of the Restoration House?"

She looked at him with a thoughtful expression but said nothing.

"You can see that this is the Lord, and I think there is something He wants you to do there. I think that was why he didn't want us to stay with Taylor."

She shook her head slowly. "But I can't be the head of that place, Keith! It's not possible. I won't even know what to do."

"The Lord will help you do what He wants you to," Keith said firmly.

Rachel chuckled, but she still looked very worried. "You had to go tell Dennis to make me the leader of that place. It's just like you, Keith." She sighed and then grinned at him. "You trust me with things that I don't even think I can do or I am ready for."

He caressed her cheek with his thumb. "It's not just me, Rachel. The Lord does the same. You don't understand how much you are capable of doing or all that I see in you."

She smiled at him, and for a long moment, they gazed fondly at each other. She finally said, "You are everything, Keith. Apart from the Lord, you are the one person who I know loves me unconditionally, even when I don't really love myself." She reached out and pulled him into a tight hug. "Can you guess what I have to tell you?"

"What is it? Is it about Olivia's visit?"

"Yes." She told him about how Olivia had come shortly after Daniel, the guard, left. She told him everything they'd talked about; how Olivia promised to bring Emily out of the house so Rachel could see her.

"She wants us to come at midnight?" Keith asked. "That's really late."

"Olivia wants to make sure that Mike and everyone in the house is asleep before she brings out Emily to us."

"Well, thank God I am going with you," Keith said, catching some of Rachel's excitement. He grinned. "It will be great to finally meet little

Emily."

"I can't wait for you to meet her," Rachel beamed. Her smile suddenly melted off her face. "After tonight, we won't be able to be together like this," she said.

He drew her close again. "Well, at least we have this night together." Sadness flooded his heart, but he pushed it away. They would still be in the same town and they would still be allowed to see each other, just not live together. Hopefully, that would be temporary. "We will make the best of this time we have together."

Rachel nodded. "I'd love that."

They returned into each other's arms and once more he kissed her and held her close, relishing the feel of her. He felt a little sad, knowing it would be a while before they would be this way again, but he pressed away the sadness and focused his attention completely on her.

THIRTEEN

"Are you ready to go?" Keith asked Rachel as they stood up from the blanket on the floor.

"Yes," she answered, quickly buttoning up her dress. Keith had found the big flashlight he packed with their clothes and it provided light for them.

It felt so comfortable and familiar to her, this particular dress. She'd gradually started wearing outfits like jeans and tops and trendy jackets when she was in Destiny, but she had sold most of them at the yard sale. All she had left were a few of her old dresses — plain gowns she'd owned before she met Keith, which she was used to wearing. And it was for the best. If they were going to live in this place, they had to merge in as well as they could, and she would not merge in wearing pants and tops.

Keith wore a white T-shirt and jeans, a little different from the slightly formal short-sleeved shirts and pants worn by the men here, but he'd probably merge in as time went on. He took her hand in his and said, "It's a good thing we are in Arizona and it's summer or we would have frozen to death in this place."

She chuckled in spite of her nervousness. "You're right. If this was Destiny, I can't imagine how we would have survived living in this place without electricity and with that entrance wide open. At best we would have caught a cold, and at worst…" She shook her head.

They stepped out of the house into the cool night. The sky was full of stars and streetlights illuminated their path. Rachel gasped when she heard footsteps behind them. She quickly turned around and fear gripped her. There were two squad guards following them. She squeezed Keith's hand in alarm and whispered, "We're being followed, Keith. By two security squad guards. We're in trouble."

"It's okay, Rachel," Keith said. "Dennis told me he would assign bodyguards to us… to protect us."

"But we don't need any guards to protect us!" she whispered harshly.

Keith shrugged. "He said it was for our protection, but I know it's actually to monitor our activities here."

She turned around. "Go away!" she said to the guards. "We don't need you to follow us anywhere!"

"No, Rachel!" Keith said. "They might be God's provision for us. Dennis is right. In spite of his true intentions, I think we need the guards, even if they will probably be reporting everything that we do to him."

"Still, I don't like it," Rachel said, but the apprehension she felt when she first noticed the guards was beginning to subside. She still felt very nervous. They were taking a great risk to see Emily now. If Mike caught them, he would make sure it was the last time she ever saw her daughter.

As though he could read her mind, Keith pulled her even closer and said, "It's okay, Rachel. The Lord will keep us safe and you will be able to see Emily without Mike knowing."

She smiled in appreciation. "Thank you. I'm extremely excited to finally get to see Emily after so long, but I'm also terribly scared. If Mike gets wind of our plans and comes out of his house to see me with Emily... I know him. It'll be the last time I ever see her again."

"Let's not start thinking of what will probably never happen."

She said nothing and they continued on, Rachel leading the way. Keith asked her about the town again, clearly trying to distract her from her worries. Each house they passed, he asked who the owner was and if she knew them personally.

"I know or at least have heard of most of the people in this community," she answered when he asked if she knew everyone in Fallow Creek. "However, I lived a sheltered life when I was with Mike. I hardly spoke to anyone or made friends with other women."

They passed Lily Hunter's parents' house, and she immediately pointed. "That house belongs to the parents of the girl I told you about. Lily Hunter. You remember her. I told you she was my childhood friend, but we stopped being friends for years until I met her again at the Restoration House. She was the one who gave me the courage to ask for that hearing with the elders, which ultimately led to me leaving Fallow Creek. Because I thought you were dead then, we might not have been reunited in Destiny if I'd not left this town." She smiled up at him. "Now that I have to go back to the Restoration House, I'm quite excited to see Lily again. She was the only friend I had there, and she was a very good friend." Rachel fell silent as she thought about Lily, the girl's bravery and spunk.

"Are you sure she's still there? Maybe she's been released and is in her parents' house right now."

Rachel nodded. "Yes, she could be, and I would be happy for her if it's true. But the thing is, if she's been released, she'll probably now be married off to some guy. She told me that was the reason why she'd been taken there in the first place. She'd refused every single suitor that had come her way, and her parents had gotten tired and angry and actually sent her there themselves."

Rachel sighed. Lily had vowed never to marry anyone, especially someone that was already married. But there was a huge chance that if she'd been released from the Restoration House, she would be married to someone who already had a wife or several.

Once again, Rachel felt overwhelmed by how much God had favored and blessed her by leading her to Keith. She smiled at him and leaned in and kissed his cheek. "I can't believe you're mine," she said.

He kissed her hair. "I can't believe it either."

They continued to walk in companionable silence, holding onto each other. Rachel's mind went back once again to Emily and she immediately began to hasten her steps. The thought of finally getting to see and hold her daughter consumed her.

They finally got to Mike's, and Rachel stopped. She looked back again and noticed the guards. She had forgotten about them as she'd walked with Keith, completely focused on him as they'd strolled through the town, talking.

"This is a big house!" Keith said, looking up at Mike's house.

Rachel shrugged and frowned. "Olivia's not out yet."

"We should go and stand right there, just at the side of the house so no one sees us until she comes out."

Rachel nodded. As they moved to the side of the house, Olivia stepped out. She was holding a baby in her arms and immediately a sob escaped Rachel's lips. She rushed forward and without speaking to Olivia, took Emily out of her arms. "Oh, my baby!" she whispered, "I've missed you so much." She kissed Emily's cheeks, inhaled her sweet baby smell deeply, and smiled.

"She's asleep right now, Rachel," Olivia said as though Rachel couldn't see that clearly. "Please try not to wake her up or she might start crying and that would alert Mike. We don't want that."

Rachel nodded and smiled gratefully at Olivia. "Thank you," she whispered, and looked down at Emily again, her heart flooding with joy and sorrow at how much she had missed her. Emily had grown much bigger than the last time she'd seen her. Rachel whispered, "Babies grow so fast." She kissed Emily's forehead and ran her fingers gently through her hair. "I can't believe you're in my arms right now."

"Why are those guards here?" Olivia whispered

in Rachel's ear, sounding terribly scared. She turned to look at Keith, who was standing near Rachel, and her eyes grew wide.

"It's okay, Olivia," Rachel said to her. "They're here because Dennis Hamilton assigned them to us to keep us safe." She turned and faced Keith and smiled widely. "Olivia, this is my husband, Keith Thorn. And Keith, this is my precious little girl, Emily."

Keith smiled at Olivia, who said nothing, only stared at Keith with a look of curiosity and wariness.

Rachel handed Emily gently to Keith and he took her and began to rock her in his arms. She watched with her heart overflowing with joy and love. Keith gently kissed Emily's cheek and smiled. He looked up at Rachel and whispered, "She's beautiful."

"Yes," Rachel said. She could already see that Keith had fallen in love with Emily. It was all she'd ever wanted and would continue to pray for. For the three of them to be united as a family.

"There's a guard somewhere at the back of the house," Olivia whispered. "I have to hurry back in now."

Rachel shook her head and took Emily back from Keith. "No, Olivia. Please give me a little more time with her."

"Any moment now, Emily could wake up and start to cry and then we'll all be in trouble." She reached out to take Emily out of Rachel's arms, but Rachel stepped back. She held up her hand. "Please, Olivia, just one more minute with her."

"Rachel, please! Don't make me regret bringing her out here for you. I have to go in right now."

Rachel said desperately, "Can't I take her with me? I mean, now that we successfully brought her out, can't I just take her..." She felt Keith's hand on her shoulder and tears streamed down her face.

"Rachel, you know that won't be possible at this time. We don't even have a proper place to stay yet, and you'll get Olivia in trouble if you take Emily away. You will be able to eventually, I promise."

"I understand how you feel," Olivia said. "But he's right. Please, Rachel. I need to go in now. Every minute I stay out here with you increases the chances of being found out by Mike."

Rachel took a deep breath, kissed Emily's cheek one more time, and slowly handed her back to Olivia, her heart breaking. She said frantically, "Can I see her tomorrow, Olivia? Please?"

Olivia shifted her feet, and Rachel pleaded with her again.

"You know how risky this is. I don't know if I'll be able to sneak out with Emily tomorrow."

"Please. It'll just be like tonight. Mike will still be asleep and I can get to see my Emily again."

Olivia pressed her lips tightly together. She finally said, "It can't be tomorrow, but Mike will be away on an important business trip on Friday. You can come then. About the same time as you did today." She added, "We can't do this regularly. Surely, you know it would be too risky."

Rachel felt like weeping, but she nodded. "Yes. I know. Thank you so much, Olivia." She held Keith's hand again and wove her fingers through his. They would not live together after tonight and who knew if they would be able to come here together again? Still, she said to Olivia, "We'll be back on Friday."

Olivia nodded and then backed away to head back into the house.

Rachel instinctively held out her arms and then folded them across her chest.

Keith smiled sadly and said, "You'll see her again on Friday." He hugged Rachel briefly. "We should go now."

"Thank you, Keith," was all she could say.

They hurried back to the abandoned building, and Rachel tried to keep her feelings under wraps. When they entered the building, she sat on the blanket and let her tears stream down her face.

Keith sat beside her and put his arms around her. He said nothing except to run his hand up and down her back soothingly.

Rachel wiped the tears from her eyes. "I feel strangely sad and happy at the same time."

"She's a precious baby," Keith said.

"She is." Rachel held Keith tight as she thought about their separation starting tomorrow. "What will I do without you, Keith?" she said. "Why do we have to live separately?" She burrowed her head into his chest.

"We'll see each other every day, Rachel," he said, but he sounded distressed as well. They had known each other for less than a year, but it felt like she had known him for much longer. Since they got married, they had not left each other's side for more than a few hours at a time. The favorite part of her day was when she got into bed beside him at night and snuggled up close to him. Now that would be a thing of the past. Not only would she be in the same town with her husband and daughter and yet not be able to see them as much as she wanted, she would be staying in that awful Restoration House that reminded her of things she did not want to remember. Worst of all, she would have to run the place. She held onto Keith tightly, wishing she could hold on to him forever and never leave his side. But that was not possible.

"I love you, Rachel," Keith said, running his fingers through her hair.

"I love you too," she told him.

He drew back slightly, kissed her, and held her tightly once more. He began to pray that God would give them wisdom and direction as they parted the next day, and that they would separately and as a couple glorify him in Fallow Creek. "And Lord, help us to be truly lights here so everyone will see your glory and grace through us and glorify your name." When he finished praying, she sighed as a supernatural peace descended on her soul.

"Everything will work out for the best in the end," he told her.

She smiled at him. She was certain of one thing. Even though she loathed the place, God was sending her to the Restoration House for a reason, and hopefully she would quickly find out what it was. And then, as Keith had prayed, she would bring Him glory there.

FOURTEEN

The Restoration House was just as she remembered it. She looked at the House and sighed. She couldn't believe she had lived here just months ago. She carried her few belongings in a small bag. This morning, before she'd left the abandoned building, she had packed her clothes into the small duffel bag that Keith had put into their suitcase before they left Destiny. Saying goodbye to Keith had been difficult and full of sadness. Even though he had assured her he would do everything in his power to see her before the end of the day, she knew there was a chance that he wouldn't be able to. Already, she missed him terribly.

"Dennis might not let you see me today," she had said to him as she'd packed her clothes into the bag.

"Nothing will keep me away from you," he'd said. "I will tell him whatever the Lord has laid on my heart. After that, I hope to settle down in the room he promised me, and then I will come to the Restoration House to see you."

"Maybe I should be the one to visit you," she said.

"I don't know that you will be safe or comfortable in that place. Dennis said it was somewhere at the back of the town hall. I think a lot of people, especially the men of this town, will be around there and probably won't take kindly to us being together in that room. It's why Dennis said we can't live together. I'm pretty sure the Restoration House where there are just women will be a better place for us to meet."

"But we'll have no privacy," she said. She threw her arms around his neck, smiled coyly, and kissed him. "And you know we need our privacy for this." She kissed him slowly this time.

He smiled when she drew back. "I know. But for now we'll have to do without."

She sighed in frustration. "That's the problem, Keith. We don't know when we'll be able to finally be alone together after this."

He told her that God would make a way and that he was sure it would not be long before the whole town got used to them. "Then we can move in together again."

"Hopefully not back to this place," she said. "Somewhere homier."

He had agreed.

She groaned as she looked up at the Restoration House again. *Stop torturing yourself with memories of that last private moment with Keith.* But she kept running their time together in her mind. It would be a long time before they had that again. She had to stop thinking about it and focus on the Restoration House and why she had been sent there by God.

Two women were outside, cleaning the windows.

There was another at the side of the house, mopping the side porch.

Rachel looked back at the squad guard, who apparently had been given charge of her by Dennis Hamilton. He looked at her, his face expressionless, and she turned around again. She sighed once more, reluctant to enter the house, and winced when Margaret stepped out.

The woman still wore her usual scowl, but Rachel was surprised when Margaret greeted her politely... at least, as politely as the woman could manage. Margaret told her to step into the house so she could bring her up on her duties as the head of the House. Clearly, Margaret had been warned by Dennis Hamilton or one of his men to be civil to her.

Rachel followed Margaret into the house and looked around the large empty space that was supposed to be the common living area where residents could gather and pass the time. Margaret had been in charge of this place for years, and she had not thought it necessary to furnish the space at all. Actually, it was probably intentional.

Margaret was not a fan of any kind of social gatherings that promised any amount of fun, or 'idleness,' as she called it. She hated to see the women congregate in a common area unless under her order. She had put strict rules in place to make sure that didn't happen. Everyone was assigned a room and each had from two to six women, depending on the size of the room. No woman was to enter another room that wasn't hers unless sent there by Margaret herself. It was one of the first things Rachel wanted to change about the place. She would ask Dennis Hamilton for money to furnish this area so it could be used as a place where the residents could just sit 'idly' and spend time together.

Rachel watched as women went up and down the stairs, many of them carrying mops and buckets and other cleaning supplies. The stairs led to the various rooms and the classrooms where the mind renewal classes took place. Two women were cleaning the stairs. Someone on the other end of the space where she stood was scrubbing the floor on her knees. When there were no classes, the women did nothing else but clean. That was another thing she was going to have to change — the numerous, unending chores.

She followed Margaret through the entire house as Margaret pointed out different parts of the house to her and their purposes. Rachel already knew it all, having lived here for weeks on end, but she nodded each time Margaret pointed out a room to her.

They went up the stairs. and Rachel stuck her head into all the rooms and made sure to smile at each woman she saw. This was something else she had to do. When she'd lived here months ago, everyone had been treated like a number and not really as a unique individual. That would change.

They finally finished touring the house. From a shelf in the hallway, Margaret picked up the annoying bell she rang when she wanted everyone to gather in one place for a general announcement. She rang the bell for what seemed like an eternity to Rachel and then told Rachel to follow her to the back of the house. It was the place everyone usually gathered to hear whatever new announcement Margaret wanted to make. It had only happened once when Rachel was here, and that was the day they were told they would start taking additional renewal classes as early as five o'clock in the morning. They'd been made to wake up before that time to attend the horrid classes. That was an unpleasant memory for Rachel.

She stood with Margaret in front of the crowd of women at the back of the house. Another woman stood on the other side wearing a similar scowl to Margaret's. Rachel looked over the women before her. They stood close together, but none of them had smiles on their faces. Hopefully, through the help of the Holy Spirit, that would soon change as well.

Rachel scanned the crowd for Lily, but could not spot her. She was very disappointed to not see her friend.

Margaret began to speak, addressing the women. She told them that Rachel would be their new temporary leader and they were to listen to her instructions. "Cecilia here will act as Rachel's assistant," Margaret added.

She continued to speak about the rules of the house, stressing about keeping the strict rules no matter who was head of the house now. "We need order in the House."

Rachel knew without a doubt that she was speaking more to her than to the women in front of them. Margaret rightly knew that Rachel planned to change many of those rules and relax some of them. Nothing the woman said would change her mind about that. She looked over at the women again, amazed at the thought that she was about to assume the leadership of this place. Just months ago, she had been one of these women, toiling away and attending the stupid renewal classes. It all felt so surreal.

Margaret kept droning on about the rules and Rachel tuned her out. Silently she prayed, asking the Lord for wisdom in order to know exactly how she would lead and how she could be a bright light in this place, directing the women to God's loving heart. Margaret finally stopped speaking and made way for Rachel to address the women.

Rachel didn't know what to say to them and once more she asked the Lord for help. She opened her mouth to speak and words poured out. She told them that things would be different now with her running the house. She did not mention exactly what she planned to change or reform because Margaret was still here and would report back to Dennis Hamilton everything she had said. She only stressed that she would do things differently from the way they had formerly been done.

She talked a little about everything, including the renewal classes, but she was careful not to say anything that would give Margaret ammunition against her before the leader of the community. She already planned to reform the lessons taught in those classes. If she had her way, she would cancel them entirely. The dour-faced teachers that taught the classes were not around today. They would be tough to handle. Maybe she would have to let them all go, but she was not yet sure it was something she had the power to do.

She told the women that the daily rhythm of

the house would be a little slower and easier from now on. She wanted to tell them that the numerous chores would be reduced, but she thought better of it. Tomorrow, though, when Margaret was not here, she would do just that. The women would only clean once a day rather than the continuous toiling they did in this place.

One thing she was sure of was that the house would be a place where women who were brought here could find refuge rather than a place most women loathed to come. "It will be a rescue house," she said, looking at the faces of the women standing quietly before her. Some of them were now smiling. She could feel Margaret's angry glare but she did not look at the woman. As long as she ran this place, she would run it how she saw fit.

"As of tomorrow, we will meet in small groups for prayer and fellowship," she said. "I want to get to know every single one of you and I want you all to start to see each other as sisters. Each of you is very special, and God has a specific purpose for every one of you."

Many of the women looked at each other with surprised expressions on their faces, but many of them were now smiling and looked hopeful, though slightly confused. It was to be expected because they had lived so long being treated like they did not matter; not just in here, but also in the town as a whole. It was likely that none of them had been told that God had a specific purpose for their lives that did not involve being married to some man who did not cherish them and probably had other wives. They'd been treated like a herd and told that unless they complied completely to the restrictive roles expected of them, their lives would be incomplete and miserable. She wanted each of them to feel special and loved by God.

"Everyone can share something from the Bible when we gather together," she said. "Then if anyone has a specific prayer request, everyone can pray about it."

The women began to murmur.

"Enough!" Margaret commanded and immediately the murmuring ceased.

Rachel frowned at Margaret's booming command but said nothing about it. It was another thing she would do differently. She would not copy Margaret's despotic rule of this place. God had placed her here, and He was the one really in charge. He would use her to do whatever He wanted.

After she finished speaking, the women slowly dispersed, whispering to each other.

"Let me show you to your room," Margaret grunted.

Rachel followed her into the house again and they climbed up the stairs. Women milled around the house once more. Some of them began to make their way towards the classes, others to their various rooms. A lot of the women entered the large renewal class where Rachel had met Lily again.

She followed Margaret down the long hallway until they came to a door. Margaret unlocked it and entered. It was the room where Rachel had been led the first day she came here. The room that contained enough cleaning supplies to last the house almost a whole year.

She followed Margaret past the shelves of cleaning supplies until they got to another door.

Margaret unlocked that door and walked into a room. Rachel entered behind her and glanced around. It was a large room. There was a huge bed on the left side of the room that looked inviting. Rachel nearly walked over to lay down on it. There was a large rug in the center of the room and to the other side, two cream sofas and the small coffee table in the middle. Paintings lined the walls and a large flower pot stood near the window. Red linen curtains hung down from the ceiling to the floor. The place was more an apartment than a room in the house. She hadn't known that this place existed, and she was surprised that Margaret lived in such a nice place. Because of Margaret's constant sour look, she had unconsciously imagined the woman living in a bare space with nothing nice around her.

Margaret opened another door which led to the bathroom, and another to the kitchen.

Rachel thanked her for showing her the place.

Margaret stood in front of her and gave her a hard look. "I know you think you have won. I don't know what you said to our leader to make him hand this place over to you." Margaret looked her over, her eyes sparkling wickedly. "Or what you did, for that matter."

Rachel bristled at the insinuation. So, Margaret thought she had given herself to that wicked Dennis Hamilton in exchange for the leadership of the Restoration House. She wanted to tell Margaret off but thought better of it. There was no point arguing with the woman. She would believe what she wanted to believe.

Other people in the town probably believe the same thing, a voice in her mind mocked.

She shuddered at the thought. Surely everyone here knew that Keith had come to this town with her. They knew he was her new husband. No one would think that way. At least not any thinking person. Margaret clearly wasn't a thinking person.

Margaret smirked. "Congratulations, then," she said meanly. "You've been able to purchase what you want with what you have. But know that this is only temporary. When you are ultimately disgraced and sent away from this town again, I will come back here because this is my rightful place." Margaret narrowed her eyes as she stared at Rachel, and then she grunted as she usually did and walked away.

After she left, Rachel went to the bed and slowly sat down on it. Even though she knew she should not be bothered by what Margaret had said, she still was. "Lord, please help me. Don't let anyone think of me the way Margaret does."

For a long moment, all kinds of troubling thoughts kept running through her mind. Finally, she became weary of them and forcefully pressed them away. She had a huge responsibility now and that would have to be her focus. She took a deep breath and knelt beside the bed. She began to pray once again. She asked the Lord to reveal to her why He'd brought her here and to help her do whatever it was He wanted her to do. Most of all, she asked that the changes she made here would be long-lasting and impactful in the little time she had.

FIFTEEN

Rachel smiled and stretched out her hand to the right side of the bed where Keith usually slept. She gasped. He wasn't there. She came fully awake and opened her eyes. *Where are you, my love?* And then her heart sank as she remembered. She and Keith would not be sharing a bed for a long time to come. She pressed her lips tightly together and groaned. She loved waking up next to him in the mornings. She loved the way he pulled her close with his eyes still closed and wrapped his arms firmly around her, filling her stomach with butterflies.

She sat up on the bed, took a deep breath, and looked at the empty space next to her. Usually she got out of bed before Keith did. She was used to waking up very early ever since she was a child because it was what most people in Fallow Creek did. After she and Keith got married, every time she woke up out of habit at about five o'clock, he whispered groggily, "Stay in bed a little longer," and then drew her close. She always sighed in contentment as she relished his touch and the feel of his body next to hers, and then once he went back to sleep again, she reluctantly climbed out of the bed to begin her day.

She loved being married to him. She loved the way he looked in the morning when he woke up, his hair messy and his eyes bleary. She loved how he kissed her before he went to his little office every day. She missed it all, even though this was their first morning apart. When would she be able to wake up next to him once more?

She sighed and got out of bed. Suddenly, she became apprehensive as she remembered the huge responsibility she had been given. She gasped as she looked at the clock on the wall. It was already seven o'clock. The Restoration House usually came alive at about six. She was the leader of this place now. She should be the first one awake, and yet she had overslept.

She began to dress up quickly, and then she felt the tug of the Spirit in her heart and sighed again. "I haven't even prayed this morning, and I'm about to rush out to start my day," she said to herself. She needed to start the day with the Lord if she wanted to make a real change in this place.

Once more, as she had done the day before, she knelt beside her bed and prayed for wisdom. She had no specific plans for the day except for the plan she'd made to meet with a different group of women daily.

She finished praying, stood up, and got her Bible from under her pillow. She started to read quickly, keeping in mind that she had to leave the room soon.

She studied the Bible just the way she had seen

Keith do countless times since she'd moved in with him, only faster. She searched the scriptures for something to share with the group of women she would meet today, but she could not seem to settle on anything. She asked the Lord for the right scripture, but still, nothing she read felt right to share.

She shook her head and finally closed the Bible. *What am I supposed to do now?* she thought as worry ran through her. *Why, oh why did Keith ask Dennis to make me the head of this place?* She had never led anything except maybe for her home daycare in Destiny.

"Lord, please help me," she said again. She stood up and quickly showered in the bathroom that Margaret had showed her yesterday. She dressed in a simple blue gown and flats. She braided her hair, grabbed her purse from the bedside table, and headed out of the small apartment to start her day. She'd already decided before she'd gone to bed yesterday that she would meet with each group of women based on the position of their rooms. She would start from the first room nearest to her small apartment and move down the hallway from there until she got to the last one. Since there was an average of four women in each room, they would be small groups and she could pay attention to each woman and get to know them really well.

Just as she began to make her way through the cleaning supply room, someone ran up to her. A girl of about twenty with a short bob. Rachel knew her face but did not remember her name. She stared quizzically at the girl. "What is it?"

"Taylor Dalton... your brother... he's looking

for you." The girl sounded breathless and way too excited for the simple message she had come to pass across to Rachel.

"Where is he?" Rachel asked, eager to see Taylor. She had not seen him since she and Keith arrived here.

"He's downstairs in the common room."

Rachel began to walk out of the room, but the girl said in a hushed tone, "I heard he is looking for a second wife." She had a wistful expression on her face. "He's the most desirable man in Fallow Creek. You're so lucky to be related to him."

Rachel chuckled. She had not heard of her brother spoken of in that way in a long time. There was a time when they were children and still very close when the girls in this town fawned over him as much as they were allowed to. Her friends told her he was the most handsome boy in town and they would marry him when they were older. Now that he was not just handsome but rich, she could see why women would say he was the most desirable man in the community.

She remembered how Lily told her she would never get married, but then had spoken about Taylor with such yearning that Rachel had been somewhat amused. She wanted to ask the girl the same thing she asked Lily then, but she immediately remembered what the girl had just said — that Taylor was looking for a second wife. She was clearly interested in being just that, even though Taylor was already married.

Rachel looked at the girl thoughtfully. If there was one thing that was most important to her other than sharing the true gospel with the women here, it was letting them know they were worth more than just being one of the wives to men who regarded them as nothing but property. She made a mental note to speak to Taylor about his decision to get a second wife and maybe try to talk him out of it. Lily had said he was different, and so had Keith because of all Taylor had done for them. And she agreed fully, so hopefully she could reason with him.

She walked away from the girl, hurrying down the hallway, ignoring the curious stares of the women in the house. She couldn't wait to see Taylor and hug him. She was sure he would wonder why she had not come to his house since she'd arrived in Fallow Creek.

She stopped for a second in the middle of the stairs and beamed at him as he watched her climbing down. She ran down the stairs and hugged him.

He held her away from him and studied her. "You look good, Rachel. That makes me happy. Now tell me what you're doing here and why you haven't visited since you came back to town. I heard you've been here for some days and you still haven't bothered to visit me."

"I'm so sorry, Taylor. A lot has happened since we came here and we haven't had the time to come to your house… even though we've really wanted to."

"We? You and Mike?"

"No, not Mike!" she said, slightly annoyed, and then brushed her anger away. "I'm surprised you haven't heard. I thought everyone had. My husband, Keith."

He stared at her with his brows raised. "You married someone else? Mike isn't your husband anymore?"

"He never was," she said wearily. He started to say something, but she stopped him. This was what she would have to deal with from now on. It would be hard to explain to the brainwashed people of this town that Keith, and not Mike, was her husband. "Mike is not my husband, Taylor," she said. "My real husband is Keith. We are married legally and in God's sight."

"You've changed so much, Rachel," Taylor said. "Anyway, why are you staying here? And why did you and that Keith guy not come over to my house to stay with me? And where is he now?" Taylor looked around the common room.

"He's not here, Taylor," Rachel said. "You know this house is only for women."

"You haven't answered my questions." Taylor looked intently at her.

She didn't know whether he would believe what she told him, but she told him the truth — that the Lord had told her and Keith not to stay with him, probably because he wanted her to run the Restoration House and Keith to start holding prayer meetings at that room near the town hall. Dennis had put her in charge here and given Keith permission to hold his meetings. "All that would not have happened if we had gone to stay in your house," she said.

Taylor blinked rapidly, the look on his face one of shock. "Wait! Did I just hear you right? Did you say you now run this place?"

"Yes, Taylor. I was just as surprised as you when I was told about it."

"And when was that?" Taylor asked, staring at

her as though she had just told him she went on vacation to the moon.

"Just yesterday," she answered.

"And you said Dennis put you in charge?"

"Yes."

Taylor folded his arms across his chest and shook his head slowly, looking at her in disbelief. "And you said God told you not to stay with me? Firstly, explain to me in detail how you were allowed to come back to Fallow Creek when you were banished and allowed to stay here with a brand-new husband in tow. Because it is unheard of, Rachel. And now you've been given charge of the Restoration House and your new husband housed at the back of the town hall. You said he's going to start holding prayer meetings in the town?"

"Yes."

"Okay. That's just crazy! Please, tell me everything!"

She walked to the bench near the door and sat down. He came and sat beside her. "It's a long story, Taylor," she said.

"I have time."

She sighed and told him everything, starting from how the Lord spoke to her about not pursuing the sole custody case and then told her to return to Fallow Creek with Keith. She told him how the Lord confirmed his word by speaking to Keith without her having to tell him anything, and then told him about Keith's encounter with Dennis and the words of wisdom the Lord had given him for the leader of the town.

Taylor gasped and shook his head, his eyes full of wonder and slight disbelief.

She continued, telling him about how Keith had negotiated with Dennis concerning where they would stay. "That is how I came to be put in charge of this place. I have to confess that I am out of my depth here. Keith is a pastor. What he's been given to do is second nature to him, but me…" she sighed. "I wish he was here with me." She closed her eyes and said, "I already miss him so much."

"Rachel, it's hard to believe everything you have just told me, and yet I know it's all true." Taylor sounded bewildered, but excited at the same time. "I wish I had the kind of relationship you and your husband have with God. I wish I could hear God's voice clearly, the way you both do."

Rachel gave him a small smile. "Actually, I couldn't hear His voice at all until I began to draw closer and closer to Him. It started when I gave my heart fully to Him after watching my husband's life and the relationship he had with God."

Taylor's forehead furrowed as his eyes searched hers. "How can I have this same relationship that you both have with God?" he asked.

Her mouth dropped open in surprise. This was the last thing she had expected to come out of her brother's visit. And yet, it was the best thing he could have ever asked. Still, she felt ill equipped to give him what he was asking for.

She turned away slightly and then turned to face him again. He was looking at her with such hunger and expectation that she knew she had to try.

She told him everything she could remember Keith telling her when she asked him a similar question to what Taylor had asked her now. She shared the gospel with him — the true gospel — not the one they'd heard since they were children. The one based on rituals and good works. Many of the people in this town tried to be good constantly, but fell short every time, while some, like Mike, had given up a long time ago and all that was left for them were the rituals.

She remembered the scripture that Keith quoted constantly, which seemed to particularly fit this time and said, "The Bible says, 'To him that worketh not, but believeth on Him that justifieth the ungodly, his faith is counted for righteousness.'"

He asked her what it meant, and she told him it meant that their salvation was not based on good works but faith in what Christ had already done two thousand years ago. Faith in His sacrificial death and His resurrection. After she finished sharing the gospel with him, she asked if he was willing to pray right now to give his heart totally to Jesus.

He nodded eagerly.

She prayed with him and then opened her eyes and smiled widely at him.

"I feel like a brand-new man," he said happily. He stood up abruptly. "I have to go and share this with my wife," he told her, and began to walk out of the house. She thought about calling him back, especially to ask him about the "second wife" thing, but he was already out the door. Sighing, she shook her head. Hopefully, now that he had received Christ into his heart, he would know better than to go ahead with his plans to marry an additional wife.

She felt as though she was walking on clouds as she walked up the stairs. Her brother had just given his heart to the Lord. She felt exhilarated, and then she remembered the responsibility that had been placed on her and the meeting she was supposed to have with the women this evening, and her joy melted away. She still had no message to share with the women.

A still small voice whispered in her heart, *What about what you just shared with Taylor?*

Immediately her heart leapt. *Of course.* She would tell them her testimony and then share the true gospel with them. Maybe this was why the Lord had brought her here.

She hurried to her room to pray and then eagerly wait for this evening, when she would meet with the women and give them the best gift anyone could ever receive — a deep, intimate relationship with Christ.

SIXTEEN

Rachel's day was full. She and her assistant, Cecilia, worked on reducing the household chores. She also went around the house, inspecting every corner to find out the things she needed to change. She greeted each woman she saw, reminding them that the group meetings would start this evening. "You're in the room closest to my apartment?" she asked a woman named Carol who she saw coming out of one of the classrooms.

When the woman confirmed that she was, she told her that she would be meeting with her and her roommates this evening. After that, she went down the stairs and immediately went to the kitchen. She walked through it, noting the meals that were being cooked for the residents of the house. Women here mostly had a restricted diet, as though eating anything other than vegetables and soup would help the women better imbibe the regular brainwashing of the place. She greeted the cook, who gave her a reluctant "Hello."

She left the kitchen again, adding "more variety

of foods" to her list of things she needed to do. All the things she wanted to implement in the house would cost money, which she had to ask from Dennis Hamilton. It would be a hard sell, but she hoped the Lord would give her favor with him.

At about five o'clock in the evening, she stood at the entrance of the big renewal class and listened briefly to the familiar tutoring going on. The tutor scowled at her, but she refused to move. As usual, the young women were made to recite quotations and scriptures taken out of context. Scriptures used wrongly to validate the unwarranted subjugation the women lived under in this town.

She could not stomach any more of the lies and walked away quickly. The classes would be the last and most important thing she would change. And the hardest. It would take a real miracle to change them, especially since many of the things that were taught were the very foundation that Fallow Creek was built on.

At about nine o'clock in the evening, when the classes were finally over and the women trooped to their rooms, Rachel smiled with excitement and nervousness. She made her way from her office, which was on the other side of her small apartment, to the first room where she would hold the first group meeting.

She entered the room before any of the occupants did and pulled out a chair from the desk at the corner. She put it in the center of the room, sat down, and looked around. It was a room similar to the one she had stayed in when she was here months ago. However, unlike her room, there were five beds here, which meant that five women occupied this particular room. She'd had only one roommate, and even then Margaret had wanted her to stay alone and be isolated because of what she termed "Rachel's rude behavior." She shuddered at what would have happened to her had she continued to stay here under Margaret's thumb. The woman had promised to make her life a living hell, but thankfully the Lord had brought her out quickly.

A woman who was about ten years older than Rachel walked into the room. Rachel knew her well because she had lived just a few feet away from the house Rachel grew up in. She looked surprised to see Rachel sitting down in the middle of the room. She sat down slowly on the bed facing Rachel and gave her a tentative smile.

Rachel smiled back. "Hi, Deanne!" she said cheerfully and told her that she was here to start the meeting. She asked briefly about the woman's parents and siblings just as the four remaining occupants of the room walked in. Again, Rachel greeted them with a smile, calling two of them by their names. She asked the two women who she did not remember their names. When they told her, she addressed them all and told them to gather together on Deanne's bed. When they did, she took a deep breath and bowed her head in prayer to start the meeting.

After she had prayed briefly, she raised her head again and opened her eyes. All the women were looking at her curiously, but she could see the hope in their eyes. "Lord, help me," she whispered, and then began to ask each of them if they had anything to say. None of them said anything, but she was not surprised. This place had a way of suppressing a person's spirit. She decided it was time to share her testimony in order to inspire them and make them hungry for the true gospel.

She began. "I know you all are wondering how I came to become the head of this place when just months ago I was banished from the town. I can truthfully say it's all God's doing. A miracle." She told them about her life with Mike, leaving out the parts that she deemed unnecessary. She told them about how they'd fled to Destiny. Most of the people in this town already knew about that. When she started to talk about Keith and falling in love with him, their eyes went wide. She knew three of the five women were married, at least supposedly married to men who had other wives. The remaining two were still quite young and single.

Undeterred by the strange looks they gave her, she continued to talk about Keith and how their relationship developed in Destiny. She spoke about being kidnapped and brought back here, about not being allowed to see her daughter. She told them how devastated she'd felt when she thought Keith was dead but did not tell them directly that Mike had caused the accident that had led to Keith's hospitalization.

The women were still looking at her with wide eyes. She continued to talk, focusing on how her relationship with God had grown the more she'd gotten to know Keith and studied his way of life. "I finally couldn't resist, and I told Keith that I wanted to know the Lord the way he did."

She told them about asking the Lord into her life and then talked about the relationship with God she enjoyed now, so different from the one she'd had before that was based on fear and self-loathing. The women seemed captivated as they listened without moving, but they still had uncertain looks on their faces.

She began to tell them of how God had spoken to her specifically about coming back here and their mouths flew open. When she told them how God had confirmed the word He had spoken by speaking to Keith in a dream, they began to whisper amongst themselves. She stopped and asked if any of them had a question for her.

Carol, the young woman with golden blonde hair and striking bright blue eyes said, "But how exactly did you hear God's voice?"

Rachel smiled and told her she was coming to that. She continued to talk about how the Lord told them to give all they had and how they had been afraid that they would have nothing. "But so far, He has provided abundantly for us," she said.

"But how?" Deanne asked.

She told them about the open door through Dennis Hamilton because Keith had given him a specific word from God. But she did not tell them anything else about it.

They all looked puzzled and Carol blurted out, "And you were made the head of this place, just like that? You married a new husband and Dennis Hamilton still let you both live here?"

"Like I said, it's all God's doing."

"And you have continued to hear God's voice clearly?" Carol asked again, looking perplexed. "How can I hear His voice that clearly?"

The other women nodded.

"It starts by having a close and loving relationship with Him. The closer you grow to God, not just in order to hear Him speak, but because you want to truly know Him, the clearer His voice will be." She looked at each of them. "He might not speak to you all in the same dramatic way He's been speaking to Keith and I, but you will hear His voice clearly in your heart and He will direct your paths."

She started to share the gospel with them, telling them how she had opened her heart and received Christ into her heart, and how her life had been forever changed. She could see the eager looks on their faces as she spoke. Soon, all of them had tears in their eyes. When she finally asked if they were ready to commit their lives fully to Jesus now, they all eagerly said "Yes!"

Again, she marveled as she led them in the prayer of salvation, just as she had with Taylor earlier in the day. After the prayer, she looked at all of them. Their faces were streaked with tears, but their smiles were huge and their eyes sparkled.

"Thank you so much," Carol said and pulled Rachel into a tight hug. The others gathered around laughing and hugged her too.

They all stayed together as a group, hugging, laughing, and simply enjoying the presence of God. It was clear they had experienced a second birth, and Rachel felt again as though she was floating on clouds. Her heart was as light as a feather and joy bubbled up in her until she couldn't hold it in. She raised a song about God's love; it was a song she had heard Keith sing more times than she could count. They listened since they clearly did not know the song, their faces awash with a supernatural light.

Finally, Rachel prayed again, thanking God for what He had done and asking Him to help the women draw closer to Him every day. Before she left the room, she told them they would have another meeting as soon as she was through speaking with the women in the other rooms.

"When will that be?" Deanne asked eagerly.

"It might not be until next week. But read your Bibles and ask the Spirit of God to speak to you as you do."

She left the room and made her way to her apartment. She crashed down on her bed, exhausted, but thoroughly happy. It was definitely one of the best days of her life. The only thing that would have completed her joy today would have been Keith's presence. He had unfortunately been unable to come to see her, just like she'd guessed. He'd insisted that nothing would be able to keep him away, but she knew how this place was. Dennis had probably held him up somewhere, somehow. Still, it did not dampen her joy. She stood up from the bed again and began to change into her pajamas. She raised her head when a knock sounded on her door.

She went quickly to answer it, and her assistant walked in.

"Yes, what is it, Cecilia?" Rachel asked.

"The guards at the gate told me to let you know that Keith is here to see you."

Her heart immediately soared with joy. Without thinking, she started to make her way out of the room, but her assistant called her back. "Where are you going?" Cecilia asked with a frown.

"To see my husband. Where else? Is he in the

common room?"

"He's not inside the house. He is outside the gate."

She stopped and turned to face Cecilia. "Why didn't the guards let him in?"

Cecilia stared at her as though she were the stupidest person on Earth. "They didn't let him in because this house is only for women and it's very late."

Rachel frowned. "But they let my brother, Taylor, in today."

"That's different. Your brother has contributed so much to this community and is well respected. Besides, he didn't come looking for you in the middle of the night."

Rachel glowered at Cecilia. It was on the tip of her tongue to tell the woman to stop being so belligerent, but she decided to let it go. There was no point anyway. She sighed heavily and then quickly went into her room and changed back into her dress.

She hurried out of the room again and down the stairs. She didn't stop until she was at the gate. She stared at the guards there and told them to open the gate for her. Immediately she stepped out of the gate, Keith rushed up to her and pulled her into a tight hug.

"I've missed you so much," he said when they pulled apart.

She put her hand on his cheek and looked into his eyes. "I've missed you as well," she said softly. "I thought you wouldn't be able to come again today."

He chuckled. "I told you that nothing would keep me away from you. Dennis held me up today. We had a lot to talk about. I'll tell you everything

soon, but I just want to spend this time with you."
He pulled her close again and kissed her.

She kissed him back and then sighed loudly in
annoyance when a guard behind her cleared his
throat. They stepped away from each other but still
held hands.

"I have a lot to tell you as well," she said. "I'm
so happy. The Lord did great things today." She
told him about how she had addressed the women
yesterday and then with joy she told him about
Taylor's visit and how he'd asked the Lord into his
heart. After that she told him about the meeting
with the women and how they had done the same.
When she finished, she took a deep breath and
beamed at him.

He shook his head, his eyes full of amazement.
"Wow! That is something!" Joy danced in his eyes.

She told him about her plans to meet with more
women tomorrow and her ideas to change a lot of
the rules in this place. "I know it'll be hard, but I
believe that the Lord is already working on my
behalf."

He said nothing, and she tilted her head and
studied him. "What's wrong?" she asked.

"You have to come in now," one of the guards
told her. "We were instructed not to let anyone out
of this place... even you. We just gave you a little bit
of time because you're the leader here. But it's late
and you have to go in."

She stared at the guard who had just spoken.
"This is my husband. Just give me five more minutes
with him."

The guard frowned. "I can't do that. We'll have
to answer to Dennis Hamilton if anyone reports

this." He pointed at her and Keith.

Keith squeezed Rachel's hand and said, "Go in, Rachel. I'll see you tomorrow, and then I'll tell you everything."

She smiled and reluctantly let go of his hand. "Tomorrow, then," she said.

He nodded. "Tomorrow." He kissed her forehead. "I love you, sweetie."

"I love you too," she whispered, and moved toward the gate. She turned back again and waved at him.

He blew her a kiss and waved.

She entered the house once more and went up to her room. She climbed into the bed after changing into her pajamas. The overwhelming joy she had felt earlier had faded some. Keith had looked worried. She couldn't wait to see him tomorrow so she could find out why.

But what if he couldn't come throughout the day until nighttime like today? What if they barred him from seeing her tomorrow?

You need to stop worrying! She couldn't control the future and there was no point worrying about it.

"Thank you so much, Lord, for everything you did today," she said as she stretched out on the bed. The joy she had felt after she met with those women earlier flooded her soul again. She thought about everything the Lord was doing now with a full heart. The day after tomorrow, she would see Emily. She would also meet with another group of women. She couldn't wait to see what else the Lord would do in the house.

She closed her eyes with a smile on her face,

and then she remembered the look on Keith's and stopped smiling. She prayed, asking the Lord to make a way so she and Keith would be able to spend more time together tomorrow. Then he could tell her what was bothering him and what he and Dennis Hamilton had talked about. Hopefully, she would be able to put a smile back on his face and together they would solve whatever problems he had.

SEVENTEEN

The next evening, Rachel had another meeting with the women in the next room and, like the night before, each of them heard the true gospel shared for the first time in their lives and received the Lord into their hearts.

She couldn't contain her joy as she left the women to go to her room. She briefly looked into the renewal classroom and sighed. She still hadn't gotten around to doing something to change the lessons here as she was still so occupied with planning for the evening meetings and trying to get to know each of the women here personally. The daily chores had, however, been reduced considerably, and some of the women had expressed their relief to her already.

"No house or building needs to be cleaned so thoroughly almost every hour," she'd said, and had smiled when they'd thanked her. She would have to make time soon to do something about these classes.

She went to her small apartment with a spring

in her step. Keith had visited her very early in the morning. He'd told her he could not stay long as Dennis was expecting him at any minute. "I still have no additional words from the Lord to tell him," Keith had said, looking a little morose. She'd held him to try to comfort him, but she knew he was tired of it all and missed Destiny terribly. "You will get something soon," she'd said.

"I hope so."

He had left, seeming happy and encouraged after their time together, and she hoped that he had received a word from God that he could share with the leader. Knowing Dennis, he would soon lose his patience and ask them to leave town. And she couldn't leave now. Not with everything the Lord was doing with her, and especially not without Emily. She felt a slight pang in her heart but brushed it off. God wouldn't let that happen. He'd brought them here and He would give Keith a word for Dennis, probably before the end of today. She was certain of that. She got to her apartment, shed her clothes, climbed into bed, and immediately fell asleep.

She jerked awake after what seemed like only a few minutes and rubbed her face. She glanced at the clock on the wall. It was seven-thirty in the morning. She had overslept again. She stood up quickly and began to straighten her bed. She raised her head when a loud knock sounded on the front door. She frowned and left her room to open it.

She gasped as Carol, the beautiful young woman in the first room who had opened her heart to receive Christ, staggered in, sobbing.

"What is it?" Rachel asked, alarmed. She put her

arms around Carol and held the young woman close. "What's the matter, Carol? Tell me."

Carol pulled away from Rachel and said brokenly, "They're sending me away from town with nothing except the clothes on my back. I'm never allowed to come back here or ever see my parents or siblings again."

"What? Why?"

She led Carol to the sole sofa in her small living room and sat beside her. "Tell me everything."

"After you told us of your testimony, how you left Mike Cadwell because you knew it was wrong to be with someone who was already married, I knew I had to do the same. My husband sent me here because I wasn't as obedient to him as he said the Bible commands wives to be. He has two other wives and I'm the last and youngest. I was supposed to be released from this place in a few days' time to go back to him, but I sent a message saying I wouldn't be going back because I now knew it was wrong to be married to him." She wrung her hands. "He went straight to Dennis Hamilton with my letter and now they want me to leave so I don't pollute the town with my rebellion."

Rachel felt sick. *What have I done?* Carol was just nineteen and had never left Fallow Creek. How would she survive outside of it?

Carol dashed at the tears running down her cheeks but fresh ones replaced them. "I don't know anyone outside this town. I have no money either." She burst out sobbing. "I'll d-d-die on the s-streets!"

Rachel held her tightly again. "You won't, Carol! I'll speak with Dennis on your behalf."

"It'll do no good. He was the one who ordered

them to send me packing."

"I'll try to reason..." Rachel jerked her head up as someone banged on her door.

"Open up!" a male voice barked. The door swung open and two squad guards barged in. They immediately strode to Carol and grabbed her by the hands.

Carol cried out and Rachel stopped. "What's the meaning of this? Why did you both just barge in here? Leave right now."

They ignored her and began to drag Carol out of the apartment toward the door.

"Stop it!" Rachel yelled. "Let her go now! I'll speak to Dennis about this!"

The men paid her no attention. They pulled Carol out the door with them, and Rachel immediately followed them out. She kept yelling for them to leave Carol alone as she followed them down the hallway and down the stairs. Carol's sobbing pierced her heart.

Many of the women in the house came out of their rooms to see what was happening, but none of them said anything. Rachel continued to follow them as they exited the house with Carol. She threatened and then pleaded with the guards, but to no avail.

"At least let her be allowed to take her things," Rachel said as they pushed Carol into their SUV.

Carol stuck her head out of the window, and Rachel winced when one of the guards shoved her inside and entered the car beside her. She was squashed in the middle of both guards while another started the car.

Rachel screamed again, ordering them to let

Carol go, but they didn't even look at her. Her heart grew heavier and heavier as the men drove away. Helplessly, she watched the car go down the road until it disappeared. She folded her arms across her chest and went back into the house. Again, she whispered, "What have you done, Rachel?"

She had only shared her testimony and the gospel with the women to inspire them to believe that there was more, and to liberate their hearts from the bondage they were in. Now, she had gotten one of them into trouble. She walked through the common room with her shoulders sagging. She would have to speak with Keith this evening and get him to speak to Dennis on her behalf, because in spite of the fact that Dennis Hamilton had made her the head of the Restoration House, he would never give her, a woman, an audience. Not unless it was like the one she had been given during the hearing, which, if she'd been honest, she would have known would end the way it had. Keith was more likely to get a better result if he spoke to the man. And it had to be now because who knew what and who would be next? She had told her testimony to almost a dozen women now. Who knew what that would inspire any of them to do? Maybe they would suffer the same fate that had befallen Carol just now. She shuddered at the thought.

She climbed up the stairs to her room and sat on the bed, staring at the wall in front of her. It had been right for her to share her testimony and the gospel; she fully believed that. However, she would have to stop for now until she could speak with Keith and get him to try to change Dennis's mind concerning the women and his harsh stance on what he termed "rebellion."

She couldn't hold her agony in any longer and began to sob. "Oh Lord, please help. Please help Carol. She has no money and knows no one outside of Fallow Creek."

Rachel had no money to give to the young woman or she would have. She shuddered again at what Carol had said about dying on the streets. "Lord, please protect her," Rachel prayed desperately once more.

She sighed heavily and stood up. There was work to do in the House. She couldn't stay here mourning for Carol forever. She would have to try to protect the other women, even with her life if need be. What happened to Carol could never happen again.

"Keith, please hurry over," she whispered as she left her apartment. "I need you now."

She went about her duties for the day mechanically, still grieving for Carol. She oversaw the cooking of the food, making sure it was much more nutritional than it usually was, went to the account room to see how the money allocated to the House was being spent and what was left of their monthly budget. She wanted to get new mattresses and pillows for some of the rooms because they were now very old and uncomfortable to sleep on. She oversaw the daily chores, now just done once a day. She tried to make sure everything was running as smoothly as it should be and smiled at each woman she saw, even though she was hurting on the inside.

She stayed away from the renewal classes today. After what had happened to Carol, she had to tread carefully. Changing anything about the classes right now was not feasible.

Finally, when it was time for lights-out and all the women had gone back to their rooms, she hurried back to her own apartment. She took her hair down, brushed it thoroughly, and changed into another dress. She glanced at her wristwatch. It was almost eleven o'clock. Soon, by God's grace, Keith would be here and she could tell him about Carol. After that, she would ask him to speak with Dennis about the plight of the women here. Keith would be sympathetic, but whether he would be able to get Dennis to agree not to send away any of the other women was something else. However, she was sure he would try.

She went down the stairs and walked out of the house. Slowly she walked to the gate and sighed wearily as the guards there turned to look at her with suspicion in their eyes. She reached the gate and asked them to open it immediately.

"I'm sorry, but we can't..."

"I'm not about to tell you again!" she said angrily. She was in no mood to be nice to these guards. "Do I need to remind you that I am now the leader of this place and was made so by Dennis Hamilton? I'm not a prisoner here, and I'm not one of the women sent here for 'reformation.' I can come and go as I please."

The guards looked at each other, and one of them said, "But those were not our..."

"Open this gate right now!"

They stared at her for a few seconds and then opened the gate for her.

She walked out of the gate and looked this way and that, praying that at any minute, Keith would come walking up to her. There was a chance he wouldn't be able to come today if he was held up by Dennis. She breathed a huge sigh of relief when she saw him briskly walking toward her, his eyes fixed on her.

He reached her, and she immediately fell into his arms. He hugged her tightly and then pulled back and kissed her.

She brushed back his hair from his forehead and asked, "How was your day, my love?"

"Still the same as yesterday," he said with tired eyes.

"I'm sorry."

He put his hand on her cheek and looked into her eyes. "Something's bothering you, Rachel. What is it?"

"Today was awful," she said, and told him everything that had happened with Carol. When she finished, she felt like breaking down. "What if more women follow Carol's path, Keith, and are sent away from the town empty-handed? What will I do then? It would be all my fault."

He pulled her into his arms again and rubbed her back soothingly. "Stop it, Rachel. You did the right thing sharing the gospel with them. What happened wasn't your fault."

"But maybe I should've just shared the gospel with them. I shouldn't have told them my testimony. I shouldn't have told them how I left Mike and married you."

"Of course you should have," he said. "You know what, Rachel? God is in control. He will watch over Carol. But I agree with you that something has to be done."

She sighed. "As much as I don't like this town and I wish the women here were free to leave and find their own lives, I don't want it to be this way. They throw women out with nothing except the clothes on their backs. That's just wrong. And worse, they separate them permanently from their families." She bit her lip and said thoughtfully, "There has to be a way I can help Carol." But there was nothing she could do to help. She didn't even know where the girl was.

"I'll speak to Dennis," Keith said. "But I don't know if I'll succeed in changing his mind." He sighed loudly and stopped talking as his face clouded up.

She remembered he'd been troubled yesterday by his talk with Dennis and asked him what they had talked about.

"All Dennis wants to hear from me is a prophetic word about his blackmailer and how to get rid of him. I tried to share the gospel with him, but he didn't want to hear it or even talk about other things. The main thing is that his patience is running out. He has made it clear that we are useless to him unless I have something worth his while. I've been praying, but I have nothing. He said that we have only a few days and, if I have no word from God for him by then, we'll have to leave the town." Keith sighed and looked up. "As if I can control how and when God speaks. I hope he listens to me when I tell him about the girls." He gave Rachel a sad smile. "But please don't get your hopes up, my love. If I get word from God about Dennis's blackmailer, he might listen to what I have to say about the women here, but if not…"

She gently brushed his cheek with the back of her hand. "I'm sorry, Keith. I know you have a lot on your plate right now and I shouldn't be bothering…"

"No, Rachel! You're not bothering me. Your problems are mine, and we have to jointly do whatever we can to help the women here."

He smiled and kissed her again. His eyes lit up. "Dennis might be tough to talk to or try to convince to stop banishing women from the town, but maybe Taylor can help. You said he accepted the Lord Jesus into his heart yesterday."

She nodded.

"He might be open to helping out. You told me that he has great influence in this town, so he might be able to get Dennis to back down and relax his rigid rules."

"You're right, Keith. Taylor does have some influence. The men here are usually not the right people to talk to when it comes to such matters, especially considering Carol had decided not to return to the man she was living with. But since Taylor gave his heart to the Lord fully yesterday, I hope he will see things differently now." She frowned. "But the Lord said we shouldn't ask Taylor for anything."

"Yes, for ourselves," Keith said. "But I think we can ask on behalf of others." He took Rachel's hands. "We'd better pray about it, though."

He began to pray, asking the Lord to reveal His perfect will in the situation and asked specifically if they could ask for Taylor's help. After he finished praying, Rachel asked, "Did you hear or sense anything?"

"No, but I feel at peace about the decision to ask

Taylor for help. What about you?"

"I'm at peace with it, too,"

"Then we should go now," Keith said. "Come to think of it, I haven't even seen your brother before. I wish we had gone to visit him before now. It's weird that the first time I get to meet him is when we have a favor to ask of him."

She threaded her fingers through his. "It's okay. I don't think Taylor would mind that much. He knows you've been held up in Dennis's study for a while." She shook her head at the worry in his eyes. "No, I didn't tell him any details of what you and Dennis are talking about. Just that you had a specific word from God for the leader."

They began to walk away from the gate. Rachel looked back when she heard footsteps behind them. A guard that had clearly been assigned to Keith followed a few feet behind. Rachel turned back to look at Keith, and he shrugged.

"Where did he come from?" Rachel asked as they walked.

"I think he was standing in the shadows somewhere," Keith said, waving his hand. "He's become somewhat of a fixture to me now. I hardly notice him."

They talked about their day in detail, and Keith told Rachel again how worried he was that he still hadn't gotten any more word for Dennis. "I keep asking for wisdom, but I haven't gotten anything else. Maybe the Lord is through speaking to me."

Rachel said nothing about that, but she knew he was worried, not for his sake but for hers. She was going to see Emily again tomorrow and was extremely excited about that, but her ability to continue to see her daughter was hinged on Dennis Hamilton's goodwill. If that ran out, they would be sent packing from the town and she would be separated from her daughter again. She pressed her lips tightly together and tried to shoo away her worries. To distract herself, she asked Keith about the new prayer meetings he was planning to start in a room at the back of the town hall — the place Dennis had provided for him.

"The meetings will start this Saturday; that is, if Dennis will still allow me to hold them. Since he's been growing more and more impatient, I don't know if he'll suddenly change his mind about them. I'm not even sure if anyone will show up. I've been telling people I meet about it, but none of them have seemed particularly enthusiastic. A few have even looked suspicious. Right now, if not for the fact that I believe it's what God wants me to do, I would say it just isn't the right time to start holding the meetings."

She didn't know what to tell him, so she just squeezed his hand to let him know she was going to stand by him and try to help him no matter what.

He smiled again and said, "I've started rambling again." He sighed. "Our focus right now is on finding a solution for the women."

They continued walking in silence until they got to Taylor's house. Rachel stepped up to the door and rang the doorbell. They waited, but when no one answered the door, she rang the bell again. After they waited another minute and still no one came to the door, she said, "I don't think anyone's home."

Keith knocked on the door repeatedly, but still the door remained closed.

Rachel shut her eyes and frowned. Where had Taylor gone at this time of night? She groaned. "This is great! Just when we need him, he's not around."

She walked to the side of the house and then around to the back and looked up. All the blinds were drawn and she couldn't see into the house. She came to the front of the house again and shook her head. "No one's here."

Keith put his arm around her. "Don't worry, Rachel. I'm sure he'll be at home tomorrow morning, and then you can speak to him about helping the women out. I just wish I could be here with you."

"I know," she said. She whispered again, "Even his wife and child aren't at home. I wonder where they all went?"

Keith took her hand. "I'll try my best to come by tomorrow morning so we can come here together again."

"Thank you," she said gratefully as they began to walk away. Hopefully Keith would be able to come here with her because she always felt better when he was by her side. Hopefully, when they came back, Taylor would be home. She needed his help right now, before another woman suffered the same fate Carol had.

EIGHTEEN

The birthing room was just a few feet away from the waiting area where Taylor stood. His wife was in there, giving birth to their child. He could hear her screams.

When she let out a particularly piercing scream, he clenched his teeth. "Lord, please have mercy. Please help her."

She'd had a difficult pregnancy and had been in labor for hours. After about eight hours of labor, he had told the midwife he wanted to take his wife out of Fallow Creek to a hospital he had seen the last time he went to the city on a business trip. He had heard somewhere that a protracted labor could have serious complications for the mother and baby. The hospital in the city would have the right medical equipment that would help Faye give birth safely.

The midwife had insisted that his wife would deliver their baby safely in the Fallow Creek clinic. He groaned as he kept pacing the otherwise empty waiting area. If anything happened to Faye or their baby, he would never forgive himself for listening to the midwife. And he would not forgive the midwife, either. In fact, he would never forgive anyone who had told him she would deliver their baby safely here even though Faye had had a high-risk pregnancy. That included her parents, some of his friends, and Dennis Hamilton.

She gave another piercing scream, and he moaned. If not for the stupid rules that discouraged men from being in the birthing room when their wives were giving birth, he would barge in there right now. As it was, he could hardly contain himself. He felt like going in there, grabbing Faye, and taking her out of Fallow Creek to the bigger hospital.

"Why didn't you do that before now?" he scolded himself, and then sighed. It was too late now. He thought about their son and prayed that Faye would be kept safe. He needed her. Their son needed her. He had sent Josh to stay with his wife's parents when Faye had gone into labor.

She had started to feel intense pain right before he'd come back from a business meeting. Half an hour later, he had driven her to the clinic after dropping their son off at his grandparents'. Hopefully, by the time this ordeal was over, they would have a brand-new son or daughter and Josh would have a sibling.

Faye screamed again, and he bit his bottom lip until the pain stopped him. *Why didn't I take Faye to the hospital hours ago when the midwife told me the baby wasn't in the right position?* The midwife had assured him they could turn the baby to the position it was supposed to be. He didn't even know if they had succeeded in doing that.

"What if she needs an operation to get the baby out?" he asked himself, his heart pounding with fear.

He shut his eyes and shook his head. *Calm down, Taylor. She will be all right and the baby will be fine, too.* But he couldn't calm down. He continued to pace the room and then blinked when he didn't hear any more of her screams. He also didn't hear the welcome cry of a baby.

He couldn't take it anymore. He marched to the birthing room and then he froze on the spot. The midwife was standing over his baby, smacking him on the bottom, probably trying to get him to make a sound.

Taylor's heart jumped into his throat, and he marched over to the midwife. "What's wrong with my child?"

The baby suddenly gave a piercing scream and he gasped. Relief flooded him. His son looked alive and well. He turned to Faye with a smile and then frowned. She was lying on the bed, unmoving. The assistant midwife was standing beside her and looking at him with terror in her eyes.

He walked slowly to the bed, his heart almost bursting out of his chest. "No," he said in alarm. "Faye, wake up. We have a son, and he's healthy and strong." He hurried to her, knelt down beside the bed, and took her hands. "Wake up, Faye! Wake up!"

He put his head to her breast. She was breathing, but she didn't open her eyes or move. He looked up at the midwives and screamed, "What's wrong with her?"

"There were complications," the midwife said.

Taylor shook his head. "But she's alive! So, what's wrong with her? Why won't she wake up?"

"She fell into a coma and we don't know how long she has."

He looked up at the women and yelled, "If anything happens to her, you'll have me to answer to."

He looked down at his wife's pale face and closed his eyes in agony. He had never allowed himself to get too close to her — the same way many of the men in this town treated their wives. But now, looking at her again, he knew that he loved her with all his heart. Nothing could happen to her... for his sake and for his sons'.

He got up quickly and lifted her into his arms.

"Where are you going?" the midwife asked, standing in his way.

He nudged the woman aside and carried his wife out of the birthing room and out of the clinic. He reached his car and then turned to look at the midwives who had followed him out. He barked at one of them, "Open the back door and let me get her in."

The assistant midwife immediately opened the car for him and he gently laid Faye on the back seat. He jumped into the driver's seat and started the car.

The head midwife came to the window and said, "It's not safe to just grab her and go."

"And it's safer to leave her there on the bed and wait for her to die?"

She started to say something else, but he cut her off. "Take care of my baby. I'll be back." He drove away as fast as he could.

As he approached the border, he spotted the

security squad guards at their usual post, their SUVs blocking the road. Usually, whenever he planned to go out of Fallow Creek for whatever reason, especially on business trips, he had to get permission from Dennis Hamilton beforehand. Today, he had no permission to leave. That would be a problem.

They all turned as he approached, curiosity in their eyes as he glared at them.

Their expressions changed from curiosity to alarm when Taylor did not stop. They jumped out of the way but pointed their guns at him. He finally stopped at the last minute because their SUVs were blocking his path.

Their leader, Daniel Bacon, came to his window and said gruffly, "Where are you going in such a hurry in the middle of the night, sir? We weren't told that you were going…"

Taylor spat out, "Look in the back of my car! My wife is lying there unconscious, almost dead. You better move these cars right now. If anything happens to her because of your stupid delay, I will make sure that whatever it is will happen to you."

Daniel's mouth dropped open, and then he sighed loudly. He went to speak with his men and came back to Taylor. "We were not told by Dennis Hamilton to let anyone through today, but because it's you, we'll make an exception."

"And hurry up about it!" Taylor barked. He had a mind to bash through these cars if not for the safety of his wife in the back of the car. He didn't care about himself right now.

He hit his dashboard and yelled when instead of the men entering their cars and moving them out of the way, they turned to stare at him. He stuck his head out of the window and glowered at them. "Get out of the way right now!" He looked back at his wife and pressed his lips together, fear flooding him. "Stay with me, Faye," he said. "For Joshua's sake and mine."

The squad members drove out of the way at last, and Taylor pressed the gas pedal hard and raced away. "Please, Faye, don't die," he said. If she survived, he would never take her for granted again. He would ignore all the rules and attitudes of this place and treat her as she should be treated — like his queen. Most of all, he would cancel his plans to marry another wife, no matter what Andrew Lowery, the father of the girl he'd planned to marry, said. He told his wife everything he was thinking, even though he knew she probably couldn't hear him. "I'll do better." he said. "I promise you."

***

Rachel's stomach twisted with worry and excitement as she and Keith made their way to Mike's house. Again, she could not help but think about the risks they were taking to see Emily. If Mike ever found out, he wouldn't let her see her daughter ever again, unless somehow she fought him in a court of law. But the Lord had said they were not to take that route.

"Lord, please help me." She hurried her steps, still holding onto Keith's hand. Thankfully, he had been able to leave Dennis's early enough to accompany her. She was grateful to God for that.

It was the middle of the night, but the streetlights

illuminated the house brightly. "I can't wait to see Emily and hold her." She smiled at Keith.

"I can't wait to see the precious smile on your face when Emily is in your arms. It made me so happy the last time we went to see her... because you were so happy."

Her happiness gradually overtook all her worries, and she beamed. "Emily is such a precious and beautiful baby."

"Yes, she is."

Rachel's steps were light as they continued to walk to Mike's house. For the first time since the day started, she felt hopeful about the future. She would see her daughter again and get to hold and kiss her. "One day, the Lord will make a way so I never have to leave Emily again," she said to Keith.

Keith squeezed her hand and smiled. Soon, they began to reminisce about Destiny, their friends there, and their wedding. "Our wedding was magnificent," Rachel said, smiling.

Keith raised his brows. "It was a simple wedding, Rachel."

"Simple?" she chuckled. "All of Destiny was at our wedding."

"Yes, because it was a wedding fit for a queen. My queen." He put his arm around her and drew her close to his side.

She smiled. There was no better feeling than the way she felt whenever she was with Keith. He made everything seem better and she still had butterflies in her stomach whenever she was with him. She looked up at his face and desire ran through her. "If only we didn't have to live apart," she said.

"I know." He bent his head and kissed her softly.

He chuckled and a mischievous look appeared in his eyes. "Maybe we should just defy Dennis and go to that abandoned house to spend the night."

She looked back and sighed loudly. She faced him and kissed him again. "Your man is still following us."

He gave a short laugh and hugged her to his side again. "I guess we can't do that, then. But don't worry, Rachel. Soon, we'll be able to move in together again. I believe that." He planted another kiss on her lips, "then we can spend as much time as we want alone." He shook his head and sighed in clear frustration. "We are newlyweds, for goodness' sake. We shouldn't be living in separate houses."

She laughed. "That Dennis is a wicked man. Doesn't he understand that newlyweds need lots of alone time?"

Keith chuckled. "I'm pretty sure he understands that concept with all the wives I've seen in that house."

Rachel suddenly stopped smiling. What Keith said took her mind back to Carol and the consequences she had suffered because she'd refused to be part of a man's harem. She looked up at Keith again and said, "When I was in Destiny with you, I began to forget how privileged I am to be married to the man I love and not to have to share you with anyone else. It's so different for many of the women here. I have to do something to change it, Keith." She had a burning desire to help those who did not want to be part of the polygamous lifestyle rampant in this community.

"I know my actions come with risks, but there has to be a way to help more women who don't want to be part of the lascivious lifestyle of the men of this town."

"We will have to pray and ask the Lord for wisdom to know how you should proceed, because just as you said, it's risky. You don't want any other girl to be sent away like Carol was."

"Like I was too," she said to him. "But I was blessed to have you waiting. Most of the women here know no one outside because their parents and grandparents totally cut off from everyone they knew in the outside world. Dennis always used to say at places like the general church services that everyone in Fallow Creek was related spiritually. He'd say, 'You have no other families outside this town. No one will ever love you the way the people here do.'"

"Wow!" Keith shook his head. "I'm so glad you left Fallow Creek when you did. I'm really glad we found each other in Destiny."

"And yet here we are, back in Fallow Creek. Sometimes when I wake up in the morning since we came here, I wonder if we've both gone crazy. This is the last place anyone should ever come back to." She shrugged. "But the Lord does work in mysterious ways. If it wasn't for Him, no one would ever have convinced me to come back here."

"Well, I'm beginning to see why God brought us here; at least why He brought *you* here, Rachel. You have a lot to do here."

"So do you," she told him. "I'm sure of that. There's a reason God revealed so many secrets about Dennis Hamilton to you."

"I know," Keith said softly, and smiled at her. "I just wish He would reveal more of those secrets to me before Dennis boots us out of town. I believe we can make real changes if we're allowed to stay."

Rachel said nothing, and they continued to walk hand-in-hand while she mused about her childhood and the way her life was growing up in Fallow Creek. For years she had dreamt and planned on how to escape the town and then she finally had. Now she was back. It would be funny if it weren't for the seriousness and risks they had taken and were still taking in order to accomplish what God had brought them here to do. One of those reasons was to see and be reunited with her daughter again.

She took a deep breath when they finally reached Mike's. They went to stand beneath the large tree on the left side of Mike's house where they would be well concealed. Rachel kept looking at the front door, willing Olivia to come out.

When Olivia didn't come out of the house after a few minutes, Rachel's heart began to pound with worry. She turned to Keith. "Where's Olivia? Where is she with my baby?"

She couldn't stay still any longer and began to walk towards the back of the house. She would try to see if Olivia's window was open and if she could spot her and get her out here. Keith beckoned to her to come back, and she turned around and told him she wouldn't be long. She left the shadows and Keith caught up to her. Just before they rounded the house, the front door opened.

Rachel gasped, fear flooding her as Mike stepped out and glared at her. Two guards also came out of the house and walked towards her and Keith, looking menacing. Mike strode to them, clapping his hands. "Well, well! You worked your magic on

Dennis and he let you back here." He scowled at Keith and Rachel. The look on his face turned to one of derision. "And you had the guts to bring him to my house, Rachel." He looked at the guards and nodded at them.

Rachel screamed when one of the squad guards suddenly grabbed her.

"You whore! You thought you could just come back here after leaving me for another man. I got wind of your plan from Olivia. Just know that you will never see Emily again."

"Leave her alone!" Keith lunged at the guard holding Rachel, but the other one grabbed him as well. He struggled to break free, but couldn't.

"You'll regret ever stepping foot on my property to try to kidnap my daughter."

"You know that's a lie," Rachel yelled. "We're not here to kidnap Emily. She's my daughter, and I have a right to see her!"

"Take them away," Mike said to the guards.

"You'll take them nowhere!" Keith's bodyguard stepped into the light.

Mike growled. "Mind your business and step away. They're trespassing on my property, and I have a right to deal with them as I see fit."

"I'm sorry, but I can't let you do that," the bodyguard said. "I have orders from Dennis Hamilton to make sure no harm comes to these two. Even this place is the leader's land."

Mike screamed in outrage. "This isn't right! A man should have the right to deal with his wife as he wants."

Rachel yelled. "I am not your wife!"

Keith began to struggle again to be free, his eyes

full of rage and fixed on the guard who had grabbed Rachel, but the other guard held a gun to his head.

His bodyguard looked at the other two guards and said, "Do you both want to answer to Dennis Hamilton, your leader? Will you explain to him why you hurt the two people who are his guests?"

The other guards looked at each other and let go of Rachel and Keith.

Mike yelled again, "This isn't right! There's no justice in this town anymore." He shot Rachel a hard stare and then shrugged. "Well, it doesn't even matter if you are free. Dennis knows, at least, that he can't force me to let you see my daughter. And I promise you, you will never see Emily again. Never! Now, I want you both off my property!" He looked at Keith's bodyguard and said, "Surely Dennis didn't also give them permission to trespass here?"

Rachel screamed. "I need to see Emily right now! I need to see my daughter this minute!"

Mike glowered at her and then turned around and walked back into his house. She rushed forward and tried to open the door, but it was locked. She sat on the front porch and put her head down, sorrow washing over her. "He can't do this," she whispered. "Keith, he can't keep my daughter away from me!"

Keith walked over to her and gently lifted her up from the ground. "I'll talk to Dennis about this, Rachel." He rubbed her back. "I promise. Mike can't keep you away from Emily. Dennis will intervene."

Rachel walked away from the house with Keith, and he continued to whisper encouraging words to her. But she knew that there was only so much that Dennis Hamilton could do. Mike was right. In this place, there was an unspoken rule that children belonged to their fathers first before their mothers. This time, Dennis might not be able to intervene when it came to her being allowed to see her daughter.

They got to the Restoration House, and Keith kissed Rachel's hair, her nose, her forehead. He finally kissed away the tears running down her cheeks. "It will turn out all right in the end, Rachel. We have to believe that."

She didn't know if that was true. What would she do if she never saw Emily ever again?

Keith gave her a tight hug and told her he would try to come back in the morning if he could. When he left, the guards opened the gates for her. She quickly made her way into the house and up the stairs.

Once in her room, she fell into her bed without shedding her clothes. This whole day had been nothing but an emotional rollercoaster. She closed her eyes and tried to sleep, but not before praying that the next day would bring much better tidings.

NINETEEN

A myriad of thoughts raced through Lily's mind that she could not process. She finally opened her eyes. She took a deep breath and then yawned. It felt as though she had just woken up from a very long, deep, dreamless sleep. She shut her eyes once more as the light from the bulb above almost blinded her. She waited for about a minute and then slowly opened them again.

She blinked in confusion and looked around her. "Where am I?" she whispered. She licked her dry lips and slowly sat up on the bed. The sound of something beeping caused her to turn. A machine of some sort was on the table beside her, and it was what was making the beeping sound. She turned away and looked around the room again. She was in a small room alone. Beside her was a long iron pole. There wasn't much else in the room. She noticed then that a tube ran from the pole to the back of her hand and it suddenly dawned on her that she was in the hospital. She had seen hospital rooms on the internet. And this room where she was definitely looked like one. She had never been inside any hospital, not even the small clinic in Fallow Creek, as far as she could remember.

Slowly, she began to recall everything that had happened in the past few days. At least, she assumed it was days, thought she felt like she had been asleep for an eternity.

She remembered being kicked out of Fallow Creek while her mother wept, and the sad look on her father's face. She shuddered as she remembered crossing the road in the strange big town she had arrived in. That was the last thing she remembered, actually. She was trying to carry her suitcase across the busy road when a car going at breakneck speed had hit her.

She groaned. *So that's why I am here.* Sadness flooded her heart as she thought about her parents back at Fallow Creek. When would she ever get to see them again? She had made a promise to herself that somehow she would find a way to get them out of that town no matter how long it took. But who knew how long that would be? She had only a few dollars left, having spent the little money her mother had given her on transportation. How was she to survive?

"Well, the first thing is to leave this place." She looked down at herself, and for the first time she realized she was not in her dress. She was wearing a blue gown that was open in the back. She frowned. *What sort of dress is this, anyway?* She gasped as fear gripped her.

"Oh no! Please, Lord. Where is my dress?" The money that was left of what her mother had given her was inside the pocket of that dress. She had to find it. She looked around the room and heaved a sigh of relief. Someone had laid her dress carefully on the chair near the window.

She looked down at the floor and made an attempt to get out of bed, but she felt too weak to do so. She sighed. "Great. I'm stuck in this place."

A lady wearing a white outfit entered the room, and her eyes grew wide when she saw Lily. She hurried out of the room and Lily frowned. *Why did that lady run away when she saw me?*

Less than a minute later, the lady in white came back with a man who looked like a doctor because of the stethoscope draped around his neck. He walked over to her with a huge smile on his face. "I see you are awake," he said. "You've been out of it for quite some time."

Lily looked up at him in confusion. "Out of it? For how long?"

"Almost a week."

Lily shook her head slowly as her confusion grew.

"You've been in a coma," the man said. He put an instrument on her heart and in his ear and listened. Then he touched her forehead. "How do you feel?"

"Like I've just awakened from a very long, deep sleep," she told him. "I feel really tired. But apart from that, I feel okay."

He nodded. "You're lucky you were brought here as quickly as you were. You sustained injuries that would cause you excruciating pain and, for other reasons as well, we had to induce a coma. Right now you're on strong pain meds to help control the pain. But I have to say you're a miracle, my dear. It may take some time, but I believe you will make a full recovery."

"Who brought me here?" she asked.

Before the doctor could answer, someone walked into the room and the doctor turned. "Well, here she is," he said, turning back to Lily. "She was actually the one driving the car that hit you, but she brought you here immediately."

Lily looked past the doctor and the nurse to the woman who had just walked in. She looked around Lily's age, but that was the only similar thing about them. She was dressed in a very elegant, expensive-looking outfit, and she looked like one of those women Lily saw online who posed for pictures in designer clothes. She had long, dark hair and a blunt fringe that almost covered her eyes, and she wore blood-red lipstick.

The woman's eyes grew wide when she saw Lily, and her face suddenly broke out in a huge smile. She opened her arms wide and strutted to Lily with a laugh. "You're awake, my friend," she said exuberantly. When she hugged Lily tight, Lily blinked in surprise, inhaling the woman's strong floral scent.

"Be careful," the doctor said. "Remember her injuries are still healing."

Lily touched her chest and only then felt a bandage wrapped around her.

The exuberant lady drew back and chuckled. "I'm so glad to see you awake."

The doctor smiled at Lily again and told her he would be back to check on her in the evening. He left with the nurse, and the sophisticated-looking lady pulled the chair that was near the window to Lily's bed and sat down.

Her presence seemed to fill up the whole room, and Lily couldn't take her eyes away from her.

"My name is Sofia with a 'f'," she told Lily with a laugh. In a very fast and cheerful voice she began to fill in the details that had led to Lily's accident. She had stopped at her favorite restaurant to have lunch and then she had got into her car to go back to the office. "I was in a hurry," she said, still smiling as though she was telling Lily about a great exciting adventure she'd just experienced rather than the accident that might have tragically ended Lily's life but for the grace of God. Yet Lily was not offended. Instead, she was intrigued by the woman.

"I saw you crossing the road with your suitcase, but I wasn't worried. I thought you would move on, but you paused in the middle of the road. I tried to stop, but it was too late. The next thing I knew, you were flying in the air. It all felt like a dream."

She leaned forward and took Lily's hands. "I brought you to the hospital as fast as I could, and I was so afraid you wouldn't make it. When you didn't wake up for some time and were later put into a coma, I thought you would never awaken. But the doctor assured me that you would. Now that you have, it's so good to see you alive and well." She let go of Lily's hands and clapped, looking excited.

Lily couldn't help but smile. This woman who had said her name was Sofia was talking to her as though they were best friends who had known each other for years, and yet they had never met.

"So, what's your name?" Sofia asked.

"Lily. Lily Hunter."

"And where do you come from, Lily Hunter?"

Once more, sadness filled Lily's heart as she

pictured her mother and father in Fallow Creek, mourning over her. She thought about her sister and about her friends with a heavy heart. When would she next see the town of her birth? She might not miss the way of life in Fallow Creek, but she would definitely miss all her loved ones. She faced Sofia fully and then, for some reason, maybe because the woman fascinated her, or because out here she knew no one, she began to tell Sofia everything about her life. She told her about growing up in Fallow Creek and her decision never to be married. She ended with her banishment from the town.

"So you were sent away when you refused to get married to someone who already had other wives?" Sofia chuckled. "So you were supposed to be a sister wife."

"Sister wife?" Lily asked. "What does that mean?"

"You come from a polygamous community, Lily. How do you not know what a sister wife means? Well, it simply means you were supposed to share a man with his other wives."

"Oh. Yes." Lily nodded. "I refused to be a sister wife."

Lily told her how she had decided she wanted to live in a big city rather than a small town like the one she had come from. She was headed for Phoenix and had stopped in this city to take another bus going there without knowing how she would survive once she got there. She told Sofia about the money her mother had given her and how she only had a little left of it. She looked at her dress hanging on the headrest of the chair where Sofia was sitting.

"Can you please hand me that dress?"

Sofia gave it to her, and she immediately dug her

hand into the pocket. She sighed with relief when she felt the money in her pocket. She put the dress aside and continued with her story. She told Sofia about her fascination with the skyscrapers and big buildings that she'd seen, which was also part of the reason why she had not crossed the road as quickly as she should have.

"So you're not angry with me?" Sofia asked.

Lily shook her head quickly. "It wasn't your fault."

Sofia grinned. "I'm so glad you don't blame me. I felt so guilty when the accident happened." Her eyes scrutinized Lily's face. "So I take it you have no place to stay?"

"Yes," Lily nodded. "I plan to look for somewhere cheap to stay and pay with the little money I have left once I arrive in Phoenix. But I don't even know if I can afford to go to Phoenix now. Maybe I'll stay here. It is a big city, after all."

"Yes, Tucson is a good place to live." Sofia kept studying Lily. "What did you do for a living in Fallow Creek?"

Lily looked away, feeling embarrassed. She had never worked for wages in her twenty-five years alive, but Sofia, who looked to be about her age, was clearly an independent career woman. From how expensive and tasteful her clothes looked, she was probably also successful in her career. They were so different even though they seemed to be the same age. Lily finally turned back to Sofia and said truthfully, "I didn't have a job in Fallow Creek. At least, not one that paid me. I did many chores, especially while I was in the Restoration House."

"The House where they take stubborn women

who don't abide to the rules of the town?"

"Yes," Lily said.

"So you don't have a job or a place to stay and very little money."

Sofia had summed up her situation rightly. The money her mother had given her would not last long at all. She had never had any personal money of her own and had only been given money to buy things like groceries from the local store. The money she had now would probably not last as long as she had thought when she'd left Fallow Creek. *Lord, help me.* She had to find a job quickly, and a house as well.

Sofia smiled widely at Lily and then asked about her qualifications or skills in case she found a job Lily was qualified for.

Lily felt embarrassed again, but she answered quickly, "I don't think I have any qualifications or skills, but we cleaned a lot back in Fallow Creek. I could be a cleaner or maid."

Sophia gave a short laugh. "No, that won't do." She looked Lily over and said, "Once you're well enough to leave the hospital, I'll assess what your real skills are and then give you a job. I'm sure I can find something for you to do. If not, George definitely will."

Lily didn't know who George was, but her heart soared with happiness and gratitude. "Thank you so much, Sofia. That means everything to me."

Sofia said, "You can stay with me until you're able to save enough to get your own apartment. Once you have a job, you'll be able to."

Lily felt too overwhelmed to speak, and for a long moment, she said nothing. When she could talk again, she thanked Sofia once more for everything.

"It's the least I can do since I was the one who put you here," Sofia said.

"But you're giving me more than I could ever imagine," Lily told her. "I've been so afraid of my future, of how I'll survive with only a little money and no place to live. But now I don't have to worry anymore."

Sofia shrugged. "Once you're released from the hospital, I'll come and take you to my house."

Lily silently lifted up a prayer of thanksgiving to God for everything. He had miraculously provided for her even though the provision had come through her accident. She looked up at Sofia and smiled. Soon, by the grace of God, she would be independent and be in charge of her own life and destiny, just as she had always dreamt about. She would be just like Sofia — beautiful, sophisticated, and successful. No one would ever tell her how to live her life again.

She took a deep breath and listened as Sofia launched into another story, this time about an actual adventure; at least, an adventure to Lily. It involved a businessman, an old boyfriend of Sofia's, and a place called a yoga studio. Lily drank in everything Sofia said and the way she said it, hoping one day to sound and look just like the sophisticated woman beside her bed. Maybe one day, she herself would have a boyfriend and go to strange places like the yoga studio.

***

Taylor drove to the clinic in Fallow Creek, feeling

completely exhausted and heartbroken. Nothing would ever fill the void in his heart again. Nothing and no one would ever be able to take his wife's place. She had passed away.

He blamed the midwife and, most of all, himself. If only he'd listened to his own intuition, the voice in him saying that it would be safer if he took his wife to the hospital outside Fallow Creek to give birth to their baby. Now he had lost her, and he would blame himself for the rest of his life. He had gotten to the hospital, but she had died just minutes later.

He got out of his car and slowly entered the clinic, body and heart aching. The only thing that would assuage this pain now, if that was possible, was the tiny baby his wife had brought into this world on her way to leave it, and his son Josh, who was at Faye's parents' house.

The midwife looked up at him as he walked into the birthing room where his wife had labored to give birth to their baby. "Where is he?" Taylor looked at the midwife. "Where is my baby?"

"What happened to your wife?" the midwife asked, looking at him with sorrow.

He barked, "Are you really asking me that? What do you think happened to her? You didn't let me take her out of here and now she's dead."

The midwife stepped back. "I'm sorry."

"No, you're not. You and everyone in this town make it difficult to leave here. I should have followed my intuition. I should have taken her out of here as soon as she went into labor." He looked around the room. His baby was nowhere around. "Where is my son?"

The midwife stared at him for a few seconds and then told him to give her a minute. She went out of the room and appeared just a minute later with a bundle wrapped in a blanket in her arms. "Here he is," the woman said, and gently handed him his baby.

He took his son and stared at him. He was wrapped in a blue blanket that almost matched his eyes. "Isn't he handsome?" the midwife said, but Taylor didn't answer. His son definitely was, but Taylor was too overcome to speak. He kissed his baby's cheek. He would never know his mother. Taylor wanted to weep at the thought, but he had no strength to do it. He looked around at the birthing room and immediately stepped out. He marched out of the clinic with a firm determination in his heart. He was leaving this town and he didn't know if he was ever going to come back.

He opened his car to enter just as Andrew Lowery accosted him. He glared at the man. He was in no mood to talk, especially to this man.

"I see your wife has given birth," Andrew said. "Now, you promised you would visit once she did. You can come to the house this evening so we can start with the marriage plans again."

Taylor wanted to knock the man's teeth out, but he controlled himself. "Do you see my wife anywhere?"

The man looked quizzically at him. "Of course not. What are you saying? She just gave birth, so she'll still be inside." He looked at the baby and smiled. "You have a beautiful baby, by the way."

Taylor glared at the man as his body shook with rage.

"So, are you coming this evening?" Andrew said.

Lord, please help me not to knock this man to the ground. "No!" Taylor said. He got into his car and drove away without looking back.

He got to Faye's parents' house and, as soon as he entered, asked for his son.

"Where's Faye? Is she still at the birthing center?" her mother asked.

He sat down on the sofa slowly as the woman took the baby from him and cooed over his son. "How come the baby is out while Faye's still there?" Faye's mother asked, still cooing at the baby. She looked at Taylor when he said nothing.

"Taylor, where is Faye? What happened to her?" he mother asked now, sounding hysterical.

Taylor went and took the baby from the woman and then told her what had happened. She let out a loud scream, and Faye's father rushed out. When Taylor explained what had happened to Faye, the man bent down and held his wife, and they wept together.

Taylor felt heartbroken for them, but he could not tarry. He went to the room where his son usually stayed whenever he was here. "We have to leave, Josh," he said. "Get all your things and let's go."

Josh began to complain, but Taylor said firmly, "Get your things now, Joshua!"

They left through the back door so Josh wouldn't see his grandparents weeping. He wanted to tell Joshua himself about what had happened to his mother.

He put the baby again into the backseat of the car, settling him in the car seat that had belonged to Joshua when he was a baby. He buckled both his sons in and got into the driver's seat. He drove off as fast as he could, just the way he had when he'd taken Faye to the hospital. He could not wait to leave this town.

"Where are we going?" Josh asked. "And where is Mommy? How come the baby is here? And what are we going to have for dinner?"

"Joshua, please, I'll tell you everything, but you have to be quiet now," Taylor said. Thankfully it was during the day and the border was not as heavily guarded as it was during the night. Still, there were squad guards there. They had stared at him curiously when he'd entered the town.

He got to the border. When one of the squad members approached him, he said bluntly, "Let me through."

"No, we can't do that."

Taylor stared at him and shouted, "Let me through now! I have some business to conduct for Dennis Hamilton!"

The guard stared at him suspiciously and then looked back and nodded at the rest of the squad team behind him.

"Thank God," Taylor murmured under his breath when the squad guards began to drive their cars out of the way.

Taylor pressed the pedal and raced out of town without looking back. He wasn't sure when or if he would ever return. Rachel was in Fallow Creek right now. She'd told him they had taken their phones at the border when she and Keith arrived. He would have to find a way to send her a message and ask her to take care of his house and everything he had until the day he returned, if ever. He would raise his children alone, because never again would he get married and put himself through the sadness he was feeling right now. He looked back at his sons briefly and then faced the road again. "Are you okay over there, Josh?"

"Yes," Joshua answered.

Taylor nodded. He still had the monumental task of breaking the sad news to his son. For a long time, he knew they would not be okay, but hopefully, soon, they would be. He would have to be both a father and a mother for his children, something he knew he would never be allowed to do peacefully in Fallow Creek, as everyone would keep urging him to find a new wife almost right away. He was not sure exactly where he was going, but he thankfully had enough money to live anywhere he wanted and be comfortable with his children.

"Lord, have your way," he said as he drove farther away from Fallow Creek to a place where he would make a new life for himself and his sons.

TWENTY

Keith hurried away from the Restoration House with his heart sinking. He'd found it difficult to tell Rachel how his day went as she was troubled about so many things — Emily, the women at the Restoration House and the town in general, and even about Taylor. Her brother and his family were still not back from wherever they'd gone.

All had not gone well today. At least, not as he'd expected.

His bodyguard, who followed him almost everywhere, fell into step behind him, and Keith sighed. He continued on, praying and asking the Lord for wisdom as he had done since the day he'd started. He had shared with Dennis a little bit about his life and his walk with God, trying to get Dennis to open up his heart to receive the true gospel. But the man was not interested in hearing anything other than what he wanted, which was for Keith to tell him who his blackmailer was. Though Keith had been praying for wisdom concerning that situation, he'd been wondering for some time what exactly Dennis planned to do with the blackmailer once he knew his identity. In some way, Keith did not want him to know, though that would not do him nor Rachel any good. He needed to get word from God for Dennis or they would be thrown out of town.

He had stayed in Dennis's office until eleven o'clock tonight because Dennis kept insisting that he tell him about the blackmailer. He had stopped asking about what God wanted him to do with the blackmailer.

Keith kept telling him he had no new word from God, but somehow Dennis believed Keith wasn't trying hard enough to get word for him.

"I won't let you leave until you have something for me," Dennis had said.

"I have nothing to tell you right now," Keith had told him.

But Dennis would not hear of it. He made sure that Keith was well fed, but that he did not leave the office. Even when he left to conduct his daily business out of the house, he told the guards to watch Keith and not let him out of their sight.

"I hope you'll have something for me by the time I get back," Dennis had said before he left Keith in the office.

Keith had groaned at how unreasonable Dennis was.

He kept asking for wisdom even as he sat in Dennis's office, but he got nothing. He went through a few of Dennis's books because he was bored and then stared out the window, thinking about the people of Fallow Creek, and then about Rachel and how much she missed Emily. She had been so full of joy when they'd gone to see Emily the first day, and he wanted her to always be that way. He'd spoken to Dennis about Mike's threats, but as he'd guessed, Dennis did not pay any attention to his words. After a while, he'd returned to his seat and continued to rifle through the book he'd been reading — a book on prayer. He marveled at how much information was in the book and how its owner seemed to clearly miss it all.

He'd soon gotten restless again as he glanced at his wristwatch and saw it was some minutes past nine p.m. Where was Dennis, and why would he not let him leave this place? He sighed heavily and leaned back against his seat. He sat up again when Dennis walked into the room.

Dennis had asked in a voice that sounded partly threatening and partly expectant if Keith had received any word for him. When Keith told him he still hadn't, Dennis sat down slowly on his seat and glared at Keith.

"Well, that means you can no longer stay in Fallow Creek," Dennis said. "I even hear that Rachel is already disrupting the peaceful lives of the women at the Restoration House."

"That isn't true,"

Dennis said firmly, "You have no more business in this town if you can't tell me what I want to know." Keith opened his mouth to speak again, but Dennis held up his hand and stopped him. "Listen, you have just two days to tell me exactly what I want to know, or you and Rachel will leave Fallow Creek and never return. And don't try to tell me just anything from your heart, because I'll know."

"I would never do that. But you know I can't

control when or what God chooses to say to me," Keith said, desperate to get the man to understand his situation for Rachel's sake. If they were thrown out of the town now, Rachel would be devastated because of Emily. In spite of Mike's threats, she still had a chance to see her daughter if she remained here. He knew her plan was never to leave this town without Emily. He wouldn't be able to stand it if they were forced to leave now because he didn't have a word from God for Dennis. At the beginning, when the Lord had started to speak to him very clearly, it had seemed like a huge blessing; now it felt like the very opposite of that.

He pleaded with Dennis to give him more time, but his pleas fell on deaf ears.

"Two days should be enough for you to do whatever it is to hear God's voice for me."

That irritated Keith. "You can try hearing Him for yourself," he said angrily.

Dennis waved his hand and looked at Keith like what he was suggesting was the stupidest thing on Earth. "You can go," he told Keith. "But very early tomorrow morning, you're back here."

Now, Keith sighed as he walked through the night after spending an hour with Rachel outside the Restoration House. The more he thought about Dennis's ultimatum, the more worried he became, and the more fervently he prayed. Rachel had seen the uncertainty and worry he felt plastered on his face even though he'd tried to hide it from her. She had known that something was wrong and had asked him about it. But he'd insisted that he was just tired.

He finally stopped praying, as it didn't seem to

be helping. Besides, he recalled that he had done nothing more than what he usually did when he received the prophecies for Dennis. He wasn't sure there was anything he could do to make the Lord speak to him now.

"But you told us to come here, Lord," he said. "Dennis is about to send us packing and still you've said nothing."

"What?" his bodyguard, who was behind him, asked.

Keith ignored him. He continued to walk very slowly because he was physically and emotionally tired. He soon spotted the town hall, which was just a few feet away from the small apartment Dennis had given to him. The place was small, but very comfortable and fully furnished. It was probably a place Dennis used when he invited visitors to Fallow Creek. It was probably because the place was near the town hall and Dennis could easily have any visitor to the town watched to make sure they didn't step out of line or break any of the rules of the community.

He continued to worry about Rachel as he walked. Apart from how joyful she had been to see Emily, she'd been so happy when she'd brought those women in the Restoration House to the Lord. But everything seemed to be falling apart with Mike threatening to never allow her to see her daughter again. And now she had stopped sharing the gospel for fear that what had happened to the girl who was chased out of the town would happen to others. To top it off, Dennis had given him only two days to deliver new information or they would have to leave. But it seemed as though God did not want to speak to him about Dennis anymore.

Dennis's insistence that he give him word from God reminded him of Balak and Balaam in the Bible. He hastened his steps and, just before he turned a corner, started when a loud thud sounded behind him. With his heart racing, he turned around and gasped. A man dressed in black had a gun pointed at him and his bodyguard was on the ground unmoving. He stared at the guard in horror and looked up at the man with the gun.

Another man, who looked to be in his late fifties or early sixties, came out from the shadows, also pointing a gun at him. He looked at the bodyguard on the ground and said to Keith, "Don't worry about him. He's not dead. We just knocked him out."

Keith stared at both of them. "Who are you?" he asked, his heart drumming.

The older man said, "I will tell you, but you have to come with us."

"Do I have a choice?" Keith asked, arching his brows. The man's words had sounded more like an order rather than a request. And they still had guns pointed at him.

Neither of the men said anything.

"No, I won't come with you," Keith said as he thought about Rachel. He preferred to be shot in the open if they were going to instead of in some secret location where his body would never be found. They probably wanted to kill him or harm him in some way because he had the audacity to come to this town with Rachel and threaten their way of life. Maybe they were even sent by Mike.

The younger man said, "You have to come with us."

"I'm not coming with you," Keith repeated boldly, even though he was trembling on the inside. "You'll have to kill me right here if that's what you want to do."

The older man stared at him for a few seconds and then put down his gun. He ordered the younger man to do the same and said, "I'm sorry for scaring you. We don't plan to kill you. I just want you to come with us because there's something very important I have to tell you."

Keith eyed both men suspiciously. "And what is the important thing you want to tell me? You can tell me right here, out in the open."

The men looked around and then shook their heads.

"I would rather tell you in private because I don't want anyone to hear what I have to say," the older man said. He looked down at the bodyguard, who was still lying unconscious on the ground. "You will have to trust us and come with us."

"No!" Keith stood his ground.

The younger man snarled. "He's not cooperating. We have to do this by force." He raised his gun at Keith, but the older man pushed down his hand.

"What if I told you that I know everything about the blackmailer?" the older man said.

Keith raised his brows and stared at the man in surprise. "How do you know about that?"

"Please come with us, and I'll tell you everything," the older man told him.

They turned around and began to walk away, and for a second Keith stood where he was. He began to follow them while chiding himself for doing so. He didn't know who these men were or what their true intentions were. Why on earth was he following them?

But he continued to follow, curiosity egging him on.

They walked for a long time, keeping to the shadows and never walking directly in front of a house. Keith kept following them while still wondering why he was doing so. He told himself it was because they had a gun and he didn't have a choice, but their guns were not even pointed at him. His curiosity had gotten the best of him. Plus, there was something urging him to follow them — something more than curiosity.

They finally got to a house similar to the others in the town but a little bigger. It was smaller than Dennis's and definitely much smaller than Taylor's and Mike's. They entered the house and Keith looked around in surprise. He didn't know what he'd expected, but it wasn't the homey living room he was in now. He was pretty sure from the look of it that the house was a family home.

His eyes shifted to the pictures that lined the walls and his heart stopped. His blood ran cold as he stared at a picture of the older man and a woman who looked like his wife. The man had one arm around the woman and another around... No, it couldn't be.

His mind went blank for a second. He turned slowly to the man. He said in a shaky voice, "Is that... is that...?"

"Yes. That's my daughter, Rachel," the man said. "Or my stepdaughter, as she always reminded me when she was growing up."

Keith turned to look at the picture again and

went closer to study it. He couldn't believe what he was seeing. The man who had pointed the gun to his head was Rachel's stepfather. The stepfather Rachel told him had disrupted their lives when they were children by bringing her and her brother with their mother to Fallow Creek, and then broken their mother's heart. Keith turned abruptly to the man and said, "So you're the stepfather Rachel's told me all about. Why did you bring me here? And how did you know about Dennis's blackmailer? In fact, how did you know *I* knew about the blackmailer?"

Rachel's stepfather faced him fully. "Because I *am* the blackmailer!"

Keith gasped and his mouth fell open. He stared at the man in shock. "You are…"

"As for your first and third question…" He didn't finish his sentence. Instead, he called out to someone named Tim.

A young man who was dressed in the fatigues the security squad guards usually wore came out of an inner room, and Keith stared at him.

"You!" Keith pointed at the guard. It was the young security squad guard who had brought him to Dennis's house the first day he and Rachel arrived in Fallow Creek. He had posted himself at the door as Keith and Dennis had talked and had been quiet and seemingly unobtrusive, almost invisible. Dennis had not even given him a second glance, except when he'd shot orders at him. After a while, Keith had even forgotten he was there at the door. Clearly, Dennis implicitly trusted his guards, but he should have known better. This particular guard was obviously loyal to someone else.

Rachel's stepfather put his hand on the guard's

shoulder and said to Keith, "Timothy here told me everything. His father and I have been very close for years, and he's like a son to me."

Keith kept staring at them, unable to speak.

Rachel's stepfather said, "By the way, my name is Matthew, and this," he pointed at the other man with the gun, "is Lester." He strode to the picture with him, Rachel's mother, and Rachel, and stood looking intently at it. After a while he turned to Keith and said, "She cut me off completely. Did she tell you that?"

"Yes, she did."

"And she probably told you that I was the devil himself and that I broke her mother's heart."

"Yes, and much more than that," Keith said. He stared in anger at the man who had forcefully brought Rachel to this awful place and had treated her mother so badly.

"I really do miss her," Matthew said, "but she wants nothing to do with me. She's always been headstrong and she remains as stubborn as ever now."

"She is not stubborn!" Keith said, anger boiling in him. "She's the sweetest and kindest woman I've ever met."

Matthew waved his hand dismissively. He kept staring at the picture for another minute and then faced Keith. "I hear that you have prophetic... or is it psychic powers? I'm still not sure which one it is. Timothy told me you know more than you should about Dennis's blackmailer but had not yet figured out that it is me."

Keith glared at him. "So now what do you want with me, and why have you been blackmailing

Dennis?"

Matthew pointed at the couch. "Let's sit down, and I'll tell you everything."

Keith sat, and the man came and sat next to him. Timothy and the other man sat on the sofa facing them. Keith looked around, wondering where the man's family was. Rachel had told him the man had married another wife and she had stepsiblings. Maybe Matthew had moved them all to another house because of this clandestine meeting. Or maybe they had all left like Rachel. He took a deep breath and began to listen to Matthew's story.

"It all started with a very close friend of mine named Nathan."

TWENTY-ONE

Keith listened with rapt attention as Matthew continued.

"Nathan lived in Fallow Creek and, as I said, we were extremely close. In fact, he and Dennis and I were best friends, and we spent a lot of time together in those days. That was before Dennis's father passed away and he assumed the leadership of this community."

Matthew frowned. "Something awful happened, which I'll tell you later on in my story, but I will tell you now that Nathan's father suddenly left Fallow Creek one day with all his family, including Nathan. Most people didn't know why, but my father told me that Nathan's dad was driven away by Dennis's father for undisclosed reasons. Anyway, when Nathan left, I was so sad, but life went on. After a few years, Dennis's father passed away and he became the leader of this community. One day, when we were all fully grown but still single, Nathan returned secretly to Fallow Creek. His father had passed away by then, and I was the first person he came to see under the cover of darkness."

Keith tilted his head toward Matthew as he talked. The older man had a thoughtful look in his eyes as he said, "Nathan came to me that night with a secret. He couldn't contain himself as he paced my small living room. He finally told me that on his deathbed, his father had told him something huge. He'd told him the reason for the quarrel with Dennis's father and why he had been sent away with his family."

Keith listened with bated breath, memorizing everything Matthew was saying so he could tell Rachel later on.

"Nathan told me that his father had discovered an original land deed of Fallow Creek. It belonged to his grandfather, who had bequeathed the land to his future generations. It's a long story, but the summary of it is that Nathan's grandfather was actually the original owner of Fallow Creek and the one who'd bought the whole place with his own money. He was a very wealthy man. He built most of the houses in this town, except for the newer, bigger ones like mine and Dennis's. Taylor was contracted to build them."

Matthew pursed his lips and then went on. "Anyway, Nathan's grandfather had disappeared just shortly after he came to Fallow Creek, and his cousin, Dennis's grandfather, took possession of everything the man owned, including the town. But he never discovered where Nathan's grandfather kept the deed."

Matthew paused for a second and continued. "Nathan's father discovered the truth — that his father had been killed by Dennis's grandfather and confronted Dennis's father about it. But his life and that of his family was threatened, and he had to flee with his wife and son."

Keith couldn't believe what he was hearing. He told Matthew what Rachel had told him about how the town had been founded and was owned by the Hamiltons. Matthew nodded. "It's the story everyone knows, but it's not the truth."

Matthew went on. "Nathan told me that day why he'd secretly come to Fallow Creek. He said he had the original deed and had come to reclaim what was his. We argued that day. I told him how dangerous whatever he was planning was. Dennis owned the security squad his father had formed and they were totally loyal to him. Nathan left angrily, and the next thing I heard was that his body had been found dumped in a river on the edge of town."

Matthew rubbed his graying beard. "I knew immediately what had happened, but at the time I had no proof. I thought about confronting Dennis directly, but I changed my mind because I knew how dangerous that would be. And so I decided to call, but since I knew he would recognize my voice, I asked Lester to help me make the call and get Dennis to confess to killing Nathan, and threaten that if he didn't, everyone in the town would know what he had done."

Keith sighed. "So that was how the blackmail began? You asked him to pay for your silence?"

"You can say that," Matthew shrugged. "There's something more, though. And that's the main reason why I brought you here specifically."

Keith didn't know if he could take any more surprises.

"Before he left my house that day, Nathan told me something else. He had fallen in love with a younger woman outside of Fallow Creek and she had gotten pregnant with his child."

Keith's heart began to race as he listened.

"The young woman was Rachel's mother."

Keith jumped to his feet. His heart felt like it would explode from his chest.

"Please sit down and let me finish," Matthew said. Keith sat down slowly and the man went on. "Nathan told me it was one of the reasons why he had to come back. He wanted to bring the young woman and their unborn child here, and he wanted to give his child his family's legacy — Fallow Creek. The town belonged to his unborn child and he had to snatch it away from Dennis."

Keith couldn't breathe properly. He took huge gulps of air to calm down.

"Nathan was not a total fool. He knew Dennis was dangerous and there was a chance that something could happen to him when he confronted the leader. He gave me the full details of the woman, telling me that if something happened to him, I was to go and bring her and her child here to Fallow Creek. I was to take care of them for him and one day try to get Fallow Creek back for his child."

Keith shook his head slowly. He tried to speak, but he couldn't.

"I couldn't bring myself to fulfill Nathan's wishes for years because my heart was divided. Dennis had been paying me a large sum of money, with which I built this house. But after a while, I knew I had to fulfill my friend's last wishes. I left Fallow Creek with Dennis's permission, telling him I was going for a protracted business deal. But I went in search of Wendy, Rachel's mother. When I found her, I was surprised to see that the woman my friend had fallen in love with had two children. And I was even more surprised when I calculated the date and realized that Taylor was not Nathan's child. Rachel was. Wendy confirmed it when she told me that her children had different fathers. Nathan was Rachel's father's name."

Keith expected his heart to jump out of his chest at any moment. He asked, "So why did you not tell Wendy that you were Nathan's friend?"

"She was so beautiful the first time I saw her that I wanted her for myself. I believed that telling her I was Nathan's friend would prevent her from warming up to me, at least not as quickly as I wanted."

"And all these years you didn't tell Rachel that you knew her real father or that she was actually the rightful owner of the land this town is built upon and most of the houses here."

Rachel's stepfather snorted. "Nathan didn't tell me his child was a girl. For some reason, I believed it was a boy or Nathan wouldn't have been so determined to leave his legacy to his child at the risk of his life."

Keith stared at Matthew in disbelief and the man only shrugged. "Daughters leave your house, marry someone else, and change their names. Your true legacy lies with your son."

Keith shook his head as he stared at Matthew. The man was a crazy chauvinist. Keith asked, "You knew that Dennis killed your stepdaughter's father and your good friend, and yet all these years you kept silent." He glared at Matthew. "You knew that Rachel was the true owner of this town and yet you told her nothing because Dennis paid for your silence."

Matthew said, "In spite of everything, I love this town and I want to see it flourish. Revealing the truth to everyone would have caused an uproar that would tear the town down, especially as its true owner is some flimsy girl."

Keith felt his anger rise again. "You call Rachel a flimsy girl! So you'd rather have a murderer continue as the leader of the town than the rightful owner because she is, as you put it, 'a flimsy girl?' So why did you decide now to start blackmailing Dennis again?"

Rachel's stepfather sighed loudly. "Lately, I've started to grow tired of Dennis's excuses. The man is drunk with power, and the security squad are at his beck and call. He does whatever he wants to in this town. I decided it was time to wrest the town from his clutches."

"So it's not the money you're really interested in. You just told him you wanted money to throw him off the scent. What you're really interested in is Fallow Creek."

Matthew smiled. "Yes, exactly."

"And what'll happen to Dennis once the whole truth is revealed about him?"

"He'll be thoroughly disgraced and removed from his position. He'll probably be sent out of town never to return again."

"And since you think the town will fall apart if some 'flimsy girl' becomes the leader, I guess you have no plans to tell Rachel she is the rightful owner of Fallow Creek?"

"Yes."

Keith's heart beat wildly in fear. "What will happen to my wife if the truth is revealed that she's really the owner of the town and the rightful leader?"

"She would be in danger," Matthew said. "No man here is ready for a woman, especially one as rebellious as Rachel, to take over as leader. No one would stand for it."

"And so you're ever ready to protect the town by taking her place and becoming the leader yourself, is that it?"

"Yes again. At least Rachel will have a relative as the owner of this town in place of her."

A scripture ran through Keith's mind. *The earth is the Lord's and the fullness thereof.* He put his hand on his forehead as his head throbbed. He didn't know what to think or do about all this information he'd been given. He wanted Rachel safe with everything that was in him, and at the same time, he wanted her to take what was hers rightfully, knowing the positive changes she could make in Fallow Creek if she had the authority to do so. He sighed. Still, nothing was worth losing her life.

Including the freedom and salvation of the people of this place? a voice whispered in his heart. He shuddered.

Rachel's stepfather said, "You understand, don't you, that you can't tell Rachel anything that I've told you today? It's for her own safety."

Keith's headache grew worse. How could he keep such a huge secret from her, and yet how could he tell her if it would put her in danger? He said to Matthew, "Will you at least let Rachel stay here so she can be with her daughter? She has big plans for the Restoration House. She wants to make changes there for the women. Will you let us remain in Fallow Creek?"

"I can't!" Matthew said. "You both have to leave immediately."

Keith shut his eyes in agony. Rachel would be devastated. He looked at Matthew and said, "Why can't you let Rachel remain here?" He pursed his lips. "It's not so much her safety you are concerned about, is it? It's that she's the rightful owner of this place and her presence here threatens your ambition to take over the town. As long as Rachel and I are here, we're a threat to you. Rachel because she's the rightful owner of this town, and me because of the gift you think I have, and also because of all you've told me. You think that one day we will expose you for the fraud you are."

Matthew stood up. He looked down at Keith. "You're right again, but that changes nothing. You have to leave now. I have begun to make plans to expose Dennis and to take control of this town as its leader. This town belongs to me," he said with a maniacal look in his eyes.

The scripture that had flashed through Keith's mind earlier flashed through it again, and this time he said it out loud. "The earth is the Lord's and the fullness thereof."

"What?" Matthew narrowed his eyes.

Keith shrugged. "A verse from the Bible."

"Yes, I know it's a verse from the Bible. What does it have to do with anything?"

Keith didn't answer. He just stared silently at Matthew while wondering what to do. After a few seconds, he said, "So why did you tell me all these things if you weren't planning on giving back to Rachel the deeds of this land and what rightfully belongs to her?"

"Because from all you told Dennis, I figured out that it wouldn't take long before you revealed everything to him, including my plans. Of course, I couldn't afford to have that happen." He sat down again beside Keith and looked into his eyes. "So what's it going to be? Will you leave Fallow Creek now with Rachel," he looked at the security squad guard and the other man who was holding a gun, "or will I have to finish off anyone who stands in my way?" He gave Keith a small smile. "That includes you and Rachel."

"You would kill your stepdaughter?"

Matthew's wicked smile was all the answer Keith needed.

Keith felt fear like he'd never known before run through his veins. Rachel had told him how awful this man was, but he doubted that she knew the depth of his wickedness. He was not as afraid for his own life as he was for his wife's. He opened his mouth to tell Matthew that they would leave the town and gasped in astonishment when a sentence flashed in his mind: *Son, you and Rachel are not leaving.* You are both are staying here.

"Lord, no!" he blurted out.

"What's that?" Matthew asked.

Keith covered his eyes with his hand. Was the Lord really asking them to stay here when their lives were in danger? How could He ask that of them?

The familiar voice of the Lord whispered again in his heart: *Have I not always made a way for you?*

Matthew said harshly, "Are you and Rachel going to leave this town right now or not? I should have gotten rid of both of you when I found out you knew more than you should, but I took pity on you. Now I'm letting both of you leave the town safely, but don't try my patience."

"Can I have at least today to try to convince Rachel to leave town with me without tipping her off as to the reason why?"

"I can't give you a day."

"You were the one who told me I shouldn't tell Rachel any of the things you said to me. It won't be easy to convince her to leave when her daughter is here. She loves me, but I'm not sure she'd listen if I told her we should leave without Emily. Maybe you could try to get Mike to let her have Emily, and then we can leave as soon as we get her." He could feel in his heart a growing certainty that he knew was from the Lord; it was a certainty that they were meant to stay. But he wouldn't tell that to the crazy man before him.

"Mike's too dangerous to approach directly. I'm certainly not going to try to take his daughter away from him," Matthew said. "I might be able to do that when I'm leader, but that will take time. Besides, if I oblige you, other men will hear of it and revolt. Your request is something I can't fulfill."

Keith groaned. Now what was he supposed to do? He sighed. "At least give me some time to talk to Rachel about leaving. Just a day."

Matthew stood up again and paced the living

room. He finally came and sat beside him again. He folded his arms across his chest. "I will give you a day, but only one. You will leave by this time tomorrow or you won't like what will happen to you. And I warn you; you must not tell Rachel or Dennis anything that I have told you today."

Keith nodded and stood up. He couldn't wait to leave the house. "I won't tell them," he said. "Now can I leave?"

Matthew waved his hand. "Go."

Timothy the squad guard escorted Keith out of the house and down the street. At the end of the street, he left Keith and turned back.

Keith glanced at his wristwatch. It was a few minutes past four in the morning. He began to hurry to the Restoration House. He doubted he would be allowed to speak to Rachel at this hour, but he had to try. Their lives depended on it.

TWENTY-TWO

The squad guards at the gate of the Restoration House stared at Keith as he approached. He reached them and asked to see Rachel, knowing the chances of them agreeing to his request was very small. But he was desperate. He needed to speak to her right away.

"We can't..."

"Open the gate right now!" Rachel's voice reached Keith.

His heart soared with relief as he looked past the guards. He smiled when he saw her taking hold of the gate bars and peering out. She had fire in her eyes.

They refused to oblige. "We can't let you leave the house at this time of night." One of them said, looking at Keith. "And we can't let him come in, either. Ma'am, we have instructions from Dennis Hamilton not to let you out until six o'clock."

"At least let me just stand in front of the gate," Rachel said. "I won't go far."

The guard who had told Rachel she couldn't go

out looked at her with a thoughtful expression on his face and then told the other guard to open the gate. "When we let you out, you can only stand right in front of the gate."

"Yes," she said.

They held the gate and she walked through and immediately went to Keith. She hugged him briefly and then looked into his eyes. "I don't know why, but I had a feeling in my heart that you were going to come by and that you had something important to tell me."

Keith's pulse quickened as she gazed at him. He wasn't sure how he was going to keep such a big secret from her, but he had to. At least, temporarily. He said, "Rachel, we need to leave Fallow Creek as soon as possible." She blinked in surprise as he took her hands and squeezed them. "I can't explain right now, but it's extremely important that we do."

Rachel shook her head slowly and removed her hands from his. "Keith, what are you saying? You know I can't leave Fallow Creek now."

"I understand, Rachel, that you want to stay because of Emily, but I wouldn't be asking this of you if it wasn't crucial."

She stared at him with a puzzled look. Finally, she said, "I can't go, Keith. I'm surprised you would ask me to. I'm definitely not prepared to leave here now, especially without Emily. It's impossible. Plus, you know what's going on in the Restoration House. You were supposed to speak to Dennis Hamilton on my behalf to help these women. Instead, you tell me we have to leave town."

Keith sighed. This was the reaction he had expected from Rachel, and he didn't know what else to say to her. There was no way she would agree to leave Emily again. And it was wrong for him to ask her to, especially without an explanation.

She took his hands again and her eyes searched his. "What's really going on, Keith? There's something you're not telling me."

He looked down, as he didn't want her to see his face. She had a way of knowing what he was thinking by just studying him. He didn't want her to find out the secret he was keeping from her. But then again, there was no way she would ever imagine, let alone know, all that had been revealed to him tonight. He looked up at her again.

She squeezed his hands. "Please, Keith. Tell me what's wrong. You always say that we became one when we got married and that your problems are mine and mine yours. We shouldn't be keeping anything from each other and you know it."

He groaned. "I can't tell you, Rachel. I have to protect you."

"You're not the one who's been protecting me, Keith. God has been protecting me, and He will continue to do so. Now tell me what the problem is."

"Rachel, I can't!" he said, feeling conflicted.

"Please, Keith. Please tell me. If you want me to leave Fallow Creek, I have to know exactly why."

He groaned as he looked at her, and then he looked up at the sky and sighed. She was right. If he wanted to convince her to leave town with him, he had to give her a good reason why. It was so hard to keep anything from her.

In his heart he knew God wanted them to stay in Fallow Creek. But he couldn't imagine how that would be possible with the threat from Rachel's stepfather hanging over their heads. He still had no prophetic word for Dennis, so they would have to leave anyway if… He gasped as he realized that he now had the answers to Dennis's questions even though they had not been revealed to him by God. Whether to share it with the man was another thing. What would Dennis do if…

"Tell me, Keith!" Rachel's words cut into his thoughts.

"Rachel, I learned something tonight that is so heavy, so huge, that I don't even know where to start."

She blinked rapidly and didn't say anything for a few seconds. Then she spoke. "Start from anywhere, Keith. Just tell me what's troubling you and why you want us to leave town."

"Lord, please protect us," he whispered, and then said, "I met your stepfather today."

"Really? Tonight?" She shrugged. "Well, he does live in Fallow Creek."

"Yes, I met him tonight. What he told me is so huge and…" he sighed and glanced up, then looked at Rachel again. He whispered as he pulled her close, "I don't want those guards to hear what I have to tell you."

She looked at the guards and then faced Keith again. "They said I can leave this place at six o'clock."

Keith glanced at his wristwatch. It was just a quarter to five. "Then we'll wait here until it's six o'clock and we can go somewhere and talk."

She looked past him as though she was searching for something, and then looked at him again. "Where's your bodyguard?"

"It's part of what I have to tell you," Keith said.

She tapped her feet on the ground. "I need to hear what you have to say now. How am I supposed to wait for more than an hour with what you just told me? That'll be torture!"

"Then let's talk about something else." He exhaled. "Even though it'll be difficult."

But they could hardly speak about other things, except half-heartedly. Keith was in no mood to talk about any other thing but what he had been told. The only thing that Rachel talked about was Emily, and Keith had an inkling why. She wanted to try to get him to change his mind and abandon his talk of leaving Fallow Creek.

But Rachel soon stopped talking and they both kept glancing at their wristwatches and looking up at the sky. They leaned against the fence, side-by-side, holding hands. There was nothing to say to each other now except what Keith had to tell her. Even though Rachel didn't know what it was, he sensed she could feel the enormity of what he had to say emanating from him. She also knew, he was certain, that he would never ask her to leave Emily if they were not in a dire situation.

Finally, when it was six o'clock, Rachel sighed and told the guards it was time. "I need to speak to my husband in private," she said to them. Before they could reply, she took Keith's hand and hurried away with him.

They walked without speaking to each other, making their way to the abandoned house where they had spent their first night together. When they finally got there, they sat on the floor with their backs pressed against the wall and their shoulders touching. They sat close to the entrance of the building so they could see each other's faces, as the light flooding in from outside was not yet bright enough to fully illuminate the place.

Keith faced Rachel. He felt like his heart was about to burst out of his chest as he ran again through his mind everything her stepfather had told him. The man had warned him not to tell Rachel anything, but how could he keep this from her? Without a doubt, telling her was the right thing to do. She was right. The Lord had been their protector since they'd come here, and they had to depend on him to continue to protect them.

"Keith, please talk," Rachel said.

Keith exhaled and then began. He told her what had happened to his bodyguard and about the men who'd held a gun to his head and asked him to follow them. He told her about seeing the picture of her with her stepfather and then how shocked he was when he realized that she was the girl in the picture.

"Was anyone else there?" Rachel asked.

"Yes, a squad guard named Timothy and the other man he had with him when they accosted me."

"Did you say Timothy was with him? The guard we saw at the border the day we came to Fallow Creek? The one who took you to Dennis Hamilton's house?"

"Yes, Rachel."

She said nothing more, and he continued. With a shaky voice, he told her that her stepfather was Dennis's blackmailer. Her eyes grew wide in surprise, and he said, "But that's not the worst of it.

There's something really, really, bad, Rachel, that I'm about to tell you."

He shifted closer to her and put his arm around her. She looked quizzically at him, and he shut his eyes for an instant. "Lord, give me strength," he said, and then continued. He told her the story her stepfather had told him, and when he got to the part about her real father, his voice grew tender as he told her everything, holding her even tighter and scrutinizing her face for signs of distress.

Her mouth fell open, and she looked like she was going to pass out when he told her that her grandfather had been the real owner of Fallow Creek. He told her what had happened to the man and how her father had decided to come back to get his inheritance for his child.

"You," Keith said.

She closed her eyes, agony written on her face.

He stopped talking and took her hand.

A minute later, she told him to go on. When he got to the part about her father's death, she cried out.

"I'm so sorry, Rachel."

Tears fell down her face as he talked about where the man's body was found. She began to sob, and he stopped talking and just held her.

For a long while, he held her and tried to comfort her as she cried. Finally, she pulled away from him and wiped the tears from her eyes with her sleeve. "Please, go on, Keith."

He gently placed his palm on her cheek and said, "Are you sure, Rachel? Are you sure you want me to continue?"

"Yes," she said firmly. "I have to hear everything

right now."

"Okay." He told her about her stepfather's real desire, which was to take over Fallow Creek and claim it as his own even though it truly belonged to her. He didn't stop talking until he got to the very end of the story. He finally said, "Your stepfather told me not to tell you. He said it was in order to protect you."

Tears ran down her cheeks, and her eyes seemed blank.

"Rachel!"

She didn't answer.

He knew she was in shock from everything he had told her. His heart began to beat rapidly. What if what he'd told her was too great for her to bear? For sure, she would never be the same again, but he prayed that what he'd just told her had not broken her. It was a lot for one person to handle in just one night. Had he made a mistake in telling her? He called out her name again.

She shifted her eyes to his and pressed her lips together. She looked like she was about to break down again.

"It's all too much," she said, her voice choked with emotion. "I don't know how I can bear it all. I find out that my mother never told me that my father came from Fallow Creek and..." She cried out again. "My whole life is a lie!"

"Shhh!" Keith drew her close once more. "Your whole life is not a lie. Certainly not your life with me. And I don't think your mother knew. Your father didn't tell her."

"I guess so," Rachel said, pulling away from Keith. "But I also found out that not only is my stepfather a lascivious fool, but that he is a greedy, heartless liar and that Dennis Hamilton is a murderer. He killed..." she stopped speaking, clearly too overwhelmed.

"Rachel... I'm so sorry." Once again, he held her close.

She pulled away from him and shook her head. "Most of all, you're telling me that Fallow Creek was really my grandfather's and not Dennis Hamilton's. And that it now belongs to me? You're saying my father had the deed?"

"Your stepfather has it now, Rachel. Your father gave it to him for you. It rightfully belongs to you."

Sadness and disbelief shadowed her face. Keith couldn't stand it. He had to find something positive in all this to tell her. "Rachel, at least the good news is that you can actually now make the changes you want in this town. We can give the town over to the Lord completely and see Him work without hindrance when Dennis is removed."

He couldn't believe he was telling her to take over the town when he had just told her an hour ago that they had to leave. Yet they were the words that came out of his mouth. The words he knew without a shadow of a doubt God wanted him to say.

For the first time since they'd gotten married, she looked at him as if he'd gone absolutely crazy. "Keith, what are you saying? We can't tell Dennis Hamilton that I'm the owner of this place. He killed my father. You know what he'd do to me."

"I'm not saying we should say anything to him now. Your stepfather is already making plans to remove Dennis. All I'm saying is that I feel like God brought us here because of all this — because He wants to change the town and use you to do it. That won't happen unless you take what is rightfully yours."

"I don't see any way my stepfather is going to succeed in forcefully removing Dennis Hamilton."

"He doesn't have to do it forcefully. I think he plans to expose Dennis as an imposter and murderer. After that, he plans to tell them the truth about the real founder of this town and show them the original deed…"

Rachel interrupted. "And he plans to also tell them that I have given him my full blessing to take over the town, doesn't he?" She shook her head. "That's why he wants us to leave immediately. You just said it, Keith. My stepfather plans to take over. How am I supposed to take charge of this place when powerful and dangerous men like Dennis and my stepfather are between me and the town? And it's not even something I want to do. All I want to change is the Restoration House."

"Is that the truth, Rachel?" Keith asked. "You don't want the whole town changed? The town you grew up in? Firstly, you won't have the power and authority to make any real changes at the House with Dennis still in charge of the town. He won't allow it. And there are other women outside the Restoration House who are still living in bondage. Men and women who haven't heard the true gospel."

Rachel put her hand on her forehead and closed her eyes. She groaned. "I know, Keith. But even if I want to make all these changes to the Restoration House, and I do, how is that possible? There is no chance that Dennis or my stepfather will agree for me to take my rightful place as the owner of Fallow Creek and definitely not become the town's leader. A woman can't lead this place." She looked at Keith and said, "Maybe if you..."

"No!" Keith said firmly. "Not me! You're the one who owns this land and who can ultimately give it over to the Lord." He sighed. "Let's try to figure out what we can do with the information we have."

"I don't know that we're supposed to do anything," Rachel said.

Keith felt a grim determination enter his heart. "I *do* know we're to do something about it. God wants to use you, Rachel. He wants to use you to change Fallow Creek. I don't think you or I have a choice." He shrugged. "Maybe we do. We can disobey the Lord and leave Fallow Creek and then ask for forgiveness. The Lord will forgive us. But is that what you really want? Do you want to live a life that is out of God's perfect will? Will you obey God's voice or knowingly disobey it?"

Rachel sighed heavily. "I want to obey the Lord in everything... but how am I supposed to do that considering everything we are up against?"

"You know what the Bible says. With God, nothing is impossible."

Rachel said nothing for a long while. He sensed she was considering their options and searching her heart, trying to figure out what decision to make. He continued to search her face, waiting for her to speak. Finally, she took his hand and her confused look melted away, replaced with a confident one. "Keith, I don't know how we're going to do any of this, but just like you said, I believe with all my heart that this is why the Lord brought us to Fallow

Creek. And since it was the Lord who brought us here, I will have to trust that He will lead us and show us what we need to do."

"So you're going to take what's rightfully yours?"

"It's rightfully God's, Keith. Not mine."

"You know what I mean," Keith said.

"Yes. We'll have to depend on God to show us the way. As you said earlier, we're already in danger."

The supernatural confidence that had been stirred up in Keith just moments ago began to melt away. He had spoken so forcefully and confidently to Rachel, but now the gravity of their situation crashed in on him. By agreeing to go in this direction, Rachel would inevitably be putting herself in the line of fire. Her stepfather had sent him away with the belief that they would leave town, but now they were deciding to stay. The Lord would have to take control concerning the threats that man had made.

Rachel touched his shoulder, and he faced her fully. "Do you have a plan, Keith? It's not like we can just walk into Dennis's office and tell him that I'm the true owner of Fallow Creek and the rightful leader, and then tell him to step down for me."

Keith's heart began to beat rapidly as he thought about what Rachel had said. "Maybe that is exactly what we're going to do," he said to her.

"Keith! Have you lost your mind?"

"I'm serious," he said. "I can't think of any other way to go about this. And I think it's what God wants us to do."

Rachel stared at him with her mouth open for a few seconds, and then she lowered her head. She looked up at him again and shook her head slowly.

"Of all the strange things the Lord has told us to do since the day He asked us to move to Fallow Creek, this one is the strangest and craziest. And also the most dangerous. You know what'll happen if this idea isn't really from God. Dennis will kill us or lock us up in a place where no one will ever find us again."

Keith covered his eyes with his hand. She was right. And this time, unlike previous times, he had not heard a clear voice. Just an impression... and an unclear one at that. He believed he'd heard from God, but what if he hadn't? He would be putting their lives in real danger. Their decision to stay here was already going to place a target on their backs. He whispered, "Lord, is this really you? Do you want us to go to Dennis and tell him everything?"

Go, he heard, not clearly, but a whisper in his heart.

"Did you hear anything?" Rachel asked.

"I think I heard 'go.'"

"Then we must go."

TWENTY-THREE

Dennis Hamilton folded his hands on the table while Keith told him everything that Rachel's stepfather had said. When Keith finally finished speaking, he took Rachel's hand as his heart drummed and squeezed it encouragingly. They were in God's hands now. He would have to do with them as He pleased.

Keith looked at Dennis. The leader had listened without interrupting as Keith spilled his guts. Now, he leaned back against his seat and stared at Keith and Rachel with a knowing smile. Keith wished the man would just say something — anything — instead of sitting there and smiling at them.

Dennis finally said, "Is that all?"

Keith furrowed his brows. "Should there be more?"

"So you're telling me that Matthew Shaffer, Rachel's stepfather, is planning to forcefully remove me as leader of this town and take over?"

"Yes."

"And you want me to hand over the town to

Rachel because she's the rightful owner. Is that what you're saying?"

Keith glared at the man. He sighed loudly and nodded. "Yes, that's what I'm saying!" he exclaimed in annoyance. He told himself to calm down. They were in a precarious position right now and they had to tread carefully. Though no matter how carefully they treaded, at this point, if they lived, it would all be God. And if not, then...

Dennis laughed heartily, as though Keith had told him a funny joke. He looked at Keith and then at Rachel and then broke out laughing again. "You want me to step aside so that Rachel here, a woman, can take over as leader of this town?" His eyes were fixed on Keith. "In the first place, I wouldn't have let Rachel into my office and given her the privilege of sitting before me if not for the fact that I've been waiting for you to give me a prophetic word. However, it seems my kindness has turned your head and now you dare come into my office and say all this to me. I don't know if you're both just plain stupid," his eyes glittered with wicked intent, "or you know a secret that you're not telling me."

"I've told you everything I know," Keith said, shrugging and forcing himself to look and sound confident, even though at this point he was scared.

"Well, let me just start by saying that it will never happen. Firstly, a woman will never be the leader of this town. Secondly, I'm not leaving my position for anyone else."

A supernatural boldness rose up inside Keith, and he said, "Male or female, bound or free, black or white, we are all equal in God's sight. This land was given to Rachel by her father, and she is the rightful owner. God wants her to take over this town, and you will step aside for her."

Once again, Dennis roared with laughter.

For the first time since they'd come to Dennis's study, Rachel leaned forward, eyes blazing with anger, and spat out, "You killed my father!"

Keith focused his gaze on her. She had sworn to remain calm while he spoke, knowing she was sitting before her father's murderer. But now, with Dennis displaying such arrogance, she could not hold back her anger any longer. "You're a wicked man! You've set rules in this town that only profit you and the people who are like you. Those you consider weak are made to suffer! You abuse power, kill anyone who challenges you, and act as though you're God. But let me tell you, you are not!"

Dennis leaned forward, his face inches from hers, and snarled, "Stop speaking right now! Who gave you the right to talk to me like this?" He looked at the door and called to the guards there. Two guards walked into the study and Dennis ordered them to take Keith and Rachel away.

One of the guards grabbed Keith's hand and the other Rachel's. They hurled them out of their seats.

Keith said angrily, "Where are you taking us?"

Dennis said, "Somewhere where no one will ever see you again. Where you will never make any more trouble for me ever again."

The guards pushed Keith and Rachel to the door, and a scripture flashed through Keith's mind. It was the same scripture that had flashed through his mind when he was speaking with Rachel's stepfather. He gasped as he immediately realized that the scripture had not been for Matthew, her stepfather, but for Dennis Hamilton. And it was for him now. Which meant that God had actually given him a word for Dennis when he was with Matthew Shaffer, the word that he had been fervently praying for. Or, at least, the part about what Dennis was meant to do about his blackmailer. The other part had been answered when he'd discovered who that was.

The guard holding Keith started to push him out the door, but Keith yanked away from his grasp, turned to Dennis, and yelled, "The earth is the Lord's and the fullness thereof! You've been asking what God wants you to do. This is His word to you."

The guard took hold of Keith again to push him out of the study, but Dennis held up his hand. "Let them go," Dennis said. His face had turned white, and he looked slightly scared.

The guards released Keith and Rachel. Dennis said with a puzzled look, "I remember when I was a little boy, about twelve, sitting on my bed one day and asking God what his specific purpose for my life was." Dennis looked up thoughtfully and then looked at Keith again. "In Sunday school, for some weeks, we had been memorizing scriptures. Something strange happened. A bright light came into my room, and I saw the form of a man standing before me, but I couldn't see his face clearly."

Dennis frowned. "The man shrouded in light quoted a Bible verse. It was because we had been memorizing the Bible in Sunday school for weeks, I knew exactly where the scripture verse was taken from. It was Psalms twenty-four verse one, the scripture you quoted just now."

Dennis studied Keith's face for a few seconds

and then went on. "The man told me never to forget that verse. He told me when the time was right, I would know exactly what my destiny in God was, and then I would fully understand why he had given me that Bible verse." Dennis ran his fingers through his beard, his eyes still thoughtful. "As I grew up, I continuously pondered on those words, and then when my father died and I took over as leader of this place, I finally understood what the Bible verse meant. I knew exactly what my destiny in God was. It was to lead this town to greater heights than my father had. Which I have done."

Keith could not believe what he was hearing. But then again, what Dennis was saying should not surprise him. Dennis and his forebears had put in place spoken and unspoken rules that guided this town, rules that were based on scriptures they had twisted to suit them.

"No you haven't!" Rachel said. "Neither did your father. You've both killed and stolen and ravaged and ruined lives. You killed my father."

"Your father attacked me and I had to get rid of him."

Keith said, "You twisted that message you got from God. Your destiny in God doesn't involve killing people and taking forcefully what does not belong to you."

"I did not take Fallow Creek forcefully. The land belonged to my father and my grandfather. Now it belongs to me."

"Now that you know it really doesn't," Keith said, "are you ready to do what God wants you to do and give the land back to its rightful owner? Back to Rachel? Because I believe that is what the man who appeared to you as a child meant when he said you would know what your destiny in God was at the right time — to give back the land that was taken unjustly. Your forefathers took what didn't belong to them, but you can set things right."

Dennis had a confused look on his face. "But this land is mine...!"

Keith shook his head. "No, it's not! It's Rachel's! You have to do the right thing. You asked me to tell you what the Lord wants you to do and this is it. If you do this, your blackmailer will lose his power over you."

Dennis blinked rapidly, and then the confusion cleared from his eyes and he narrowed them. "No, that's not what I will do!" He looked at the guards, who were behind Keith and Rachel. "Tie their hands and take them to the car! They're going to take a drive with me. And gag them. I'm tired of their words."

Keith and Rachel struggled as the guards gagged them and tied their hands behind their backs. Keith yelled at the guards to let them go, but they ignored him.

Keith strained to be free as the guards bundled him and Rachel into one of the black SUVs parked in front of Dennis's house. Two armed guards sat at both sides of Rachel and Keith, squashing them. Behind, four other armed guards entered another SUV. Dennis sat in the passenger seat next to the driver.

The driver began to drive away, and Keith wondered where they were being taken. All the guards in this car and the ones behind were armed, and they all looked like they had a specific mission. His breath suddenly caught in his throat as he realized where they were going. They were heading to Rachel's stepfather's house. They were going to pay the man a deadly visit.

Keith looked out of the window. The clouds were darkening. Lightning flashed, followed by thunder. Clearly a storm was brewing, as though the elements wanted to match the storm that Dennis and his squad guards planned to unleash.

His eyes suddenly widened in terror as a truck approached at top speed, about to ram into them. The SUV swerved just before impact, and the truck veered off the road. About a dozen men with guns jumped out of the truck. One of them was Matthew Shaffer.

Keith sucked in his breath. *An ambush. Oh, Lord! Please help us!*

Dennis and his men opened the car door and went out to meet them. Matthew Shaffer had probably learned or guessed that Keith had gone to Dennis instead of leaving town with Rachel and knew what would happen next if he didn't act first.

Keith strained to be free. Unfortunately, he and Rachel were in the middle of all this. Both sides were prepared for battle, but no matter who won, he and his wife would still be in danger. But maybe... just maybe, if Rachel's stepfather won, they might have a chance to get out of this alive. A loud gunshot sounded, and a side window of the SUV shattered. Keith winced. That was if a stray bullet didn't kill them first. He struggled again to get his hands free to help Rachel, but he couldn't.

Rachel began to struggle again, her eyes bulging. He wished he could comfort her in some way, but there was nothing he could do except look at her and try to tell her with his eyes that no matter what, they were in God's hands, and He alone would decide how everything turned out today.

The rain began to fall down heavily. The sound of thunder mixed in with the sounds of unending gunshots. Keith could not look outside. He couldn't stomach the violence taking place.

For a long time, the battle continued with a barrage of gunshots. Then it suddenly stopped. Keith bowed his head, praying and asking the Lord to take control. He didn't know what would come next. Would Rachel's stepfather come and take him and Rachel way and either kill them or send them out of the town, or would Dennis come back and just get rid of them without a thought? He prayed for a third option — that God would miraculously deliver them.

The car door opened, and the guards who'd sat beside them earlier entered the car again. Keith groaned as Dennis got back into the car with the driver.

Dennis turned and said to one of the guards, "How many did we lose?"

"Two. Patrick and Len."

Dennis faced Rachel. "Your stepfather has been captured. He's in the car at the back. He will take a drive with us."

Rachel grunted.

Dennis laughed. "You want to know where I'm taking you? You'll see when we get there."

The driver started the car again and began to drive. They got to the town's border and then turned left. They finally came to a secluded place, a grassy field with a few trees around, and the driver stopped. The SUV behind also stopped. The guards dragged Keith and Rachel out of the car. Dennis and the driver got out as well. A guard held an umbrella over Dennis's head. He walked in front with the driver, while Keith and Rachel were pulled along by the guards. The rain kept pounding down on them, soaking Keith. He looked over at Rachel. She was soaked through. They finally got to a river and stopped.

Dennis turned around and looked at Keith and then Rachel. "This is where we dumped your father's body, Rachel," he said, his eyes fixed on her. Again she struggled to be free, but couldn't. "Now this is where both your bodies will be dumped." He looked past them and said coldly, "And his as well."

Keith didn't need to turn to know he was speaking about Matthew Shaffer.

"Bring him here," Dennis said to the guards standing behind Keith and Rachel.

Matthew Shaffer was dragged to where Dennis was, a gun held to his head.

Dennis said, "Now tell me where that deed is." He shook his head. "I thought we were friends, Matthew, but it turns out you were the one blackmailing me all this time, and now you were planning to forcefully remove me as leader of Fallow Creek so you could take over." Dennis narrowed his eyes. "If you tell me where the deed to Fallow Creek is, your life will be spared and all forgiven. But if you choose not to," he nodded at the guard that had the gun to Matthew's head, "you will forfeit your life."

The guard cocked his gun and Matthew

shuddered visibly and closed his eyes.

Keith felt queasy. He was going to throw up at any minute. He squeezed his eyes shut and prayed for mercy.

"Tell me now!" Dennis shouted.

"It's in the cellar of my house," Matthew said in a shaky voice. "There's a wardrobe there and in it a safe. The deed is inside the safe."

"And where is the key to that safe?" Dennis asked.

"In the bottom drawer of the portable closet in my bedroom. Underneath a pile of books."

"If I find out that you lied to me..." Dennis nodded at one of his men. "Go and get me that deed."

The guard immediately got into one of the SUVs and drove away.

Keith turned to look at Rachel. She was shivering. Worry coursed through him. The rain was still falling heavily. He prayed silently that she would not catch a cold. His own clothes now stuck to his body and he was drenched by the rain. The ground beneath them was becoming muddy and waterlogged. He looked at Dennis. The man was holding an umbrella and looking at Rachel with hatred.

Keith's heart began to pound again. Dennis was not just postulating. He was going to kill them.

They stayed under the rain, and Keith soon began to shiver as well. A car drove up behind him and he turned. The guard Dennis sent to get the deed was back. He came out of the car and walked to Dennis with an envelope in his hand. He handed Dennis the envelope, and the leader opened it and slowly brought out a long piece of paper, holding it carefully under the umbrella. His eyes scanned the paper and he nodded. He looked at Matthew Shaffer. "It appears this is indeed the original deed."

"Now will you let me go?" Matthew glowered at Dennis.

Dennis ignored him and faced Keith. "Now that I have the deed, I have no need for any of you."

Rachel made loud sounds again, and Keith felt nauseated. Once again, he prayed for mercy.

Dennis nodded at Rachel. "You want to say something, don't you?"

Rachel nodded.

He beckoned to one of the guards. "Remove the gag from her mouth."

The man did his bidding, and Rachel coughed as the gag was removed.

"Now tell me what you want to say."

Rachel coughed again and said, "Please... please let my husband go. He won't make any problems for you. He'll simply go back to the town he came from. It's me who is a threat to you, not Keith."

No, Rachel. Keith shook his head vehemently. There was no way he was going to leave her here.

"How noble," Dennis said. "Unfortunately, I can't do that. Keith already knows too much." His eyes suddenly glittered, and he gave a maniacal laugh. He focused his gaze on Keith. "You know what, Keith? I'll let you go on one condition. As you know, I care greatly about God's will for my life. If you just tell me something different, tell me that God's will is for me to continue the good work I'm doing in Fallow Creek and to continue to lead the people here, I will let you go. It will simply be a confirmation of what I already know to be true. In fact, I will let Rachel go as well."

Rachel spat out. "You evil tyrant! You think…" She moaned loudly when a guard gagged her again.

"Now, Keith, you want Rachel to be free, don't you? You want to go back to your little town with Rachel and continue with your lives. I need the confirmation and peace that a word from God will give me. If you just tell me that God wants me to continue as the leader of this place, I promise I will let you both go." He ordered a guard to remove Keith's gag and untie his hands.

Keith looked at Rachel and then closed his eyes in anguish. He felt like his whole world was shattering. The man wanted him to lie, to tell him what he wanted to hear. But how could he make up just anything and say it was from God? And yet, he wanted Rachel to live. He wanted to live and grow old with her.

He cried out in agony. "Lord, forgive me!" He had to tell Dennis what he wanted to hear. He opened his mouth, but he couldn't bring himself to say what Dennis wanted him to say. How could he lie in God's name?

"I'm waiting," Dennis said.

"Lord, what do I do?" Keith cried out again. His heart twisted and all strength drained away from him.

A Bible verse suddenly flashed through his mind: *I will sing unto the Lord, for he hath triumphed gloriously. The horse and his rider hath he thrown into the sea.* He felt an overwhelming peace settle over him. He had to say the truth no matter what the consequences were. He looked up at Dennis and said, "I can't tell you what you want to hear because that is not what God has said. I've told you what

He's told me. He wants you to step down so Rachel can take her rightful place. He wants you to give the deed of this place to her."

Dennis chuckled and then frowned deeply. "That means you'll both die. Starting with Rachel." He nodded at one of the guards, and the young man came and pointed the gun at Rachel's head.

Keith began to pray earnestly.

The man pressed the gun to Rachel's head and cocked it. Tears poured down from Keith's eyes, mixing with the rain, and he shut them tightly. "Lord, I can't bear it." Everything in him died as he waited for the explosion.

He sensed a light flash and a loud explosion sounded. His heart twisted in agony. *Rachel!* But the explosion was not from a gunshot, but the clapping thunder. He opened his eyes as another flash of lightning brightly lit up the sky and then the sound of thunder. Dennis fell to the ground. All the guards were lying on the ground a few feet away, and the man that had been holding a gun to Rachel's head was at her feet, a smoking big hole in his forehead. He'd been struck by lightning.

Keith stared at the guard in disbelief.

Dennis's eyes were open, and he was struggling to get back to his feet. He rose weakly but fell again, the muddy ground too slippery for him. Some of the other guards started to stir and then began to try to stand. They looked dazed.

Keith grabbed the envelope containing the deed from Dennis's hand. Dennis snarled and struggled to rise again but Keith looked past him and his heart pounded. The river was beginning to overflow and rush towards them.

Commotion broke out, and the guards tried to flee, but they fell each step they took.

Panic raced through Keith, and with shaky hands, he untied the rope around Rachel's wrists and quickly removed the gag from her mouth. "We have to run!" he said to her as the river raced towards them. He took her hand, and they ran as fast as they could.

Keith looked back and gasped. Dennis and his men were gaining on them, while the river pursued behind. He ran faster. The screaming behind caused him to turn around again. His heart seized with terror at what he saw. The flood had gained on Dennis, the guards, even Matthew Shaffer, and was pulling them into the churning river.

He and Rachel continued to run with the flood still on their heels. "We have to run, Rachel! As fast as we can!" he screamed.

They ran, but the flood kept coming until it was nipping at their heels. It suddenly began to recede. The rain stopped pouring down and became light showers. Keith and Rachel stopped running and turned around again. Keith looked at the river, which a moment ago had been angry and foaming but was now mostly still. His heart pounded in terror as he thought about everyone it had just swallowed.

"Do you think they're all dead?" Rachel asked, her voice filled with dread.

"I don't know," Keith said. He shut his eyes as relief like he had never known flooded him. "All I know is that the Lord saved us miraculously today... in every way."

He put his arm around her as she was still

shivering and turned her around. "We have to go and get warm before we catch a terrible cold."

She looked at his hand. "What do you have there?"

He held out the envelope containing the deed to Fallow Creek. He couldn't understand how he'd had the presence of mind to take the envelope from Dennis when the flood was approaching. He handed it to Rachel. "I believe this is yours."

She took it slowly, her eyes full of disbelief. Gradually, a smile settled on her lips. "No, it's not just mine. It's ours."

He grinned and held her close again. They began to make their way to the Restoration House while Keith pondered on everything that had just happened and how God had saved them. "I don't know whether to be thankful or terrified," he told Rachel.

"I guess both. At least, that's how I feel."

He nodded. Rachel had the deed now. They had an open door to bring a change to this town. There was a lot to do as they would have to work to uproot years of mental and physical slavery, especially of the women in this community. But all that depended on how the people here received Rachel.

He stopped and kissed her, and they continued walking to Fallow Creek. To their destiny. To whatever God had for them in the coming days.

A LOOK AT:
THE EDGE OF DESTINY (BOOK 3)

**INTRIGUE, ROMANCE AND THE LOVE OF GOD –
AUTHOR OF THE SISTERS OF ROSEFIELD, EMMA
EASTER, INTRODUCES A NEW SET OF FLAWED
AND LOVEABLE CHARACTERS IN THE DESTINY
SERIES.**

Back in Fallow Creek, Rachel and her husband
Keith are overwhelmed by the amount of people
that have continued to leave the community since
she has stepped into the leadership role.

Lily is a reserved and conservative young woman
who escaped life in polygamous community Fallow
Creek. She is living with her friend Sofia and voices
her concern over her lifestyle choices, but Sofia
doesn't want to hear it and instead Lily decided to
move out.

Shortly after moving out, Lily meets Taylor, a
wealthy businessman, widower and former member
of the Fallow Creek Community. He finds himself
deep in thought as he prepares for his upcoming
business trip to Tucson, Arizona. He thinks of his
late wife and how he wishes he had spent more time

with his family instead of being so wrapped up in making plans for marrying a second wife. Taylor and Lily's relationship quickly grows and leads to a proposal no one saw coming...

COMING JULY 2020

ABOUT THE AUTHOR

Like the characters in her stories, Emma Easter juggles a range of identities.

In the low-income community where she works, Easter is known as a family medicine physician who treats patients of all ages and backgrounds.

College friends see her as an accomplished musician, having studied and mastered five classical instruments—but behind closed doors, she's just as comfortable rocking an air guitar to Creed. And when she isn't giving her heart, soul, and sanity to her three young children she's indulging in her most secret identity of all: meeting new characters, crafting fresh plots, and exploring every corner of her imagination.

Across all these different roles, one cohesive thread has tied everything together: her faith and love of Jesus Christ.

Find more great titles by Emma Easter and Christian Kindle News at https://christiankindlenews.com/our-authors/emma-easter/